# The Fourth State of Matter

## of Matter

*Valence Chronicles Book One*

by

D'Arcy Arden

**The Fourth State of Matter**

Contact Information: info@thewildrosepress.com

Cover Art by *Jennifer Greeff*

The Wild Rose Press, Inc.
PO Box 708
Adams Basin, NY 14410-0708

Visit us at www.thewildrosepress.com

Publishing History
First Edition, 2021
Print ISBN 978-1-5092-3611-4
Digital ISBN 978-1-5092-3612-1
Published in the United States of America

**Space is cold, the sex is hot, and the rebellion is right on target...**

Pet fumbled his drink, creating a clink of glass against glass and spilling pink droplets onto the table's surface. He had encountered Décor Preservation Services once before, at his first auction, when they evaluated his quality and determined what price to charge his buyers.

"And what does DPS want with us?"

Desmodian sounded too calm, considering the tremor Pet felt running through the hand on his head.

Vige scoffed. "Really? A trio of dirty ship-dwellers running around with one of their precious décor, and you don't think they're going to intervene?"

"We've done nothing wrong." Xavis ruffled his feathers again, filling what little space remained in their alcove. "Pet was transferred to us legally. Anyone can check the license."

In a different situation, Pet would have stroked the feathers back down, but he was too scared to do more than stare dumbly from person to person.

## Dedication

Thanks to my parents, who support me in everything I do, and to my dogs who encourage me by lying in bed watching me write.

# Chapter One

*Now*

The ship hit turbulence. Walls rattled against their bolts, and a secondary navigation screen flickered. Observation windows at the front of the room showed an endless field of asteroids and other less-natural space junk. More than once, the ship avoided collision by the kind of narrow margin that would send most people into a panic.

Pet barely noticed. He was too busy riding the lap of one of the pilots. His back pressed against Brog's chest, and his legs were spread wide to brace against the chair. The position gave him leverage to control their pace. Behind him, the pilot groaned, and broad hands dug into Pet's hips. Sharp teeth nipped his neck, careful not to break the skin, as he impaled himself on his partner's aroused cock over and over.

He loved the feel of hot flesh penetrating deep within, stretching his ass open until he thought he would fall apart. The coiling in his gut pushed him further and further toward his peak, pulling his partner along as well. He could spend his life doing nothing else, and if he had his way, he would.

"Hey, Brog, we'll be landing soon." Xavis not-so-subtly eyed the carnal act happening only feet away. He showed no sign of surprise, but rather a healthy dose of interest, evident by the arousal tenting his pants.

They needed at least one person controlling the ship, or else he would have joined them.

"What you tellin' me for?" Brog pulled on Pet's hips, thrusting deeper than before. "Tell Des."

Pet gasped as his feet slipped from the chair. He flailed helplessly as Brog took over, lifting him up and slamming him down without mercy. Each impact hit harder and with more intensity as the pilot's cock repeatedly found Pet's prostate.

Pet whimpered under the onslaught, barely able to breathe around his need to come, but not yet ready to tip over that edge.

"I already know." A fourth person stepped into the control room. Desmodian, the ship's captain on record, stopped first to check the readings over Xavis's shoulder. Then he turned toward Brog and Pet. "The Penumbra Belt's tricky on good days. You may want to wrap it up."

Brog's rhythm increased, pushing them both closer to the edge.

Pet squirmed and reached toward Desmodian, barely able to speak as the air was repeatedly driven from his lungs. "Help."

With the top half of his face covered by a bony mask, Desmodian had little expression to read. Yet the warmth of his smile couldn't be mistaken as he cupped the back of Pet's head and drew him forward.

The kiss was hot and demanding. Desmodian's tongue slipped past Pet's lips and filled his mouth in a way that never failed to make him shiver. His body clenched around the arousal thrusting inside him, and a moment later, Brog came with a low groan. Hot, wet breath painted the back of Pet's neck as Brog recovered from his high. Only then did Desmodian pull away, tongue slipping free from Pet's mouth with obvious reluctance.

Just as Pet was about to argue over his own unsatisfied state, an alarm wailed on the navigation screen.

Xavis turned it off. "Solar flares are disturbing the atmosphere. This is gonna be like surfing a gravity wave."

"You better hope it's not—" Desmodian jumped behind the controls. "—or we'll crash through the damned asteroid instead of landing on it."

Brog tossed Pet into an antigravity bubble at the side of the room, then joined the other pilots.

Pet floated in his bubble of weightlessness, bouncing softly against the malleable shell and drifting sideways back to center. Safer than the best seatbelt, the structure stood unaffected by turbulence.

Though not the grandest ship, the *Vanguard* could outfly most. She had a crew of only three, but three of the best.

A year of watching the trio meant Pet recognized the controls they used and how seamlessly they maneuvered with very few words spoken between them.

Desmodian retracted the outer panels used during descent to slow the ship's velocity.

They fell faster, but the panels were protected against the unusually hot entry.

Brog plotted a shallower course, giving them more time to decelerate.

Xavis steered the ship, dodging the Penumbra

Belt's wayward asteroids and debris.

Even weightless, the turbulence sent Pet ricocheting harmlessly off the sides of his bubble. He lost sight of what the trio did next as he turned flips in the air, but a moment later, the shaking stopped. A swooping sensation filled his stomach. They had pulled up for the final descent.

Landing pads hit the ground with a jolt, and the ship gave an unhappy groan as its weight settled into place.

Only when everything fell silent could Pet hear his own laughter as he floated upside down. He didn't remember when it started, but he had no intention of stopping.

"At least someone's having fun." Xavis scowled, but his words rang with affection.

Yes, he was having fun. The last year had been more fun than his entire remembered life. They called him Pet, but a pet was better than an object, which he had been not long ago. It wasn't the life he expected. Even if he had known what would happen the day three rough ship-dwellers stormed into his life, he wouldn't have changed a thing.

# Chapter Two

*Then*

Before being called Pet, he was known only by the number on his sales tag. 2689 blazed above him the day he went up for auction, and the number stayed with him ever since.

He lived with eleven other human décor. Every day, they woke up on their twelve identical cots aligned in perfect order like little dolls ready for dress-up. A ringing bell announced their Curator exactly two minutes before she stepped through the door.

As a species, Vunqril weren't much larger than humans, but their long, thin proportions made them seem taller. Their opalescent skin shimmered like the inside of a seashell.

To 2689, their facial features looked stoic and cold. Not that he expected any warmth. He was décor, the equivalent of furniture that decorated the homes of the rich. No one smiled at furniture.

Life changed forever the day Curator unexpectedly ordered them to wear a new costume of white silk and silver bangles with an elaborate crystal headdress.

Excited chatter bloomed amongst the décor as soon as Curator left.

2689 ignored them in favor of folding the silk to drape properly over his arms, until 3155 elbowed him in the side.

"You think something's going on? This outfit is more elaborate than usual."

She had been bought around the same time as him and was the closest thing he could call to a friend, although décor never got very friendly.

He shrugged, then groaned when the silk slipped out of place.

1834, the most experienced of the décor, called for silence. "It's not our place to question Owner. Only to look beautiful."

The room quieted, but 2397 kept whispering to 3155, close enough for 2689 to hear.

"I was stationed near Owner's office yesterday and heard something about guests coming today. They must be important."

Even the whispering ceased when Curator returned. Décor didn't speak and didn't make eye contact. They acted only as artwork.

Since he spent every day standing around the estate, 2689 was intimately familiar with the building. He knew which corners got drafty in the winter and which windows provided the best view in the afternoon. To his disappointment, Curator posted him to the main dining hall. Its windows overlooked the front of the estate, including the long gravel drive, the garage full of land vehicles Owner never drove, and a landing pad for ships.

These were the kinds of things Owner wanted guests to marvel over, but 2689 preferred the back of the estate with its acres of untouched land and beatific lake in the distance.

In this part of the Vunqril's planet, architecture

tended toward flat sprawling designs with sudden peaks, like the beeping of a heart monitor. The dining hall sat at the top of one of these spiraling pinnacles. It had a good view of the estate's front lawn, but that didn't make it any less boring.

2689 sighed and took his assigned position in the eastern corner of the room, accompanied by three other décor. At least the dining hall remained a neutral temperature, so he would be comfortable.

Staff bustled about, setting the table with the best plates, dusting the already spotless chandelier, and swapping out the usual curtains for the expensive velvet ones. Years of walking past décor every day left them blind to 2689 and the others.

He couldn't be too angry since Vunqril all looked the same to him. The only difference he could find was the number of spires jutting from their heads, marking their social status. Even Owner would have been unidentifiable if not for the veritable crown on his head.

Thoughts of Owner seemed to summon him, for a moment later, he stepped into the dining hall. A cloud of irritation billowed around him as he inspected the table.

"These place settings are uneven, and the glasses are supposed to be a finger's length from the plates."

The staff bowed as they fixed the problem, taking a ruler to the table and measuring everything twice.

Owner's twitchy Assistant never strayed far from his side, questioning without ever challenging him. "Sir, why're you so concerned? Our guests are mere ship-dwellers. Surely they don't deserve this much effort."

Owner's hard stiletto feet struck a rhythmic tattoo

as he paced the room, pointing out more miniscule flaws. "I could only find one crew willing to make my delivery to the Partition system. That gives them power over me, and I refuse to bow to ship-rats. The moment they step onto my land, they will be reminded of their place."

Owner and Assistant passed 2689's corner. He kept his eyes soft, neither looking at them nor looking away as he straightened his spine under the weight of the headdress.

They were out of hearing range from the staff but forgot that décor had ears. It was a common oversight.

"Can we trust such an important shipment to these kinds of people? If they search the cargo…"

Owner waved him off. "They won't notice anything. Everything's labeled as it should be. They have no reason to be suspicious."

Owner and Assistant left, and without their disruption, the staff finished preparations in less than an hour. Once done, the staff also disappeared. Only 2689 and the other décor remained to appreciate their work.

The waiting gave 2689 time to think. Owner's fortunes rose and fell so irregularly he suspected it came from questionable means. It was the first time those suspicions had been confirmed, yet that made no difference. No one would listen to décor any more than they would listen to the dining table.

Instead he turned his thoughts to more exciting news. Their guests were ship-dwellers. A divide existed throughout the galaxy—between landowners, who lived on a planet, and ship-dwellers, who spent their lives traveling through space. Owner never hosted ship-dwellers before, so 2689 had no idea what to expect.

His assignment to the dining hall suddenly turned advantageous. A proper host always fed their guests, and 2689 would get a good look at them so long as he wasn't caught staring.

Years spent as décor taught 2689 how to entertain himself in his head. As he waited, he composed music he never voiced, letting his thoughts wander between the notes.

Oh, what was the commotion outside the window? People scurried over the estate grounds, looking like colorful insects from his vantage several stories above. Servants, staff, security, and even Owner all blended into a single migration to the landing pad.

A ship appeared in the planet's orange sky. It approached much faster than most ships dared.

Was he about to witness a crash?

Just before it hit the ground, the ship expanded like a starburst, slowing abruptly, and barely stirred the dust when it landed.

In all of 2689's admittedly limited memory, Owner's property had never hosted a ship like the one gracing them now. It looked patchwork, like an old blanket made from the pieces of its predecessors. The name *Vanguard* stood out in large letters on the side, paint chipped and faded but still prominent. Four triangular arms extended from a spherical center. The arms stayed clustered to the back when it flew, but when it landed, its arms spread like a starfish lying at the bottom of the ocean. It seemed to be trying to take up as much space as possible. Neither the color scheme nor the materials matched.

2689 loved it.

He couldn't see who disembarked. Hopefully they

were as interesting as their ship implied. They would never talk to him but would at least provide something new to look at.

An unusually long time passed after the ship landed before the doors to the dining hall opened. Owner should have entered first, leading the guest into the room as he acted the perfect host. Instead, the guest entered with Owner trailing behind.

The promises made by their guest's ship didn't disappoint. The person who strode through the door was the most curious individual 2689 had ever seen.

It was an Ocan.

He knew of the species by name, but rumors didn't prepare him for reality.

Ocans were known for the size of their bodies, the size of their personalities, and the size of their appetites. Evolved from a shark-like creature, the blue-gray skin looked thick and tough as rubber. His broad, flat face boasted a wide mouth and intensely orange eyes set in round sockets. Thick neck muscles connected to two impressive sets of shoulders, supporting the alien's four arms. The smaller inner pair of arms matched the proportions of his body, while the outer pair hung oversized and edged in spines.

The only thing more impressive than the Ocan's size was the number of guns he carried. One for each hand and a fifth larger weapon strapped to his back.

"Fuck. What's with all the white? Is there any other color in this place?"

Owner glanced back at Assistant, looking for an appropriate reaction to their guest's outburst. Their plan to assert dominance over their guest had already gone awry.

They likely never stood a chance.

"I don't know, Brog. I kind of like the white," someone said from above.

Décor didn't move, so 2689 couldn't move his head to look up, but he strained his eyes far enough to see who spoke.

A Scaacax perched in the window near the ceiling. Male, judging by the lack of shirt. He jumped from the sill and glided to the floor on a pair of feathered wings.

Owner sputtered as the Scaacax landed in front of him. "That window was locked."

The Scaacax ignored him and joined the Ocan. "This place is kind of like being stuck inside a seashell."

Seeing the pair next to each other reinforced how strange it was for different species to work together. Ships were usually crewed by homogeneous groups. The only thing these two had in common was the fact that they walked on two legs.

Despite being significantly thinner than the Ocan, the Scaacax's flame-colored wings gave him a larger silhouette. A strip of burgundy hair ran down the center of his head and blended into the red feathers on his shoulders. Pale yellow skin turned dark and rough along the lower limbs and ended in hands and feet of sharp talons. They looked like the kind of appendages that belonged on a bird of prey, not a sentient being.

To complete the odd look, eyes of solid purple spit fire and sparks.

2689 could almost feel the static creeping up his skin.

Brog, the Ocan, claimed a seat at the dining table. The chair groaned under his bulk. "Bein' inside a seashell's a good thing?"

The Scaacax shrugged, feathers shivering with the movement. "I'll never fit inside a seashell any other way." He slouched into another chair, kicking up his feet on the table and knocking over the meticulously placed dishes.

Brog grinned at his companion, showing off a mouth full of sharp teeth. "You're a weird one, Xavis."

" 'Course I am. I hang out with you morons every day."

During this exchange, Assistant slipped from the room.

Ignoring the departure, Owner squared thin shoulders and stepped to the head of the table, though he didn't sit. "Gentlemen, thank you for coming on such short notice. This is a time-sensitive job I have for you."

The pair didn't appear to hear him. Xavis, the Scaacax, was too busy spinning a plate on its edge while Brog tried to knock it over by tossing silverware.

Owner kept going. "It's just a supply run and should be simple, but unfortunately the destination has turned dangerous."

Brog leaned back in his chair when he finally succeeded in sending the plate crashing to the floor. "Sounds sketchy. What you think, Des?"

2689 never saw the third individual enter the room. Judging by Owner's shocked reaction when they spoke, neither had he.

"It certainly does."

The third guest stood just inside the doors, leaning against a war hammer as tall as himself. With a hide of green scales, whatever species he evolved from must have been a mix of lizard and cat. A mane of indigo hair fell to his shoulders, framing a face mostly covered by a bone-white mask. Small horns jutted from temples and shoulders, and a long thin tail with six spines at the end swished behind his legs. A thin frilled membrane connected the underside of his arms to his sides, like webbing that evolution hadn't finished weeding out.

A name hung at the edge of 2689's tongue. He had to search far back in his memory to a short info-vid once watched during his limited free time. Oh, a Dhen'in. That species rarely interacted with others outside their homeworld, and he never expected to see one up close.

The Dhen'in addressed Owner without looking at him. "Mister Stiril, you were scarce on the details for the job when you contacted us. What exactly do you want us to do?"

Owner took the disregard with atypical grace. "I have goods that need to be delivered to the Partition system. It requires a capable crew."

Still standing in the doorway, the Dhen'in regarded Owner coolly over the top of his hammer.

At least, his body language implied a cool look. The bony mask covering the top half of the Dhen'in's face had no eyeholes for him to show expression. Or maybe it was part of his face. 2689 didn't know enough about Dhen'in to be sure.

"Don't play coy, Mister Stiril. We're your only option. The Partition system is ravaged by interplanetary war. No one flies there. Whatever you're delivering must be important."

Owner stared down the Dhen'in across the length of the table, shoulders back and head up. "I make my money in agriculture. Many Partition colonies rely on suppliers like me to keep them fed. Transporting cargo out so far was difficult during the lull in the war, but recently the fighting has grown worse. If you can't make the trip, a lot of people will starve."

"My heart bleeds." Brog tipped back on two legs of his chair. "They should've thought 'a that before startin' a hundred-year war."

Remarkably, the chair didn't snap under Brog's weight.

"Speaking of food." Xavis looked up from where he'd been toying with the pieces of broken plate. "We're in a fancy dining room. Shouldn't there be fancy food to go with it?"

Owner latched on to the new conversation topic like a drowning man to the ocean's only piece of driftwood. "Yes, of course. You must be starving after living off ship rations."

"The food on our ship is just fine." The Dhen'in's tone could have indicated insult or amusement. There was no way to tell without an expression to match. "But we've gone through the trouble of coming here. A meal isn't too much to expect after that."

He strode down to the other end of the table, hammer striking the floor with each step and leaving a mark on the stone. At the head of the table, he claimed the primary chair. The hammer stood on its own at his side, upright despite the top-heavy design.

Owner stepped aside, eyeing the hammer with a nervous glance. "Of course. My staff have already prepared a meal. We can discuss the details of the job once you've eaten."

Servants, unseen until needed, appeared out of the

shadows as Owner left. They placed food on the table.

The trio ignored them in favor of bitching about their host.

"Fuckin' grounded." Brog gave the chair a rest and fell back onto all four of its legs with a bang that made the servants jump. He pulled a knife from his belt and stabbed a shwan fruit from its platter, eating straight from the blade.

Xavis forewent utensils entirely and shredded a hunk of meat with his talons. "Can't see the stars for the clouds, that one."

2689's stomach squirmed. Décor never felt hunger because they never consumed food or drink. Artwork didn't take bathroom breaks, after all. Upon becoming décor, their systems were changed to only consume a special nutriment that absorbed completely and created no waste. It made them as close to an object as a living being could become.

This never bothered him until someone ate in front of him. Nostalgia for something he never experienced seemed impossible, but the trio made food look like fun.

Ignoring the napkin provided on the table, Brog wiped his mouth with the back of one hand. "We really takin' this job, Des?"

Unlike the other two, the Dhen'in didn't immediately fall on the food. Instead he took up a nearby goblet, but one sip left him sneering at the drink. "He's offering good money, and it's nothing new. Hell, most of the people that hire us are arrogant landowners. If they could fly a ship, they'd do their own dirty work."

Xavis snorted. He crouched in the chair with feet

perched on the seat, so his cold humor landed on his own knees. "Landowners? Work? They don't know the meaning of the word. Like to see that pompous fool survive one day out in the Stardust. Maybe then he'll have something worth complaining about."

The three shared a laugh, their amusement ringing off the walls with an authenticity 2689 hadn't heard in years. Their every word and action felt so raw and real. Now that he saw the newcomers, how fake Owner and his usual guests seemed. The airs they put on, even with their so-called friends, seemed hollow by comparison.

A hunger opened in 2689's gut, not for food, but for living interaction.

# Chapter Three

*Now*

Despite the turbulence, their ship took no damage. The *Vanguard* was a tough bird not easily knocked from the skies and had navigated the dangers of the Penumbra Belt many times before. Made from asteroids, ship debris, and other space junk cast off from inhabited planets, the Penumbra Belt formed an ever-growing ring around civilized space. Its many crevices and hidden pockets became a haven for wayfarers, ship-dwellers, and those who belonged nowhere.

The *Vanguard* paid frequent visits to a popular club called the Gravity Well on one of the belt's larger asteroids. It was dirty yet colorful, filled with a thousand different faces, each hiding a different story.

Pet always enjoyed their time at the club, but first he had to get off the ship.

The way the *Vanguard* landed, with the main part of its body pointed upwards, made for awkward disembarking. The ship's generated gravity kept him feeling upright even when the ship faced the sky. This gave the peculiar illusion of falling sideways when he stepped from the hatch into the asteroid's artificially enhanced gravity. He fell on his face the first time he tried to make the transition, and after a year of practice,

Brog still caught him when he stumbled.

Even the largest asteroids in the Penumbra Belt had limited space, so ships crammed together on the landing pad. Novice pilots could be spotted by the number of new dents in their ship. The *Vanguard* usually stabilized itself by spreading out its four limbs. In the tight space, this wasn't possible, and instead the arms swung all the way around to cluster at the front of the ship facing skyward. The position took up much less room but also made for a precarious landing. It spoke of his trio's skill that their ship hadn't gained a single new scratch.

Brog led their group through the maze of docked ships. "Got here just in time for the evenin' rush."

"Perfect timing then." Desmodian kept one hand on Pet's shoulder, making sure he didn't get lost among the chaos.

Just past the landing pad, pop-up stands crowded together in a makeshift market. They sold everything from parts that looked ripped right out of a ship's console to live creatures kept in cages. A booth even sold toys and clothes for children, with the wares sorted according to the number of limbs the child had.

One attention-grabbing booth glittered in the ship-light. It sold common trinkets, with pearlescent jewels that never stopped shifting color.

Xavis joined him at the booth and picked up one of the pieces. "Kaleidoscope pearls. Not rare, but still beautiful."

"One of the costumes Owner made us wear had these on it. I liked that one, but a guest mocked how cheap they were. Never saw that costume again."

He didn't mean the story as anything more than a

remembered moment from his past. So it shocked him when Xavis handed over credits and picked out one of the headpieces. Two delicate chains encircled Pet's head, and a third ran over the top. The probably fake gold complemented his light-brown hair, while a single teardrop-shaped kaleidoscope pearl hung at the center of his forehead.

It wasn't the first time his trio bought something for him. He came to them with nothing. Yet they rarely indulged in unnecessary extravagance for themselves. Their clothes were industrial and featured function over fashion.

In direct contrast, he wore a pair of semi translucent harem pants made of fine purple silk, and a short open vest with gold-chain clasps along the front. He even got to pick the outfit for himself. His eye had been drawn to the vest because of its gradient colors. The transition from bright orange to dark purple, almost black, reminded him of a sunset.

With Owner it had been different. The Vunqril dressed his décor in expensive outfits to display his wealth.

Fake gold and a single kaleidoscope pearl displayed nothing except an acknowledgement of something Pet liked.

Neither Brog nor Desmodian commented on Pet's new jewelry when they left the booth, though Desmodian took a moment to admire the pearl.

Pet stared up at his boney mask since there were no eyes to meet, waiting for a sign of approval. It came in the form of a small smile.

Then they continued through the crowd toward their destination.

As expected, the Gravity Well buzzed with prime-hour business.

A puff of incense hit Pet in the face when they first stepped through the door. The smoky floral scent did little to cover the club's natural mix of sweat, alcohol, and burning fluorescents.

Rusty neon lights lined the walls and ceiling in swirling patterns. The chairs looked like clumps of red-brown moss grown into the shape of furniture, while the knee-high glass tables resembled blocks of ice.

Only the bar at the head of the room distinguished it as a club. The long slab of metal had probably been taken from an old ship. It stretched the length of the wall, with stools made of the same metal lining one side. Patrons filled the stools and spilled over to mingle among the low chairs and tables. A single tender manned the bar. It would have seemed short-staffed, but the bartender had more arms than eyes. Considering they had a dozen eyes, it was an impressive sight. They served multiple drinks at a time from the pipes covering the back wall while never looking away from a customer.

Desmodian led their group to a table at the back of the club with a perfect view of the rest of the room without being easily observed themselves. People naturally stepped out of his path, parting around the trio without needing to be asked.

While Desmodian claimed one of the moss chairs, Xavis perched on the ledge behind the chair instead. His wings didn't fit conventional furniture. Their ship had furniture built for him, but the Gravity Well served too many customers from too many races to cater to them all.

Brog tested the other chair, and the moss dented under his hand. He shook his head and sat on the floor.

A chair remained open for Pet, but he chose to remove the cushion and lounge near Brog with his elbows propped on the low table. This put him at the center of the trio, surrounded by a sense of security and peace.

The club's music had a heavy, amplified bass that cut easily through the chatter of so many voices and vibrated the table under Pet's arms. How pleasant it would be to lie across the surface and let the music travel through his body. He probably would have if the club's owner hadn't chosen that moment to approach them.

Vige was an Echoid from the Theta Remidian system. With her face like a deep-sea fish's and a transparent skull cavity, she wasn't a woman easily overlooked.

The trio had known Vige for years before Pet came along. They gave her the minimalistic greeting typical of old friends who had exchanged too many words to bother coming up with new ones.

Echoid eyesight suffered in bright lighting, an unfortunate handicap for the owner of a place featuring so much neon, so Pet supplemented his own greeting with an eager wave.

Her smile toward Pet was friendly, frightening teeth and all. "I see you boys still have your pretty decoration."

"Unless you know something we don't, he's not going anywhere." Desmodian nodded an invitation toward one of the empty chairs.

She sat and patted Pet's head.

Other people touching him usually made his skin crawl, but as a friend she could be tolerated. Especially when she placed a drink in front of him.

"The pink stuff." He immediately snatched it up.

On their first trip to the Gravity Well, he had regretfully turned down the drink she offered him. Despite his explanation that décor couldn't eat normal food, he feared he had insulted one of the trio's important contacts.

The second time they returned, however, she offered him a new drink specifically invented for him out of nutriment. It had a sweet taste, a distinctive pink color, and partially imitated the effects of alcohol. He hadn't had stimulants since becoming décor after he reached adulthood.

Desmodian leaned forward, bracing elbows on knees as his six-pronged tail brushed Pet's arm. "Is this your plan, Vige? Give him free stuff when we come here to keep us in your debt?"

"No debt. I make money on the deal. Every time you bring your lovely little Pet, I get more business. People come in just to see if rumors about the ship-dwelling décor are true."

She patted Pet's head again.

Xavis and Brog left the talking to Desmodian, watching the rest of the room while he spoke with Vige.

"Speaking of rumors, have you heard about a Class 1 colony ship called the CS *Trailblazer*? It disappeared on its voyage, and we've been hired to find it."

The music changed to a different song with an even heavier bass that created ripples in Pet's drink. Neon lights flashed, people danced or fell over drunk, and Vige calmly leaned back in her moss chair. Her hand left Pet's hair to steeple her fingers in front of her as she thought.

"Is this the ship from Oculi 5? The one meant to start a new colony out in the Stardust and bring some culture to us backward ship-dwellers?"

"That's the one. We know it left the Penumbra Belt, but not where it went after that."

Vige shook her head slowly. "The ship didn't come through this area of the belt, but it passed near Munk's Place. He seemed to think it was headed for the Iota Cloud."

This answer brought forth a variety of curses from his trio, and Pet tapped Brog's arm for an explanation. His trio looked worried, and that in turn made him worry as well.

Brog's scowl lessened when he answered Pet. "The Iota Cloud is a tricky bit of navigation. The ionized gas messes with the equipment, visibility is zero, and it's full of hydrogen pockets that'll toss the ship around."

A few feathers floated to the ground as Xavis ruffled his wings in a clear sign of anxiety. "The fact that there's been no distress signal also worries me. Either they're dead, or they're out of range for their beacons. That should be impossible, unless they tried a hyperspace jump in the middle of the cloud and got kicked to the other side of the universe."

Vige stroked Pet's hair again, and she watched him while speaking to his trio. "This sounds like a difficult job. Flying where no one else can is your specialty, but what about the poachers that hang around the cloud? Your little Pet would be too sweet a temptation for those kinds of criminals. It would be safer if I kept him. Temporarily. My business will increase, and he'll be out of your way."

Desmodian brushed her hand away to replace it with his own. "He's not in our way. He's safest with us, even out in the cloud. You know this. You're angling for something. These kinds of games aren't your thing, Vige. Spit out what you want to say."

A new quieter song kicked on over the club's speakers, as if giving Vige a stage to confess whatever thought bounced around in her transparent head.

"Munk told me something else. Someone's been asking about you." She trailed off, hesitating over the rest of her information.

"What kind of someone?" Desmodian's hand tightened on Pet's head.

Not enough to hurt, but Pet felt the outline of his new jewelry against his scalp.

"A pair from Décor Preservation Services."

Pet fumbled his drink, creating a clink of glass against glass and spilling pink droplets onto the table's surface. He had encountered Décor Preservation Services once before at his first auction when they evaluated his quality and determined what price to charge his buyers.

"And what does DPS want with us?"

Desmodian sounded too calm, considering the tremor Pet felt running through the hand on his head.

Vige scoffed. "Really? A trio of dirty ship-dwellers running around with one of their precious décor, and you don't think they're going to intervene?"

"We've done nothing wrong." Xavis ruffled his feathers again, filling what little space remained in their alcove. "Pet was transferred to us legally. Anyone can check the license."

In a different situation, Pet would have stroked the feathers back down, but he was too scared to do more than stare dumbly from person to person.

With obvious effort, Desmodian stilled his shaking hand and removed it from Pet's head. "Whether his ownership is legal or not won't matter. If they want to take him, they'll find a reason. But we'll deal with that if they show up. For now, we're heading into the Iota Cloud. Not an easy place for them to track us."

Brog snorted with an explosive sound, half laugh and half despondent sigh. "With our luck, they'll try anyway, and we'll have to save their asses too."

Vige didn't agree with words, but her eye roll spoke for her. "Well, they're not a problem for now. Relax while you're here, and get ready for your next journey."

She left the table, but her empty seat remained, as did the tension she brought.

It didn't last long before Desmodian cut the silence. "You heard her. Relax. In a couple hours, this asteroid will be in a better position for takeoff, and we'll be gone."

That was advice Pet could take. In one hefty swallow, he threw back the rest of his drink. The imitation liquor hit his system with a warm rush, and he swiped up the sweetest dregs from the bottom of the glass.

Before he could finish it, Xavis swooped forward. He wrapped his mouth around Pet's finger and sucked it clean. "Thanks for the treat."

Pet pushed him away.

Xavis laughed, pressed a kiss to his cheek, then disappeared into the rafters. Scaacax were too heavy to fly long distances, even with their wingspan. The club's rafters hung just close enough for him to reach with a jump and a few good flaps.

Someone from another winged species Pet didn't recognize waited for him up there. Unlike Xavis, their wings were made of skin and bone, and they had an unpleasant hollowness under their eyes, as if their bones were trying to absorb their flesh.

"Who's that?"

Desmodian barely looked up, but his lip twitched in annoyance. "Someone Xavis knew before we met."

"Are they bad?"

It was a regrettable question. The tension pulling at Desmodian's lip spread through the rest of his body. Like a lake freezing to ice, his emotional landscape suffered a sudden unforgiving winter.

"They're fine as long as they don't try to sell Xavis anything unwanted."

"Bastard already knows what'll happen if he does." Brog's threat didn't bring the thaw, but rather a harsh wind to the already bitter season. With a huff he pushed away from the table to search out his own drink.

Several people waiting by the bar scurried out of his way.

Unused to dissension between his trio, Pet looked to Desmodian for assurance.

Realizing Pet was watching, he hastily drew a cloak of spring around himself. Without visible eyes, he usually at least pretended to look at people. The fact that he didn't this time hinted of the desolation still raging within.

"Just something from the past we prefer not to talk about. Don't worry about it. There's another long trip ahead of us. Enjoy having your feet on the ground for a time."

Normally Desmodian would be just as eager as everyone else to relax before starting a new job, but to Pet's surprise, the Dhen'in stayed in the corner and pulled out a holographic tablet. The information it contained must have been important because it stole his attention immediately.

As dismissals went, it was a polite one.

Pet found his own entertainment on the stage.

A dancer called his name from where she was wrapped around a pole. The club lights reflected off her chrome finish, giving her a natural costume.

He waved and leaned over the edge of the stage. "Hey, Oi. That's a new move."

As a robot, Oi could contort her body into positions organic dancers only dreamed of. Her head hung toward the ground as she clung to the pole with her hands behind her back and her legs open in a full split.

She waved at him, now clinging by only one hand. "Come here. I'll show you."

He kicked off his shoes and joined her, earning a discord of whistles and jeering calls. When he drew near, the most interesting part of Oi's design activated. She was programmed to imitate the shape of whoever was closest to her. Usually this meant one of the customers. With Pet on stage as well, her body rearranged itself into a metallic version of human.

Pet stayed toward the bottom of the pole while Oi moved higher up. Having only practiced a couple times during previous visits, he had no hope of pulling off the same complicated moves she could, but Oi was accommodating. She simplified her routine, and together, the two of them kept pace with the pounding music.

By the end of the song, Pet's arms and stomach trembled from the strength needed to support his own weight. Sweat dripped from his forehead, but he felt lighter than before. Everyone watched and enjoyed him. It was an aspect of being décor he found appealing, so long as they looked at him the right way. Owner and his various guests had looked at him with cold eyes, admiring him only for his value. The audience in the Gravity Well looked at him as something desirable.

They also didn't require him to stand still all day.

Oi landed beside him on surprisingly heavy feet. "Looks like you lost one of your boys."

She pointed him toward the bar, where an Apha girl flirted with Brog. The pair left with drinks in hand and disappeared into the club's back rooms.

"He'll be back." A spike of ugly emotion pierced him, and he rubbed at his chest as if to brush it away. What was this feeling called? It wasn't jealousy. The Apha girl posed no threat to him. She looked like a combination of armor and plant. It gave her long legs and wide hips, but an indistinct upper half. Pet wasn't blind to what he had. His looks were his best asset. He never would have become décor otherwise.

Oi's metal face twisted into a synthetic smile more real than most organic expressions. "With you around, he'll definitely be back. Apha have a reputation for being like, crazy in bed, but I know her. She doesn't fit the stereotype. He's going to be so disappointed."

Pet shared her smile, but it felt more manufactured than Oi's entire existence. He found a name for his current emotion, and it unsettled him.

Possessive.

Knowing it would turn out badly didn't change the fact that someone else got their hands on one of his trio. He needed to cull this emotion. Décor didn't possess. They got possessed. Unlike his previous owner, his trio treated him as a person, yet he remained an object in the eyes of the law. People enjoyed an object, but they didn't commit to one.

Oi handed him a nutriment drink as she took an oil break for herself.

The cool glass dripped condensation over his fingers as he sat on the edge of the stage, trying not to look at the door to the back rooms. Checking the clock, he counted down the time. The *Vanguard* would leave for its next job in a few hours. From his own experiences with Brog, he and the Apha girl could get up to a lot in that much time.

The problem wasn't that Brog wandered but that he wandered for something he could just as easily get with Pet. A quickie in the club's back room was nothing new. Pet had given Brog the exact same thing on their last visit.

An unfamiliar voice broke him from his thoughts just before he started a mental spiral that didn't lead anywhere good.

"So you're the pretty décor everyone's talking about." The stranger drew closer, placing a hand on Pet's knee. "I thought they were joking when I heard about décor that spreads its legs for ship-dwellers. How much for a private show?"

By intergalactic standards, the stranger could be considered attractive. Pet didn't recognize the race offhand, but their skin glittered like fish scales and a ring of naturally growing jewels crowned their head. Along with four legs and an athletic build, they presented an alluring appearance, though impossible to categorize as male or female.

It wasn't the first time someone propositioned Pet since leaving his previous owner. Living with ship-dwellers gave people ideas about his use. Usually he turned them down immediately, but this time he hesitated. If Brog could go off with someone else, then so could he. Plus, unlike what Brog was doing with the Apha, it would at least be a new experience for Pet.

The hand crept a little higher, taking his lack of *no* as a *yes*.

Across the club, Xavis's purple eyes burned as they watched him.

The Scaacax had returned from the rafters to perch near Desmodian's chair, where the Dhen'in sat motionless.

Even without seeing his eyes, Pet could feel when Desmodian met his gaze. It felt like a knife scraping over cloth until it caught a loose thread. He waited in tense silence to see if the sharp edge would move on or unravel everything.

With a slight nod, Desmodian leaned back in his chair.

Someone watching the exchange would have missed the motion, but Pet spent enough time studying his trio to know it was unvoiced approval to act how he wanted.

Pet considered going off with the stranger, but the hand inching precariously high on his thigh sent a shiver of disgust crawling over his skin. He jerked his leg away from the unwanted touch and stood. "I'm not for sale."

The stranger jerked back from his abrupt rejection, but it didn't deter them for long. They followed Pet, their four legs easily climbing onto the stage. "Come on, pretty. I promise you'll like it. You're supposed to make people happy. It's your job."

"No. It's not." The stage only had so much room, and Pet retreated from the stranger until his back hit a wall.

Stout hands planted themselves on either side of him.

"Leave him alone." Oi hovered nervously a few feet away, her body automatically shifting to match the stranger's form. Wherever she came from, she must have been coded against conflict, because confrontation brought out her insecurity.

The stranger's breath washed over him. Any inclination Pet may have had to go off with them died the moment the scent of burnt meat invaded his nose.

His trio would have handled the situation easily, but Pet had never tried such an act before. From what he knew of four-legged races, their genitals were usually situated between their back legs. Bracing his hands against the wall, he dropped to the floor and kicked at the stranger's underbelly. He connected with something soft that caused the stranger to collapse and curl into a pathetic ball.

"Bitch." Tears welled in their eyes as they struggled back to their feet. Before they could do anything more than shout, a brightly colored wing blocked their path.

Xavis stood shorter than the stranger, but his wingspan made him the largest being on the stage. "He said *no*."

The emotion flashing through the stranger's eyes was unfamiliar to Pet. Even on a foreign face, unpleasant emotions usually looked similar. If he weren't already on the floor, Pet would have run from the dangerous unknown in front of him.

The stranger lunged for Xavis but was pulled abruptly short by a hand on their wrist.

Sometime while the stranger and Xavis stared each other down, Desmodian climbed onto the stage unnoticed. He carried his hammer with him as always but made no effort to use it. Not even when the stranger rounded on him. Instead he kept a tight hold on the stranger's wrist and twisted it in a way that sent their whole body lurching sideways.

Two of the stranger's four knees collapsed and their free hand braced against the floor.

Before the stranger could push themself upright, Desmodian pinned their hand to the stage with the handle end of his hammer.

Delicate tendons straining as they were ground into the floor made Pet wince and grip his own hand in sympathy.

With the weight of the hammer focused entirely on such a delicate area, all fight drained from the stranger immediately.

"That wasn't a smart move." Desmodian stood calm and victorious over his kneeling opponent, no longer bothering to hold onto their other wrist.

"You get it every day when most of us have never even seen décor. How's that fair?" They tried to tug their hand free. It moved barely an inch.

Even that small possibility of freedom disappeared

when Desmodian pressed down harder with the hammer.

The stranger gasped and collapsed to all four knees.

"Nothing in this universe is fair. Fairness is not guaranteed, but I can guarantee you'll get your ass kicked when you mess with something that doesn't belong to you. He said *no*. It means no."

Pressing down one last time, Desmodian then released the stranger's hand from the floor, ignoring the entire club full of people watching them. He knelt in front of Pet, who remained pressed against the wall. "That was a good kick. People will hesitate before approaching you again."

Behind him, Xavis chased the stranger from the stage.

The unwanted contact and subsequent aggression left Pet's skin tingling in unpleasant ways. Desmodian reached for him, and Pet flinched in expectation of another touch. As much as he wanted his trio, he already felt overwhelmed.

The touch never came. Instead, Desmodian's hand hovered before him in the air, waiting for him to close the distance on his own.

With a deep breath of relief, he accepted the hand and allowed Desmodian to pull him off the floor. Before they left the stage, Pet made sure to say goodbye to Oi. The robotic girl looked more shaken than he felt, and she'd shifted back to a human shape. It would be a shame to let the incident affect their friendship. After a minute assuring her that he wasn't mad over her inaction, they parted on positive terms and a promise to dance together again.

They reclaimed their seats in the back corner, Xavis making more fuss than anyone. "Where is Vige? She doesn't usually let people get away with this kind of thing in her place."

"Hopefully taking care of something more important." Desmodian's tone promised anger if that weren't the case. When he sat back in the moss chair, he kept his arms open, inviting Pet to join him without insisting.

After a moment of debate, Pet took the offer and settled onto Desmodian's lap. Physical touch felt much better when it was his own choice, and the naturally cool temperature of Desmodian's scales helped soothe his overheated skin.

In ironic punctuation to the whole event, Brog stormed out of the back room a moment later, slamming the door behind him. "Disgustin'. Better off drinkin' myself stupid." His grumbling continued during his trek across the club until he rejoined their group. "What'd I miss?"

Xavis leaned against Desmodian's chair and extended one talon to lightly stroke Pet's cheek. "There was a bit of an incident, but we're fine. So, how was it? You weren't gone long."

The disgruntled look on Brog's face should have been answer enough. Xavis may have been teasing, or maybe he asked on Pet's behalf.

Either way, Pet wanted to know.

"Apha are usually more fun, but that one just lay there expectin' me to do all the work. Like tryin' to fuck a dead fish." He almost collapsed into a chair until he remembered to sit on the floor instead. The concerned look never left his face. "Hey, Pet, you okay?"

He reached out but flinched when Pet pulled away.

It was useless to be mad at Brog. Yet, the image of Brog enjoying someone else's flesh lingered in his mind the same way a stale taste lingers on the tongue. No matter what he told himself, he couldn't cleanse his palate of the thought that, while Brog had been touching a stranger, another stranger had been touching him. It felt like Brog and the stranger somehow swapped places, turning the Ocan into the stranger he used to be.

## Chapter Four

*Then*

2689 watched as Owner's guests indulged in the worst display of manners. The servants and even some of the other décor struggled to keep the disgusted looks off their faces, but 2689 loved it.

Xavis finished first, gnawing on a stripped bone as he waited for the others. "It'll be a long job. We'll be stuck here for two days just getting the ship ready. Then it'll take weeks to reach the Partition system. We're talking at least a month's commitment."

From the head of the table, Desmodian flicked a half-eaten vegetable at his winged companion, knocking the bone from his mouth. "We've taken longer jobs. Harder ones too. Hell, we spend more time out in empty space than any sane person should. What's a month as long as we're getting paid for it?"

Brog slammed his empty drink on the table, having forgone a goblet to partake directly from the pitcher. "This swill barely counts as water, but I wouldn't mind spendin' two days planetside. There's plenty to satisfy, at least."

Orange eyes met his own, and 2689 would have cursed were he allowed to speak. Being caught staring was a cardinal sin for décor. The affronted guest would demand retribution from Owner for such an insult. 2689 needed to look away, try to lessen the damage already done, but those eyes, with their deep round sockets and pinpoint pupils, held him captive. For the first time in years he felt real again.

One of Brog's arms shifted under the table, palming himself while maintaining eye contact, causing blood to rush to 2689's face.

Noticing his companion's actions, Xavis turned in his seat to stare at 2689 as well. "You talking about the décor? They're certainly pretty. And the house is full of 'em. Might even be able to satisfy you for more than five minutes."

Desmodian laughed so hard he hunched over his mostly empty plate. One hand carelessly upended his still-full goblet, spilling its contents across the table.

The other two shared a look. Xavis seemed amused, but Brog scowled and crossed both sets of arms. "Hey, Des, want to fill us in on the joke?"

The Dhen'in finally looked up with a cruel smirk twisting his lips. "Don't get your hopes up. They're décor. Legally they're objects. Like this table. Or those curtains. Meant to look pretty, not do anything. Fucking one would be considered the same as fucking a lamp."

Neither Brog nor Xavis spoke until the Scaacax shrugged his feathered shoulders. "It wouldn't be the strangest thing you've done."

Two of Brog's four fists slammed on the arms of his chair, and something cracked. "Hey, we agreed to never bring that up again. I was drunk."

2689 would have been terrified if someone yelled at him in such a way, but Xavis responded by flicking the shell of a ginger seed at Brog.

The Ocan flinched when the shell bounced off his

forehead, just a tiny jerk backward, but it convinced his chair to give up the fight. With the loud rip of splintering wood, the chair collapsed and sent him sprawling.

The sight of six strong limbs flailing amongst a rain of splinters caused a new sensation to expand inside 2689. It started in his stomach, just under his solar plexus, and traveled up through his lungs and out his mouth. So that's what laughter felt like. It was more unpleasant than he expected. The explosive sound kept coming, even after he clapped a silencing hand over his mouth. His stomach convulsed and his lungs forgot how to function until he was nearly crying from the need to breathe. Yet, he didn't dare remove his hand in case any more unwanted sounds came out.

Everyone in the room stared at him with surprise and judgment. Not just the guests but the servants and other décor gaped as well.

2689's breathing struggled back to normal as the reality of what he had done sank in. The crystals on his costume shook as he trembled, catching the light and giving away his panic.

The rules never specifically forbid décor from laughing at guests because it was so obvious it didn't need saying. If the trio complained, Owner would get rid of 2689 on the spot. He would be reauctioned, stripped of his current number, and become something new.

2689 may not be a person, but he liked who he was, nonetheless. He didn't want to lose the modicum of identity he'd managed to gain since he was last purchased.

To his relief, the trio didn't rush off to Owner, but

they didn't forget the outburst either.

A grin split Xavis's face as he teased his companion. "You should make a living as a comedian, Brog. Even the décor is laughing at you."

Brog shot Xavis a rude hand gesture as he clambered off the floor and kicked the chair's remains out of the way. "At least I'm bringin' 'em some joy. Can't be much fun standin' around all day. Seems insane to me. This house is full 'a the prettiest ass I've ever seen. You tellin' me these rich fucks don't enjoy 'em at all?"

"What can you say? Rich people have weird tastes." Desmodian shrugged as if unconcerned, but a smile lingered below his mask.

Conversation returned to their upcoming job as Brog pulled over another chair.

2689 breathed again. The staff and other décor would tell Curator and Owner about his mistake, but hopefully he would be forgiven since the guests didn't seem to mind.

By the time Owner returned, the sun had nearly set, and the trio's interest turned to more mundane topics.

In that time, 2689 got himself under control. He never had anything that needed controlling before, and it took some practice. The laughter never returned, but he feared it still lurked deep inside him, waiting for the most inopportune moment to reemerge.

Owner hesitated at the sight of the shattered chair, but he managed to walk past it with only a slight twitch in his eye. "I'm glad to see you're enjoying my staff's hospitality."

The servants disappeared as soon as they were mentioned, as if hearing their name banished them back to the shadows.

If only 2689 could follow them.

The goblet that had been upended earlier still lay in its own puddle. Desmodian raised the wasted goblet to Owner in a toast. "As comfortable as our own ship."

Unlike earlier, Owner never came within reaching distance of the trio, choosing instead to hover on the farthest edge of polite conversation. "That's good. If it will help get the job done, then please make yourself at home while you're here. Which...will be how long, exactly?"

Desmodian shared a glance with each of his companions as if they were conversing, though no words ever left their mouths. "Two days before we're ready to leave. The Partition system favors electronegative pulse weapons. The *Vanguard* has never been tested against these before. We'll need to update our shields to make sure we can survive the crossfire of their war."

"Two days." Owner repeated the number to himself like someone taking up running for the first time, counting the miles ahead of them. "All right. I'll have my people get the cargo ready for loading in two days. Until then, ask my staff for anything you need."

Owner's stiletto feet tip-tapped him right back out of the room.

"You think he knows we know he's terrified 'a us?" Brog took one last pastry puff from the decimated tray.

Before he could eat it, however, Xavis swiped the dessert and stuffed the whole thing into his mouth. He had to swallow before he could speak. "Terrified is wrong. More like disgusted. He's probably going to spend the rest of the night disinfecting himself."

It may have been a joke, but Xavis was probably right, which only made it funnier. The laughter that still lurked inside 2689 threatened to return, and he bit down hard on the inside of his mouth to silence himself.

Servants reappeared and escorted the trio out of the room. They also maintained a barrier of distance between themselves and the ship-dwellers, though a less obvious one.

With his eyes facing forward, 2689 couldn't be sure, but he thought at least one of the trio stopped to look back at him. He could feel the weight of their gaze against his skin.

Another hour of standing in an empty, messy room, and décor were finally allowed to seek their own meals. A secondary kitchen lay behind the main kitchen for staff's personal use. Behind that lay a tertiary kitchen set aside for décor. It held only a table and no cooking appliances, yet they called it a kitchen for lack of a better title. Décor never cooked, to avoid the risk of burning their skin. The staff brought their nutriment already prepared.

Décor also never ate in front of others. It broke the illusion and reminded people that no matter what the law said, décor were still biologically alive.

Just like their perfectly aligned cots, 2689 and his fellow décor sat in a neat row. No one spoke while staff presented them with twelve identical bowls of twelve identically bland meals. It took effort to make nutriment appealing, and the kitchen staff had no effort to give. Nutriment was meant to keep décor alive. It wasn't meant to be enjoyed.

Several hours spent indulging in the aroma of

warm spice that had wafted from their guests' lavish meal made the bland mush sitting in 2689's bowl particularly unappealing. He watched the spoon slowly sink below the gray surface. At least he couldn't remember the taste of real food to know what he was missing.

The staff left, allowing the décor to finally eat. Quiet conversation started between friendlier individuals. Friendships were hard to build while pretending to be inanimate, but a few of the younger ones that were bought at the same time managed to stay sociable. No one fell on their meal like the trio had. Everything stayed on the plate. They couldn't risk staining their expensive costumes.

The others seemed content to ignore 2689 until 1834 addressed him.

"You moved."

The already minimal chatter died. As the most experienced décor in the estate, 1834 held authority in matters amongst themselves. 2689 never had a problem with her before, but he had also never failed on such a spectacular level.

He didn't try to defend himself as she continued her lecture. No one wanted his opinion.

"Not only did you make eye contact with the guests, you laughed at them. You're lucky the ship-dwellers are too stupid to be insulted."

2689 kept his gaze on his plate. "I'm sorry. It was a mistake. They took me by surprise."

In an unexpected show of support, 3155 spoke up from her place on his right. "We were all a little surprised. I only saw them for a moment, but I barely kept my composure when they walked past. I can't imagine spending the whole afternoon with them. They're not the kind of guests we're used to."

As much as 2689 appreciated her kind words, they made little difference to 1834.

"That doesn't matter. We reflect Owner's wealth and status. Your imperfection harms his reputation. Since the guests were only ship-dwellers you can be forgiven this time, but Curator will be speaking with you, 2689. Expect to spend the evening in deprivation to clear your mind."

2689 ducked his head. If it was only 1834, he might have argued, but not with Curator on her side. For décor, their Curator had almost as much authority as their Owner. If an evening spent in a sensory deprivation chamber would mitigate his mistake, he would do it. Some supposedly found sensory deprivation to be a pleasant way to meditate. He wasn't one of those beings.

As he finished his meal, an idea occurred to him. The next bite he brought to his mouth, he let a bit slip from the spoon. Anyone watching would think it landed back on the plate, but it hit the edge and some dripped onto the table. The sight of that small stain hidden under the lip of his plate brought more satisfaction than he expected. He couldn't get away with more, but he had left behind a mark for someone else to clean.

When the meal ended, all twelve décor filed out of the tertiary kitchen and headed toward their recreation area. The small room at the very back of the estate held things to keep them entertained during their brief downtime before sleep. This included a few games, a selection of info-vids, and a screen programmed with a restricted list of movies. Nothing too stimulating that would inspire outbursts. They needed to remain blank canvases without excess emotion or opinions.

To no one's surprise, Curator waited by the door.

She silently motioned for 2689 to join her. He complied without a sound and stepped out of line to wait beside her as the others went inside. Most avoided even looking at him, but 3155 made eye contact as she passed.

The door closed, and 2689 wished he were on the other side of it.

Curator finally spoke. "Do I even need to remind you what you did wrong?"

2689 shook his head, knowing better than to speak.

Her judgment came swift and abrupt. "Three hours in deprivation. So long as Mister Stiril's business with these ship-dwellers goes well, that will be all. You can spend the time contemplating how lucky you are. Go now. Someone will fetch you when your time is up."

He turned and left. Like their entertainment area, the deprivation chamber also lay at the far end of the estate. Unfortunately, it was the other end, so he needed to traipse all the way across the considerable property.

The servants' hallways were built into the walls to keep them out of sight, so they had no windows. This was unfortunate, as the night sky was one of his favorite sights.

The Vunqril's homeworld lay in a system with many other planets, and their distant bodies added color to the silver-dotted stars.

2689 tried to remain calm as he marched to his fate. The sensory deprivation chamber would do no harm. He would get in, lie there quietly, and in three hours, he would be done. Yet he couldn't shake his apprehension. He hated deprivation. It made him feel like he was losing a part of himself, and he didn't have that many parts to begin with. The silencing of all his senses soaked into his brain and stopped his thoughts. It would be days before the music in his head played again.

2689 walked as slow as possible, trying to delay the inevitable. He wanted a pleasant memory to hold on to while in deprivation. Maybe keeping his brain active would stave off the silence. The only problem was, he didn't have many pleasant memories. Not many unpleasant ones either, but the trade rarely seemed worthwhile.

There were no other staff in the usually busy hallways. Even halfway to his destination, he remained alone. Everyone must still be busy cleaning up after the guests or else avoiding them. It was a unique opportunity. With Owner and Curator nowhere around and the staff all busy, no one would notice if he slipped into the main section of the estate to look out one of the windows. The sight of the stars might be enough to sustain him.

Before he could talk himself out of it, he pushed through a door that led into the library. With no way of knowing how long he would be alone, he headed straight for the nearest window. He only needed a moment, but when he pulled back the thick curtain, his heart sank. The weather, it seemed, had also been offended by his mistake. He found no stars.

Only a sky full of clouds.

## Chapter Five

*Now*

Pet stayed curled in Desmodian's lap, letting him and Xavis decide what to tell Brog. Hopefully they would downplay the incident. The Ocan could have a quick temper, and Pet didn't want any more fights breaking out because some idiot got handsy.

Desmodian spoke with the even measure of someone carefully choosing their words. "Just give it a minute. He had a bit of a scare. Handled himself well, but it was still unpleasant."

Realization dawned ugly on Brog's face. "What? Who was it?" He jumped up and turned in circles, hunting for the culprit.

"No one worth mentioning. Don't worry about it." Desmodian's arm tightened a little more around Pet, but he showed no other reaction.

Surprising no one, Brog couldn't be so easily disarmed. "Where is Vige? I want the bastard castrated. How could she let something like that happen in her club?"

"Because I was busy saving your sorry hides."

Vige appeared out of the crowd like the predatory fish she resembled. Next to Brog's anger, she looked fragile, but she stood before him with a calmness that belied her strength. "I've got bad news, boys. Those

DPS people who were looking for you are here. I just got the heads-up. They've got your ship under surveillance and are on their way to the Gravity Well. They must have tracked you."

Xavis bristled at her accusation. "No one can track our ship."

The agitated feathers brushed Desmodian's face, and he smoothed them out of the way. "No, but they could keep an eye on our preferred rest stops around the Penumbra Belt. It was only a matter of time."

Brog pulled a gun from one of his holsters. The safety stayed on, but it added dramatic emphasis. "They're not taking him."

Desmodian stood and pushed Pet toward Xavis. "Legally they can't take him without cause. They'll have to investigate us first. Xavis, take Pet to a back room for now. Brog, you'll stay here with me. If they're looking for us, then we let them find us. No reason to look like we're hiding something."

"He says, as we're literally hiding Pet from them." Xavis's joke fell flat, and he led Pet away without further comment.

Pet released a sigh when Xavis chose a different room than Brog had used. Too bad he couldn't light that place on fire as well, but Vige would probably frown at that.

With his trio's appetites, Pet had seen many back rooms. However, it was the first time he'd been in a back room for such an unpleasant reason. Wings wrapped around both of them as he and Xavis sat on the bed. He expected a long and boring waiting game, but Xavis pulled out a holographic tablet. By manipulating a code of numerical jargon, Xavis tapped into the

Gravity Well's security cameras so they could watch what happened in the club from the safety of their room.

Barely two minutes passed before a pair of Yce DPS agents stepped through the door. Members of that species were notorious for their refusal to leave civilized space. Disapproval showed in every line of their bodies. Their naturally pinched expression, with pursed lips and an upturned nose that reached above their eyes, was amplified by the affronted looks on their faces as they observed the club.

The pair seemed to be a male and a female, judging by the male's darker burgundy color compared to the female's dusty red. They stood at least half a foot taller than most patrons, but their shoulders were barely wider than their heads. To combat this disproportion, they wore robes with wide shoulder panels and long hems that reached the floor. The robes created an illusion that they floated rather than walked.

They stopped at the bar first, and the female spoke to the bartender as the male watched her back.

"Hold on." Xavis toyed with the screen again, diving back into the code and mixing more numbers around. When he returned to the security feed, the image came with audio as well. Some noise leaked through the door to their room, and the same sounds repeating from the tablet created a delayed echo.

In the time it took Xavis to fix the security camera access, the DPS agents spotted Desmodian and Brog in the corner.

Brog had dragged over one of the metal barstools, giving him something more stable to sit on. He and Desmodian looked completely relaxed as the government agents approached.

"Captain Desmodian?"

Standing, Brog would exceed the female agent's height, but not by much. With him seated, she towered over everyone.

Desmodian swirled his drink without looking at her. "That's what it says on the ship's license."

"We wish to speak with you and your crew."

"Well, you've found two of us. This is Brog."

Following Desmodian's lead, Brog gave the agents only a brief acknowledging nod.

The female agent extended her hand halfway toward Desmodian and suddenly stopped. "Oh. You're both part of the *Vanguard*'s crew?"

"That a problem?"

"No, no." Her face shifted through several interesting shapes as she tripped over what to say next. "You're just...I was just surprised. Normal ships aren't usually crewed by more than one species."

If Brog had eyebrows, he would have raised one at her. Instead, his flared nostrils conveyed the same sentiment. "Normal ships?"

"I mean, crews with multiple species are usually..." Whatever she was about to say would likely not be received well, and she was smart enough to stop talking in time.

Desmodian finished the thought for her anyway. "Crews with multiple species are usually criminals, cast off from their own societies."

"Yes." She looked like it physically pained her to agree. "I didn't mean..."

Desmodian cut her off. "You didn't mean to insult us. You're not the first. Won't be the last. Now stop standing there awkwardly. Sit down and say what you're here to say."

Her partner remained standing at her side as a silent pillar while she seated herself in the empty chair. She traced over the mossy texture as though not sure what to make of it.

"I suppose you know why we're here. I'm agent Nauzeia. This is my partner agent, Irih."

Brog laughed, and both agents jumped. An Ocan's rough timbre could be unnerving even when they were speaking normally. Laughing, they made some truly unsettling sounds.

"Your parents didn't like you, did they, Nausea?"

"Nau-zey-a."

Her correction only made Desmodian join in Brog's laughter. Their amusement bounced between them like light reflecting off mirrors, brightening the whole exchange.

It also made Nauzeia flinch. "Do you mind? We have serious matters to address."

Her partner laid a hand on her shoulder. "Don't get so upset, Nauzeia. They're just doing it to get a reaction out of you."

The laughter stopped, but Brog's grin remained. "Yeah, Nausea. Lighten up. It's all in good fun."

The female agent frowned over the continued mispronunciation of her name, but she settled her robes about her legs and composed herself.

"We've been sent by Décor Preservation Services to talk to you about item number two-six-eight-nine— the décor that recently came into your possession."

"You call a year recent?" Brog managed to convey both condescension and genuine curiosity.

"Private sales are harder to track. And the records were a little uncertain. It only recently came to our attention."

Desmodian finished his drink and placed the empty glass on the table, letting the hollow clink echo. "Uncertain how?"

Nauzeia turned to her partner, Irih, who placed a tablet beside the glass. The tablet projected a holographic display of complicated government documents.

"First off, the records didn't specify your occupation." As she spoke, the pages of information scrolled by faster than anyone could read. "You're in cargo transportation?"

The light of the moving holograph threw flickering shadows over Desmodian, making it look like something sinister writhed under his scales. "We do a little of everything. Transport things. Find things. Hunt down wayward criminals. Navigate across dangerous tracts of space. Anything that requires a crew capable of flying where no one else can."

"I see." Nauzeia tapped something into the screen. It stopped scrolling and took the sinister edge from the shadows. "How did you come to acquire item number two-six-eight-nine?"

Brog and Desmodian shared a look.

Pet could read the memories passing between them of the events that brought him under their ownership.

In the end, Desmodian provided the cleaner story. "He was a gift. We were employed by his previous owner. Mister Stiril hired us to take food rations to refugee colonies in the Partition system. The active warzone is not an easy place to navigate. He was so

51

happy with our work, he let us pick our own bonus." Desmodian managed to provide all the right details, while making the story sound completely different.

If only life with his trio didn't need such lies of omission.

His distress must have shown on his face, because Xavis pulled him closer. "Our story only matters to us."

Back on the screen, Nauzeia had a different reaction. "Of all things, you picked décor?"

Desmodian shrugged while Brog answered. "You've seen plenty of 'em. You know how pretty they are. Why not pick one?"

All Yce had a fleshy tubule extending from either cheekbone to connect at the back of their heads. It related to their breathing, and hers swelled when Nauzeia became agitated. "Décor do not belong on a ship. These are delicate works of art. They need a stable environment and proper maintenance."

"And you don't think we can provide that." In a similar manifestation of annoyance, Desmodian's tail twitched around his legs.

Nauzeia gazed around the club, staring at the rust clinging to the neon and the dusty working-class patrons. "I have my doubts."

Brog's grip tightened on his gun.

With deliberate intent, Desmodian tapped at the shaft of his hammer sitting idly beside the chair. He didn't take up his weapon but succeeded in drawing the agents' attention away from Brog's obvious threat. "We're aware of the maintenance décor go through."

The female agent settled slightly, though the male still looked nervous. "Nonetheless, a ship is too unstable for such a delicate object. Plus, I'm sure you've found that décor is expensive to maintain. We've been sent by DPS with an offer to buy item number two-six-eight-nine. It'll be best for everyone. The décor will be resold, and you'll receive fair payment to buy something more appropriate for a ship."

Her partner tapped the tablet, switching the display from government documents to a single glowing number.

The string of zeros sucked Pet in like a hypnotist. So that was his price? He'd always wondered but never found the courage to ask.

In an action so quick Pet never saw him move, Desmodian picked up his hammer and smashed the tablet.

The holographic numbers sputtered out with a crunch of metal and plastic.

Lifting the hammer, the Dhen'in revealed the remains of the obliterated tablet as well as a deep crack running through the table. He then calmly sat back down and returned his hammer to its place at his side. "A fair price? I know the average worth of décor. That's not even half, and ours is more than average. Don't come here thinking ship-dwellers will gladly lap up whatever you deign to give us."

Irih squared off against Desmodian. As the only one standing, this made him the tallest of the group, but his dominant height didn't automatically give him dominance over the situation. "You want more?"

"No. We don't want anything. As the legal owners of *item number two-six-eight-nine*, we're not obligated to sell." Desmodian spoke Pet's item number with contempt, though the agents probably mistook it as displeasure over their offer.

Nauzeia frowned at the broken tablet, struggling to come up with a response, but her partner had no such difficulty. "Offering to buy the décor from you was a generous solution. If you won't accept it, the décor will be confiscated instead, and you'll get nothing."

Pet waited for another outburst. The direct threat seemed much worse than not offering enough money.

However, rather than pick up his weapon again, Desmodian laughed softly.

The sound resonated inside Pet's head, causing the same discomfort as hearing a wrong note in a familiar song. Laughter should only mean joy, but there was nothing joyful about Desmodian's expression. Pet hated it when a person's expressions and emotions didn't match. He had a hard enough time navigating social landscapes and didn't need the added difficulty of people contradicting themselves.

Luckily, it only lasted a moment before Desmodian stopped laughing and settled back into displeasure.

"No. You won't."

Irih's already high nose pinched even higher in contempt. "Excuse me?"

"You won't be confiscating anything. According to décor ownership laws, an observation period is required before décor can be confiscated and only if justifiable cause is found. You can't just come in and take what you want because you don't like ship-dwellers."

"That's not…" Irih started.

Desmodian cut him off. "It is. Look it up if you don't believe me. Décor ownership laws. Section thirteen, paragraph three, subparagraph two. Listed under repossession clauses."

Irih looked like he was going to argue anyway, but

Nauzeia dragged her partner away. A whispered conversation broke out between them as they huddled in a corner of the club.

Still keeping an eye on the agents, Brog leaned over and said something to Desmodian too quietly for the security cameras to pick up.

Xavis had no way to increase the audio, but he did provide Pet with another solution. "If I'm reading their lips right, Brog is asking Des when he became such an expert on décor ownership laws. Desmodian is saying about an hour ago, when Vige warned us."

"You can read lips?" Even after a year, his trio kept surprising him.

Xavis preened under the praise. "It's easier with people I know well. I don't have much experience with Yce, so the agents are more difficult. They're mentioning numbers...oh, they're debating offering more money. I kind of hope they try. That'll be fun to watch. But...they've decided that's not going to work. The female is saying something about observation. Probably saying they'll have to go through with the observation period. The male is saying something about authorities. Wait...he's suggesting they leave and bring back the authorities. Oh. Oh, I do not like that."

"Why not?" Pet watched the screen closely, trying to match people's mouth movements to their words. At best he could match the occasional syllable but never full words.

"If they need to bring the authorities, that means they aren't the authorities. DPS sent a pair of art conservationists to deal with us. Probably expected us to take the money. Which would be fine, except for the weapons strapped to their hips. There's no way they have any real training with those things. Morons will end up shooting someone if we're not careful."

The agents on screen continued to argue while trying not to look like they were arguing.

"So they're dangerous?"

Xavis's arms tightened around him. "I wouldn't turn my back to them. Hopefully it won't matter. Neither seems keen on straying outside of civilized space."

The agents came to some sort of decision, which left neither of them looking happy, and they returned to the table.

Nauzeia sat and Irih stood once again, while the destroyed tablet went ignored. "We're willing to stay and give you your observation period."

As with the tablet, they also ignored Brog, who returned the sentiment by glaring at them.

Pet expected Desmodian to be put out by their answer, but he only showed delight. "All right. We have to get going to stay on schedule, so make any preparations you need to now." He rose.

Both agents protested. "Leave? What do you mean leave?"

With a sigh Desmodian sat back down, fingers tapping impatiently against the arm of his moss chair. "You need to observe the décor in our home. Well, our ship is our home. Plus, the observation period can't interfere with an owner's livelihood, and our job requires us to travel. We've been hired to find a missing colony ship, so we're headed to the Stardust."

The agents gaped, but Nauzeia found her voice first. "You want us to travel out past the Penumbra Belt?"

"We don't want you to. This is your option. Take it or don't."

Xavis tugged on Pet's arm. "Come on. Desmodian wants us on the ship before them."

Desmodian had said no such thing. "How do you know?"

In a flurry, Xavis stowed away the tablet and stood from the bed. "His hand. He's tapping out a code. We should teach you sometime so you'll know for emergencies."

He carefully checked outside the door before urging Pet to follow.

"But why are we going back to the ship at all? Why not let me meet the agents and show them I'm fine?"

They hugged the back wall, and Xavis tossed the bartender a few credits as they slipped behind the bar. "You'll meet the agents. No choice about that. But you'll do it on our turf. Harder to snatch you off the ship."

Beyond the bar, they pushed through a door marked *Employees Only*. Hopefully Vige wouldn't mind after she had gone through the trouble of warning them nor be upset about the cracked table. "Would they really try to steal me?"

The door opened to a side alley. Limited space on asteroids meant buildings pressed against each other, and alleys catered to the narrowly inclined. Pet's shoulders brushed both walls, and Brog would never fit even if he turned sideways.

Once they reached the main road, Xavis grimaced over the feathers he lost from their literally narrow escape. "Normally they couldn't just take you, but they've already shown a reluctance to stick to the law when it comes to ship-dwellers."

Back in the market, they pushed through the crowd, trying to hurry without drawing attention. Just as the *Vanguard* came into view, Xavis pulled him behind the booth selling kaleidoscope pearls.

"Vige wasn't joking about the ship being under surveillance." Xavis peered back over the booth. "I count three DPS agents. Probably more hiding somewhere. Must've planned to grab you on your way back to the ship."

Until that moment, Pet had assumed having the law on their side would protect them. It seemed the law didn't mean the same thing to ship-dwellers it did to landowners.

"What do we do?" Pet judged the distance to their ship. So short compared to the vastness of space, yet still too far.

The smile Xavis shot him calmed the knot of anxiety growing in his stomach. "We have a saying— those who forget how to look up remain grounded. In this case, it's going to be literal."

They kept their heads below the booths as they moved toward a nearby building.

Pet nodded to the kaleidoscope pearl seller, who pretended to ignore them.

At the far side of the market, Xavis herded Pet up a maintenance ladder. The rusty metal bit his skin and left red streaks across his palms. The top of the building stood level with the *Vanguard* but significantly farther away.

"You don't have a problem with heights, do you?"

Before Pet could answer, strong wiry arms scooped him up. He clamped his hands over his mouth to keep from screaming as Xavis jumped off the edge.

With a jolt, Xavis's wings opened, and their fall turned into a controlled glide. They soared over the heads of the unaware agents until Xavis's talons caught the *Vanguard*'s outer paneling.

"You should stay out of the way until we know what's going on." He set Pet down right on top of the main observation windows, then opened a maintenance hatch and jumped inside.

Pet followed, stumbling over the sudden lurch sideways as he transferred from asteroid gravity to ship gravity. Talons caught him and set him back on his feet. Although grateful for the assist, he wished his struggles weren't so predictable.

Once certain Pet had regained his balance, Xavis ran off to the control room to get the ship warmed up and ready to leave.

Join him? No, better take his advice. Pet headed for their bedroom instead. The room didn't come from any of the original ships used to make the *Vanguard*. A sunken pit dominated most of the floor, lined with a mattress and filled with pillows and blankets. There was no other furniture, but each of the room's walls held an alcove for personal belongings.

They had renovated when Pet came along and carved a recess into the ceiling. Xavis moved his stuff up there and freed the alcove on the far right for Pet's use. It didn't hold much yet. Just the clothes they bought him and a few trinkets. He came to them with nothing but, over time, slowly filled the shelves with evidence of his life.

Without his trio present, the room felt huge. Pet climbed into the sunken bed and burrowed under the blankets. Amongst the pillows, he found a music box Brog picked up for him on a trading colony shortly after he joined the *Vanguard*. He had been toying with it earlier and forgot about it in the chaos of landing on the asteroid.

He wound the key on the bottom of the box, and a tinkling melody filled the empty room. One of the notes hit flat, but he loved it anyway. Not just for the music but for the spinning galaxy dancing on top.

Rings inside rings inside rings rotated around each other in a perfect replica of their galaxy. Civilized space, surrounded by the Penumbra Belt, surrounded by the Stardust, where the poorer colonies lived, and most ship-dwellers came from. Past that lay the Great Black, the space outside their galaxy, not yet explored and where the universe's mysteries remained. Lastly, the Void sat at the center of it all. This part of space hadn't existed fifty years ago. No one talked about it, yet some random artisan decided to include it on a music box.

The door to the bedroom opened, and Desmodian stepped in, carrying a box under his arm. "I picked up some things on the way back. Feel free to take a look if you want, but first come to the control room and meet our guests. They'll be traveling with us for a while."

Lost to his sense of curiosity, Pet peeked into the box. Desmodian made a hobby of collecting old books. The subject didn't matter, so long as it was made of paper. He claimed it reminded him of where he grew up. Apparently most Dhen'in carried a fervent distrust of technology, so there had been books everywhere. Whole libraries filled with them and available for anyone to read. Supposedly a similar system once existed back on Earth.

Before he left, Desmodian stopped him at the door and ran a hand over Pet's cheek. "It's going to be all right. These agents are on our ship, so they play by our rules. They won't be confiscating you so easily."

This did help, although not enough to assuage Pet's fears. Voicing his doubts would give them power. Instead, he stood on his toes for a kiss, which Desmodian eagerly supplied. The kiss only lasted a minute, with Desmodian's tongue briefly slipping between his lips before retreating, but it provided better reassurance than any words.

When they parted, Pet trailed Desmodian to the control room. He stood at the door and startled when he looked down. He had brought the music box with him. Turn around to return it and buy more time before facing the agents, or keep it and stand his ground? If he had to confront the agents, he wanted to get it over with. So, he clutched the music box tighter and stepped through the door.

In the control room, Xavis already sat in one of the navigation chairs, busily tapping away at screens. He barely looked up at the others as he encouraged the ship to leave the asteroid as fast as possible.

Desmodian claimed his own seat while Brog loomed over their unwanted guests, practically breathing down their necks.

Irih shifted to the other side of his partner to put himself farther from Brog's reach. "Is it supposed to shake so much?"

No one answered him.

Pet looked longingly at the windows. The initial takeoff was his favorite part of every trip. He loved watching the ground fall away as they ascended to a higher existence. The agents wouldn't take that joy away from him.

Ignoring them completely, he headed for the windows and pressed himself against the glass. The agents didn't notice him at first and continued asking his trio questions that were never answered. Then they fell silent and tensions rose behind Pet's back.

They had spotted him, but he kept his nose pressed to the glass as the ship gained speed.

The market became a miniature replica of itself.

"Item number two-six-eight-nine." Nauzeia stepped into the observation pit.

The asteroid grew smaller. He could see both its horizons. Soon it didn't even fill one of the windows as it fell into the background of the surrounding space junk.

When he could no longer differentiate the landing site from the rest of the asteroid, he turned from the window toward the agent. She towered over him in a way even Brog did not. Technically the Ocan stood taller, but the agent never met his eyes. Instead her gaze wandered his body. His trio did that too, but his eyes were part of the package. Facing the agent was like going momentarily blind. As if he had no eyes to meet.

Before he could come up with a response, Brog interrupted.

"Come on, Pet. Turbulence on the way in means turbulence on the way out."

One of four arms wrapped around Pet's waist and hauled him off his feet. He dangled limply in Brog's grip, content to be carried away from the uncomfortable interaction.

"No, wait." Nauzeia tried to stop him.

Brog tossed Pet inside the antigravity bubble.

The female agent could protest all she wanted, but only one of his trio could release him from the safety of his bubble.

As the ship gained speed, the agents gave up arguing and strapped themselves into a pair of spare seats in the corner.

It was the most accommodating Pet had seen them since they first stepped into the club, and they no longer looked like they were about to burst out of their own skins. Did their anxiety stem from actual worry over him? It was a pleasant thought, but they were more likely worried over his condition and potential loss of value.

Mere seconds after their safety belts clicked, the ship took a sharp turn to the left. The agents sagged against their seats.

His trio barely budged.

"What was that?" Irih rubbed at his chest where the belts probably bruised.

Lights blinked and screens flickered, giving an impression of dizzying activity even as no one in the room moved. In all the digital chaos, Xavis's explanation almost went unheard. "It's the Penumbra Belt. Stuff's always flying around. We have to move quick."

A gesture from Desmodian caught everyone's attention. "Speaking of quick, we're entering a cluster. Better hold on."

Pet snickered inside his bubble. Clusters—areas where rocks and metal collected densely together— littered the Penumbra Belt. Usually it was easier to go around, but sometimes, just for fun, they cut through. It was also a good way to introduce unsuspecting agents to the rigors of space travel.

The ship rolled, dipped, and dove. An asteroid rose large in the observation window, moments from crashing into them. The agents shouted in fear, but after a tap of the controls, the *Vanguard* spun out of the way just in time to avoid collision.

Counterpoint to the agents' yelling, his trio hollered with delight as they put the ship through its paces, challenging each other to more and more difficult maneuvers.

Even after a year of flying, Pet never lost his joy for the ride. He bounced around his bubble, enjoying the weightless gymnastics.

"What is that sound?" Nauzeia's demand lacked authority since she looked green from the erratic motion. It wasn't a good color combination with her red skin.

His trio looked around in confusion. Nothing sounded out of place on the ship.

Brog turned in his seat at the controls to face her. "What're you talkin' about?"

"That twittering sound."

The ship took another hard maneuver. The agents cursed while Pet laughed. He ricocheted off his bubble and did a somersault in the air.

"That sound. Right there."

"Oh…oh, that's depressing." Xavis sighed and his wings drooped until they pointed at the floor.

It sparked a need in Pet to provide comfort, but that was impossible while inside his bubble.

Brog jumped up from his chair, but immediately sat again as the ship swerved. "Seriously? You've never heard one of your precious décor laugh?"

Nauzeia clung tighter to her safety straps. "It's not a sound humans usually make."

"Maybe not around you."

After that, maneuvering through the cluster lost its joy. His trio brought the ship to a level course. It would take several days to leave the Penumbra Belt, but for now, the path before them lay clear.

"Was that necessary?" Nauzeia doubled over with a telltale hand covering her mouth.

"If you hurl, use the waste receptacle, or you're cleaning it up." Xavis pointed her toward a compartment conveniently near her chair.

To her credit, she never used it, but she did give it a considering eye.

Irih scoffed as he too clambered from his seat but got tangled in the straps. "Ship-dwellers. Irresponsible. Treating this like a damn carnival ride."

The idea of either agent ever attending a carnival was laughable.

They watched Irih struggle to free himself for a minute before Brog reached over and untangled him. "What're we supposed to do? Panic every time we hit an obstacle? This is space. This is what it means to fly."

Irih kicked the last restraint away, nearly getting tangled in it again. "And it's exactly why décor don't belong here. Space is dangerous. Ramshackle ships like these are dangerous. The way you live is going to destroy the priceless work of art you somehow got your hands on."

"He's fine." Brog waved the agent off and jerked a thumb at Pet. "He's having more fun than anyone."

While this was going on, Nauzeia had willed the

green from her skin and no longer looked to be in danger of revisiting her last meal. She stood and smoothed the wrinkles from her floor-length robe. "We will see about that. Now that the excitement is over, we can ascertain the condition of item number two-six-eight-nine. If you could release it from that…contraption?"

His trio looked uneasy, but Pet already knew what was coming. He expected it from the minute the agents showed up. To head off the inevitable argument, he knocked on the bubble and asked for release with his expression if not his words. Speaking around the agents felt unnatural. They had no interest in his voice, and he had no interest in giving it to them.

At least his trio trusted him enough to release him even without knowing what would happen. He placed his music box in Brog's hands and stepped up to the agents. In a small act of defiance, he met the female agent's eyes as he undressed.

"What're you doin'?" Brog jumped to his feet, sending a tremor through the metal floor.

The ship's architecture had been built to withstand even an Ocan's bulk, but that produced an impressive effect. The agents flinched, giving Brog a wary eye as they pulled tools from the bag strapped to the male agent's hip, right next to his gun.

"We're inspecting the item for damage. Décor has never been tested long-term on a ship. There's no telling what kind of damage it may have."

The last of Pet's clothes dropped to the floor, and he obediently opened his mouth.

The agents worked in tandem. Irih set a familiar instrument in his mouth, like a tongue depressor that hooked over his lips. At the same time, Nauzeia ran her hands over his limbs, looking for imperfections.

An internal shiver of disgust passed through him, but outwardly he showed no reaction. He needed to pass inspection. The slightest mark would be a loss of value. It was illegal to adorn décor with piercings or tattoos, and scars could land an owner in court.

The tool in his mouth beeped. Irih removed it and scowled. Could he tell what Pet had been doing with Brog just a few hours ago? To most people, sex with décor seemed so ludicrous that the condition never came up.

"Readings are the same compared to his results a year ago." There was an obvious note of disappointment in Irih's voice.

It took a little more time for Nauzeia to finish her inspection. "No obvious signs of physical damage either."

They likely would have moved on to a more detailed assessment, but Desmodian interrupted by physically inserting himself between Pet and the agents. "Great. Now that you know he's healthy, we'll let you settle in. You'll be with us for a while, so get comfortable."

Xavis's wingspan worked even better to cut Pet from the agents, bisecting the control room with a wall of feathers. "I can show you where the guest bunks are."

The agents hesitated, but they had confirmed Pet was still in one piece. The rest would come with time and cooperation, so they followed Xavis out the door. In their absence, the control room felt much larger.

Sighing with relief, Pet reached for his discarded

clothes, but Desmodian stopped him.

"Don't bother." His hand trailed down Pet's back and cupped his ass, pulling him to Desmodian's side. "Brog, you'll take first shift at the controls. Keep us on course."

"What, why me?" Brog crossed one pair of arms while still holding Pet's music box with the other. It looked ridiculously small in his hands.

"Because you've had enough tonight, and some of us haven't had their fun."

The grip on his ass tightened, and Pet groaned, pressing closer to Desmodian. It amazed him how quickly he could go from zero to aroused.

"Ah, fine."

The control room had been built so the trio could easily swap places. Their individual chairs lay on tracks, which Brog used to slide himself across the room until he sat behind the main control panel.

Yet, before Desmodian and Pet could leave, Brog stopped them. "Hey, Pet. You okay? I didn't get to ask earlier."

Tempering his growing arousal, Pet pushed away from Desmodian and sat on Brog's lap. "You left."

Most of Brog's body was a dark blue-gray, but certain parts of him faded to paler tones, including his chest, stomach, and most importantly, his face. When he blushed, it showed as a band of bright cobalt in the same place where a human's nose and cheeks would be, but which lay flat on an Ocan.

"Yeah, sorry I wasn't there when that bastard put his hands on you. Forgive me?"

Not sorry for going off with someone else. It was in Brog's nature to seek pleasure wherever he could.

Pet wished he could keep his trio to himself, but they owned him, not the other way around.

His voice still felt tied up. Was there a way to speak without words? He turned the key on the music box so Brog's very first gift sang between them.

He feared the meaning of the action wouldn't translate, so he leaned forward and added a kiss. Nothing too heated—it would be cruel to start something he had no intention of finishing—but enough to convey his acceptance of Brog's quirks. Insatiable appetites and all.

Then he returned to Desmodian's side, leaving the music box with Brog to keep him company during his time alone at the controls.

## Chapter Six

*Then*

2689 waited at the window longer than he should, hoping the clouds would be merciful. He only needed them to part long enough for a brief look at the stars. Yet, the weather had no mercy to spare that night, and the clouds remained an impenetrable blanket.

That was the moment, standing in a library as mockingly white as the moon he couldn't see, 2689's life changed. Hands grabbed his shoulders, spun him around, and pushed him against the cold glass. Clouds dulled the light coming from the window but couldn't dull the intensity of Brog's orange eyes staring down at him.

"Was hopin' I'd see you again. After the way you watched us earlier, I knew I'd find you if I looked."

Panic throbbed like a second heartbeat right behind 2689's ribs. Any landowner would have been offended by his actions in the dining hall, and he had been wrong to assume ship-dwellers would be different. He opened his mouth to beg forgiveness, but no words came out. He rarely spoke to anyone not décor and usually only one-word answers. Conversation was a skill he'd forgotten, and it didn't magically return when needed.

Standing to the full height of his spine, he barely reached the middle of Brog's chest. Thick arms caged him against the wall on either side. Heavy with corded muscle, one arm could snap him in half, and the blue-gray alien had four. Yet, Brog didn't look upset. When one hand cupped his face, it nearly covered the whole side of his head. The worn leather of Brog's fingerless gloves pressed against 2689's cheek as a thumb stroked his lips.

Not even Curator touched décor. How long had it been since 2689 last felt skin against skin? His eyes fluttered closed, no longer concerned if the Ocan was upset with him as he leaned into the warm hand.

"Pelek stole your tongue? Ah, well, words ain't needed." Another arm wrapped around his waist and pulled 2689 away from the wall.

He flailed on the very tips of his toes as he pressed against the Ocan's chest. In his search for balance, he grabbed onto a pair of dual shoulders so broad he had no hope of getting his arms all the way around.

Brog bent toward him, stopping with an inch of space between their lips.

No one had been so close to him since his last inspection. It had been clinical and detached, and 2689 retained no memory of the inspector except that they existed. This felt nothing like that memory. The one inch of air between him and Brog sparked with tension. 2689 felt the space more keenly than any physical touch he had ever known.

People admired décor from a distance. They never got so close. The ship-dwellers may have made provocative comments in his direction, but he assumed they were as empty as everything else in a décor's life.

"You're starin' again." Brog moved even closer.

Less than an inch now. Barely a distance worth

measuring, yet 2689 could have counted every atom. The intent was obvious. He understood kissing in theory, enough to know their lips needed to touch. However, Ocan didn't exactly have lips. Their broad mouths slashed across their faces and hid sharp teeth.

The hard light in those orange eyes made one thing very clear. Brog wouldn't breach that last inch on his own. As the less experienced of the two, the decision belonged to 2689. Proper décor would politely excuse themselves and go to the deprivation chamber as instructed. Yet, he remembered the delight he felt leaving a stain on the tablecloth after being scolded by 1834. That small act of defiance felt so good. He wanted a larger one. Staff had probably already cleaned the tablecloth. What Brog offered couldn't be washed away so easily.

He consented and closed the distance for the kiss. It was sloppy at first. Their different-sized mouths mismatched, and their noses didn't align. The slight mounding above the Ocan's lip would barely classify as a nose without deep slit nostrils, while 2689's more pointed one kept getting in the way.

Still, it wasn't unpleasant. Their breath mingled and sent a heatwave through him. Then a tongue pushed its way into his mouth and the kiss improved drastically. He relaxed and let Brog take the lead, allowing that larger mouth to devour him.

Another hand slipped down his hip and between his legs. He yelped at the contact on such a sensitive place. His surprise broke the kiss, and he fell back against the wall. Feelings like electricity danced just under his skin. Strangest of all, the flesh under Brog's hand hardened.

Brog laughed but didn't let go. "There's a sound. Now we just need words. What's your name?"

The blush on his cheeks had nothing to do with the hand moving between his legs, and he turned away from the question.

Brog, however, wouldn't be deterred. He pushed closer and pinned 2689 to the wall. "No sense gettin' shy now. Not when I can feel how aroused you are."

The hand between his legs gripped tighter.

Aroused? Was that the name of the feeling? His cock twitched under the touch, even through the silk. It inspired more electrical sparks. So that was what pleasure felt like. His breath came in short pants, but he managed to string words together.

"Two-six-eight-nine."

"What?"

The hand stopped moving, and he whimpered at the loss of stimulation. "I'm item number two-six-eight-nine."

Wide eyes regarded him the same way staff had watched the trio eat, enthralled by their own disgust.

"Fuck. You're really considered an object." The male breathed deeply, thin nostrils flaring in a toothless snarl. "Fuck it. Don't care. But I'm not callin' you two-six-whatever. What was your name before that?"

He gripped Brog's hand, which still cupped his face, needing both of his own to encircle the wrist. The pulse in that wrist beat steadily under his fingers. He didn't want the Ocan to pull away, but his reply would upset the male. "I...don't..." He couldn't answer. His name before his auction was gone. "I'm just two-six-eight-nine."

It was more words than he had spoken to non-décor

in his entire remembered life. The effort left him exhausted yet satisfied. He liked knowing he could carry his half of a conversation like a real person.

Teeth flashed in Brog's sneer this time before he quickly schooled flat features into a neutral expression. It lasted only a moment, but the lighter color of his face emphasized the brief slip of emotion. "Right. Feels like you're avoidin' somethin', so I won't ask. Though I'm not referrin' to you by a damn number. You're gonna be my cute little pet tonight, so that's what I'll call you. Step up from furniture, at least. Sound good?"

2689 had no response. His throat already felt tired from the short conversation. He tried, but his vocal cords shredded the words into nonsense.

Brog's thumb stroked his bottom lip again. "You can just nod, if you want."

Still gripping the other's wrist, 2689 nodded eagerly.

That was all the assurance Brog needed. Bending, he hooked arms around 2689's waist and threw the smaller male over his shoulders like a limp sack.

As Brog walked off, 2689 put up no struggle as he hung upside down. The floor looked dangerously far away, and he braced himself against the massive back to keep from swaying with each step. Hmm, the Ocan had a tail. Oddly small compared to the rest of his body, the thick stumpy appendage didn't even reach his knees. It twitched under 2689's watchful gaze, and he snickered at the unexpectedly cute sight.

The laugh turned into a yelp when fingers pinched his ass, right at the sensitive crease of his thigh.

"What're you gigglin' about back there?"

"Nothing."

2689 settled down, content to be carried. He barely understood what the Ocan intended to do with him, but he didn't care. Whatever they were going to do, he had a feeling he would enjoy it. He didn't even care when Brog's shoulder spines snagged his fine silk. Curator would throw a fit if 2689 damaged such an expensive outfit. An hour ago, the very idea would have sent him spiraling, but now he had much better prospects to think about.

They pushed through a door. Based on his view of the carpet, this was a guest room he had been inside before. A guest once insisted on having their own private décor. It had been an awkward night, standing in the corner while the guest slept, trying not to breathe too loudly.

His world turned dizzying circles when Brog flipped him over his shoulders onto a soft mattress. It felt too low for the height of the guest beds. Vunqril culture emphasized luxury, but even their excess didn't meet Brog's needs. At least three beds had been cannibalized. Their mattresses and bedding spread over the floor to create a bed large enough for several Ocans at once with space to spare.

The sheets formed a veritable ocean around Pet, and he luxuriated in the soft material.

Glisfur was the softest textile on the Vunqril's planet and some of the finest in the universe.

The linen sheets he used each night had been acceptable before. Now that he knew what he was missing, his cot would never be comfortable again.

The mattress dipped as Brog planted a knee on either side of his legs.

"This shit is gettin' in the way."

Hands tore at his clothes, uncaring of the delicate material. The sound of ripping cloth sent 2689's pulse racing, and he encouraged Brog to do it again. Once the silk and bangles were gone, only the headdress remained. 2689 handed it over to see what the Ocan would do.

Brog studied the expensive crystals for a moment, then tossed it over his shoulder.

The headdress hit the floor. Soft carpet did its best to cushion the fall, but 2689 still heard the crunch of breaking crystal. It was a soft but chilling noise. So caught up in the pleasure of rebellion, he hadn't stopped to think about the consequences.

His fears crumbled when Brog kissed him again. The Ocan's weight pressed him into the mattress. Naked to the quartet of wandering hands, 2689 writhed and mewled into the kiss.

Their exchange of pleasure enthralled him completely, to the point he forgot to breathe. He gasped for air when they finally parted.

Above him Brog also looked flushed. "Fuck, I'll never understand these rich grounded. How do they live in a house with you every day and keep their hands off? Such a waste. You've never been touched before, have you? I'm the first."

"Never." He would have agreed even if it meant lying. Anything to get those lips back on him. That he could say what Brog wanted to hear by speaking truth only made it better.

He grasped for the face hovering so tantalizingly close, but two hands pinned his wrists to the mattress, while a third fisted in his light brown hair.

"Nope. No rushin'. This flesh deserves to be

savored."

That mouth descended on him again to suck at his throat. He flinched at the prick of sharp teeth, but they never broke skin. By the time Brog reached his chest, 2689 resembled a puddle more than a human. The pleasant sensations left him loose in every joint. A shockingly pink tongue lapped at his nipple, and 2689 arched his back to press his chest into the attention.

Brog chuckled and nipped the hardening bud. "You're so responsive. Damn. I can't wait to see you come for the first time. You're gonna feel so good. You can't even imagine. So, so good. Gonna make you scream."

That brought 2689 up short, even as Brog's questing mouth moved to his stomach. Scream? Why would he scream? It sounded like a bad reaction, but everything so far had felt good. He didn't want bad. He wanted more good.

Hands left his wrists, letting him clutch the head nuzzling into his stomach. He traced the main fin on the back of Brog's head and the secondary one at the back of his neck. Their firm structure gave 2689 something to hold onto as Brog kissed the junction of his thighs. Lips and tongue tickled the sensitive skin but never touched his throbbing arousal.

When Brog spoke, the vibration of words against his skin made 2689 squirm.

"Good Pet. You want more, right? Say you want more. Say you want me to fuck you."

"Fuck me?" 2689 had heard of sex before but never in such crude terms. It made the act sound more carnal, and more real.

"Fuck, yes. You're gonna come apart on my cock,

and I'm gonna enjoy every moment."

A tongue trailed up the underside of 2689's cock, and the noise that came out of him sounded more like an animal than a person. He covered his mouth. For years he barely spoke, and suddenly he was making brand new noises.

His hands were pulled from his face and pinned back to the mattress. So many hands everywhere, it wasn't fair. Brog had four, and Pet barely knew what to do with his two.

"No, don't quiet yourself. Those sounds are mine. Don't hide them."

The mix of frustration and stimulation made 2689 keen, but this time he didn't hide the noise as he thrust his hips against Brog's face. He wanted more. Despite not knowing what he wanted or how to ask for it, he wanted more.

"Damn, you smell good. You taste good. It's like you were made for this. If I didn't know better, I'd say this wasn't your first time. Fuck, your first time. Hold on, Pet. I gotta stop, or we'll both regret it."

A sudden rush of cold air snapped 2689 back to reality and he found himself alone on the bed. It had been so warm with Brog covering him, and he shivered in the empty air. Forever seemed to pass before the Ocan returned, though it couldn't have been more than a minute.

Brog soothed him and reclaimed his place over 2689. "Hush, Pet. I'm not goin' anywhere. Just had to get somethin' for you. I'm not an easy ride for someone's first time, but this should help."

The sheets slid against him as Brog grabbed his ankles and pulled him closer. Four arms meant Brog could spread his legs wide and still have hands free to uncork the bottle he retrieved.

He coated the fingers of one hand with a pale, milky oil. "This has a muscle relaxant in it. It'll make things easier until you learn to open up for me."

His explanation sounded like a promise for the future, but 2689 didn't have time to think about that. Not when Brog leaned forward, forcing his legs farther apart, and kissed him. At the same time, his hand slipped down to 2689's ass, rubbing oil between his cheeks and around his hole. The oil tingled and mixed with the shock of a touch where no one else had ever touched before. It couldn't be called pleasure, but something inside him fluttered.

Brog swallowed the sounds being made as his fingers pressed against 2689's hole. "Fuck, you're tight. I can't even get one finger inside."

It took another minute of rubbing the oil against 2689's skin before Brog's finger finally pressed past the rim. 2689 squirmed at the invasion, not sure if he was trying to pull away or push closer. The finger pushed farther and farther, stroking his inner walls and coating the oil inside. The more his muscles relaxed, the deeper the digit was able to go, until it reached all the way to the last knuckle.

"How's it feel, Pet? Havin' somethin' inside you for the first time?"

2689 tried to answer, but the finger brushed against a spot that whited out his vision. He screamed and clung desperately to Brog's shoulders with shaking hands. His whole body trembled from the sudden pleasure sparking through his veins.

"That good, huh? But this is just the beginnin'. I've

only got one finger inside you. It's gonna get so much better. I promise."

Brog continued to torture that pleasure spot. Better? How could it get better? 2689 never imagined something this good. Any better might kill him.

A second finger pushed its way inside, straining inner muscles until the oil took effect. It didn't hurt but didn't feel good either, and 2689 found a new reason to whine.

A well-timed kiss from Brog tipped the clash of sensations back to the positive side. His fingers thrust in and out, hitting that pleasure spot each time and making 2689 forget that discomfort ever existed.

The oil eased the way until each thrust pressed inside without resistance. A third finger joined the first two while 2689 was busy pressing his hips back against the intrusion, trying to get more pressure on that spot that made his whole body light up.

"You're good and open for me now, Pet. You ready to have me really inside you? Ready to sing for me? Cause you will. You'll sing like a little fuckin' songbird."

2689 answered by pulling him into another kiss, and Brog laughed against his mouth. The fingers pulled out and he whimpered at the emptiness they left. Then the kiss ended too, and he nearly cried.

"Hold on, Pet. One last thing."

Brog quickly shed his own pants. The plain industrial cloth held up much better to the rough handling than 2689's silk. Underneath his clothes, Brog didn't look so different from a human. Same basic parts in the same basic places, but the Ocan's stiff cock stood much larger. Flushed a darker blue-gray than the rest of his body, it had a ribbed shaft and a bumpy ring around the rim of the head.

Its size and shape made 2689 tremble and not entirely from anticipation. How could that possibly fit inside him?

"You'll be fine, Pet." Brog wrapped 2689's legs around his waist. "I promise, you're gonna love it."

His spread legs struggled to accommodate the width of Brog's hips. Brog's shaft pressed against his hole, and 2689 twisted his hands in the sheets to ground himself.

"Relax, Pet. Open up and let me in."

2689 could barely breathe. He tried to relax, but his efforts failed.

One set of Brog's hands braced on the mattress by his head while the other kept 2689's hips at the right angle. Then, after prompting him one more time to relax, Brog thrust inside.

2689 screamed as he was speared on the massive cock. Discomfort edged toward pain, and he began to hyperventilate. Décor weren't made for these kinds of acts. He was in over his head, and now the monster invading his body was going to destroy him.

Large fingers stroked his hair and wiped the sweat from his forehead. "You're fine, Pet. Calm down and just feel. Your body's already adjustin' to me."

Deep breaths filled his lungs with much-needed air. It was true. The strain was already easing. Apparently, his body was smarter than him, because it opened around Brog as if it knew what to do despite the fact he had no clue.

Reassured he wasn't about to be torn apart, he finally relaxed, and Brog claimed another inch. Each ridge along the shaft caught his rim as they pushed inside, and the knobs around the head massaged deeply into his walls. Then the knobbed head ground against his pleasure spot, sending ecstasy licking up his spine. He tensed, which only pressed the head harder against that spot, increasing his pleasure even more.

"Fuck, Pet. You're clenchin'around me so much. Fuck, you're tight. Never taken a human before. Didn't know it'd be this good."

He pulled out a little, letting each ridge drag on the way out, before thrusting back in farther than before. The force slid 2689 up the sheets, and Brog pulled him back, keeping him impaled on his cock. An inch out and another few inches in, he slowly forced his way deeper.

2689 trembled. Each thrust drove the air from his lungs, and he had only enough time to get it back before it was knocked from him again. His noises became breathless grunts, and his head spun from the overwhelming mix of feelings. Arousal pooled hot in his stomach, pulling tighter with each thrust. The building tension left him wanting. Though he didn't know what he wanted, he hoped Brog would give it to him.

On one thrust, Brog's cock met resistance inside him. It wasn't all the way in, but the easy slide disappeared.

"Hold on, Pet, this is gonna be rough. But you can take it, can't you? You can take me."

Only one response summed up everything 2689 felt. "Please."

Below his line of sight, Brog shifted his hips to a new angle, all while continuing to stroke his face.

"Yeah, you'll take it. You'll take all of me, and you'll love it. Now, deep breath."

2689 did as he was told. He was good at that. Brog gripped him tight and pulled him closer while thrusting forward. The thick cock pushed past the resistance and reached so deep he swore Brog was fucking into his very soul. His trembling refused to calm down as Brog finally bottomed out. The hot flesh inside him pressed against his walls, stretching him open and filling him completely as fire and ice flooded his veins at once.

Brog gasped against his neck. "I'm all the way in you. Fuck, you're pulsing all around me. Can you feel it? Can you feel how much you turn me on? I can feel you."

One of those busy hands gripped 2689's cock, stroking the already throbbing flesh and coaxing out drops of pre-cum. Never letting up the stroking of his hand, Brog pulled out until only the knobbed tip remained inside.

The tug of each ridge as the shaft slid out made 2689 clench down harder to keep it inside. He whimpered when he was left nearly empty. It didn't last long.

A moment later Brog thrust all the way back in.

2689 screamed as all his best spots were stimulated at once and he was suddenly filled. It repeated, all the way out and all the way in. Impaling him over and over as each thrust came a little harder and a little faster.

"Oh, please, please, please," 2689 chanted in time with each brutal invasion. His legs ached from being forced open so long, but he barely noticed because his whole being had narrowed to the feel of his hole being pounded.

"Please, what? What d' you want, Pet?"

The pleasure pulled tighter. Something was building inside him. His breaths came in short gasps, skin tingling down to his fingertips as his insides felt all mixed up in the best way. He couldn't speak.

Brog seemed to know the answer anyway. "Don't worry. I know what you want. You want to come. You're gonna come for me. Come on my cock. I want to see you unravel."

Their pace increased. Each thrust bled into the next until 2689 couldn't distinguish one from another. He clenched down on the turgid length inside him, and the extra pulse of pleasure turned the tension in his belly one notch tighter.

"Come on, Pet. Come for me. Don't hold back." Brog growled as he pounded into him, drowning out the slick sound of flesh moving against flesh.

Another hard thrust, and the tension in 2689's belly snapped. He tumbled over the edge of a mental cliff into a fog of ecstasy. His back arched, and hot liquid erupted from his cock. The pleasure seemed to go on forever, and the liquid kept coming out. Each escaping drop dragged more pleasure with it.

Finally it ended, and he collapsed against the mattress. He rode the high created from pleasure and exhaustion.

The whole time Brog never stopped thrusting inside him, though not as hard as before. It was a gentle slide, only meant to remind him of the connection.

"Told you, you would sing for me."

That explained the scratch in his throat. He hadn't even heard himself screaming through his first orgasm.

The sound of a door opening interrupted the

lingering euphoria trapped under his skin. 2689 caught a glance of fiery feathers beyond Brog's bulk.

"What're you doing?" Xavis quickly closed the door behind him.

Brog glanced over his shoulders, which gave 2689 a better look at the room beyond. "Fuckin' a lamp. What's it look like?"

Xavis didn't seemed surprised and merely shook his head. "Should have known. Even after what Des said. You're insatiable."

A predatory smile slunk across Brog's face, putting sharp teeth on full display. "I'm not the only one. You're about to bust outta your shorts."

2689 leaned farther around Brog to see more of Xavis. True to Brog's word, Xavis had a flush on his face and a prominent erection straining the front of his pants. What had caused it? No one had touched the Scaacax. 2689 stared, entranced by the proof that someone could feel such pleasure simply by looking at him.

A hand caressed his face, distracting him from Xavis to focus on the person still inside him. Orange eyes flicked between him and Xavis with a calculating gleam and 2689 shrank back into the mattress. He'd been caught staring again.

Brog abruptly pulled out and flipped 2689 around onto all fours to face Xavis.

Warmth covered him, better than the best blanket, as Brog draped over his back to whisper in his ear. "Look at 'im. All hot n' bothered just from the sight 'a you gettin' fucked. Seems a shame to leave him sufferin' like that."

Those words couldn't mean what they sounded

like. 2689 looked back at Brog over his shoulder. "I can have more?"

Brog's smile curled until it showed teeth and he gripped 2689's hips from behind. "You can 'ave all you want."

A hollow feeling opened in 2689's gut. Since nutriment never made for a pleasant meal, he never understood the way people described hunger. He never felt so famished he lost control of himself. Seeing Xavis's reaction to him, he felt it now. A gaping pit opened inside him at the idea that he could inspire not only appreciation, but desire. He wanted to inspire more.

It should have been no surprise when Brog thrust back inside from behind, but 2689 had been too caught up in his newfound desires to pay attention. Still sensitive from his first orgasm, he collapsed under the onslaught, but Brog kept him upright. A hand in his hair tipped his head back so he was looking at Xavis as he was taken.

"Look at 'im, Xavis. Look at that perfect pink mouth. Tell me you don't want to mess it up." For emphasis he ran a thumb over 2689's lips, at the same time making him gasp with an extra hard thrust.

So soon after his orgasm, 2689 had no hope of getting hard again, but his spent cock gave an interested twitch.

A hand of wicked talons replaced Brog's grip and traced over 2689's lips.

"Yeah, I do." Xavis's eyes had no pupil or iris. The solid wall of burning purple made it hard to judge what he was thinking.

2689 had always assumed sex to be a private

affair—something done behind locked doors but never discussed or shared. Yet Brog didn't hesitate to fuck 2689 in front of his companion, and Xavis showed no reservations about joining.

Since he was wearing only a pair of cutoff shorts, it took no time for Xavis to undress. He knelt on the bed, aroused cock level with 2689's face. Although thinner than Brog's member, which continued pounding him from behind, its length was still impressive. It also lacked the ridges and knobs that Brog had, but the pale yellow skin had a distinct sheen as if already wet.

Not sure about the sudden change in their situation, 2689 looked back at Brog again.

"It's all right." Brog slowed his motions so he could talk without grunting. "Our crew has always been close. We share everythin'. You've been so good to me. Would be a shame not to share your pleasures with 'im too."

Xavis tipped 2689's face back toward him. "Open your mouth, pretty. I promise you'll like it. I produce my own lubricant, and it also acts as an aphrodisiac. It'll heighten your pleasure even more."

The idea of even greater pleasure held appeal. It seemed the more he got the more he wanted. Making up his mind, 2689 opened his mouth and shyly stuck out his tongue. The first brief lick to Xavis's cock proved the truth of the male's claim. It tasted mildly sweet, and the moment the lubricant touched 2689's tongue, an electric jolt went through his system. His cock, which had struggled to harden again, sprang to attention.

Brog and Xavis's laughter merged over his head, and 2689 lost track of who was speaking.

"Oh, yeah, he likes it."

"He's gonna like it even more."

Lining up his cock with 2689's mouth, Xavis pushed the head between his lips.

2689 wanted more of that sweet taste that sent arousal singing through him. He sucked eagerly, taking Xavis's cock until it hit the back of his throat. Then Xavis pulled out and started thrusting, imitating in his mouth the carnal act happening between 2689's legs.

When Brog sped up and fucked him in earnest again, his mind broke into pieces. Not sharp dangerous pieces like a broken mirror, but rather like puzzle pieces. They had been forced together in a way that didn't fit, and now that they were separated, there was space between for a larger picture.

He needed more. His desires resembled hunger. Maybe they could be satisfied the same way. Taking the initiative, he pulled Xavis closer and let the length slip partway down his throat.

Xavis shouted and his hips stuttered. "Oh, fuck. He's swallowing me. There's no way he's a virgin."

As if rewarding 2689 for his effort, Brog sped up.

"He is. Or he was. Our little Pet's just a natural."

Talons tangled in his hair and Xavis fucked his mouth the same way Brog fucked his ass. Rather than moan or grunt, the Scaacax chirped and cawed with the pleasure of each thrust.

2689 found a rhythm in the dual assault that allowed him to push into one then the other. A mix of oil and pre-cum dripped down his legs, and Xavis's excess lubricant overflowed down his chin. His own sweat and body fluids added to the mix as well. He was an even greater mess than the dining table after the trio's meal. Years spent remaining obsessively perfect made the mess feel like the most scandalous part of their act.

Just imagining others' reactions to his current state made him shiver. 1834 would be appalled. Curator would probably faint on the spot. Owner would take it as a personal insult. The thought caused a new wave of heat to settle in his stomach and abruptly tipped him over the edge. Orgasm wracked his body without mercy.

"Whoa, he came again."

Just as Xavis was marveling over him, 2689 sucked him hard and lapped at the sweetest parts of his cock.

Xavis threw back his head and moaned.

"Not just a natural. He's a little slut." Brog thrust from tip to root and back again, filling 2689's ass over and over and meeting only pleasant resistance.

Was he a slut? The raw carnality came easier to him than anything in his remembered years. If that made him a slut, then so be it. Both Brog and Xavis reveled in him, so he must be doing something right.

It came as no surprise when Brog finished first. Thrusting deeper than ever, his cock swelled and his whole body went rigid as he came.

Rush after rush of heat filled 2689's belly, making him groan. If only it would never end, but it did. Brog's hips gave a few more shallow thrusts, riding out the last waves of orgasm before falling still.

Thankfully he waited to pull out, for 2689 wanted him inside as long as possible.

Soon after, Xavis came as well. The Scaacax trilled his pleasure as he filled 2689's mouth and poured his seed down his throat.

It had a saltier taste than the lubricant, but still not

unpleasant. 2689 swallowed what he could, but most of it spilled past his lips and down his chin to land on the sheets below.

He wished he could join them but wasn't up for a third orgasm so soon after his second. When they pulled free, his shaking limbs gave out. He collapsed and turned onto his back to avoid suffocating against the mattress. The two stayed near him, hands caressing his fevered skin as they all caught their breath.

"You know they could hear you all the way down the hall."

2689 tipped his head just enough to look toward the speaker. The third member of the trio leaned casually against the wall.

Out of the three of them on the bed, Brog recovered the fastest. "Desmodian. How long you been there?" He barely even sounded winded.

Desmodian shrugged. "I caught the best parts of the show."

"And you didn't join in?" Xavis somehow managed to convey a raised eyebrow with only the sound of his voice. His wings shifted and unfurled in the avian version of a feline stretching after a pleasant nap.

"Didn't want to interrupt your fun. So? How was he?"

Brog and Xavis shared a look. "You could find out for yourself."

Gentle hands caressed up 2689's legs. One on each side, they grasped behind his knees and opened him in invitation for their comrade.

2689 whimpered from the overstimulation.

Desmodian stopped halfway to the bed. "Sounds

like he doesn't want to."

"Oh, he wants to." Brog stroked 2689's stomach, spreading the mess around. "Trust me. The little Pet can't get enough. He's just worn out. We worked 'im pretty hard."

A taloned hand caressed 2689's face. The rough skin created pleasant friction against heated cheeks.

"Come on, Pet. Don't you want to know the kind of pleasures Des can give you? It's nothing like what we've given you so far."

2689 caught his breath and observed the alien waiting at the foot of the bed. The fact that he waited for consent, despite the obvious arousal tenting his pants, caused an unpleasant pressure to well up in 2689's chest. From the moment Brog first approached him, even with their forceful nature, all three made sure he wanted to be taken before they took. It was more consideration than anyone else gave him. Most assumed he had no wants.

If sex with him was anything like the other two, then wanting Desmodian wasn't the problem. What would the green scales feel like? Was it possible to kiss Desmodian with the mask covering his face?

The problem was his stamina. He already felt wrung dry and doubted his ability to last a third round. Hopefully, the trio would forgive a lackluster performance. He nodded and beckoned to Desmodian.

The Dhen'in didn't need to be told twice, and he eagerly claimed the open space between 2689's spread legs.

Supported on either side by Brog and Xavis, 2689 moaned at the press of another body against him. Desmodian's clothes sported odd cutout sections, allowing random patches of scales to slide against 2689's skin. The scales didn't feel how he expected. Slightly cool to the touch, the surface was bumpy yet smooth like hundreds of little finely polished stones.

The sensation sent shivers coursing down to his bones as Desmodian kissed him. It was an odd experience. Desmodian's upper lip, covered by the edge of the mask, remained hard and motionless. The bottom lip, however, had a soft human shape that easily molded to him.

2689 pressed into the kiss, sucking at the bottom lip and tentatively licking the top one.

At first the tongue sliding between his lips didn't surprise him, until it kept going. He shouted into the kiss as the tongue filled his mouth and slipped down his throat. It thrust in and out, almost like being fucked again, cutting off his air with each press forward and letting him breathe only when it retreated.

Desmodian's lips ended their kiss well before his tongue. Even when he pulled away, his tongue slowly slithered from 2689's mouth, tasting as much of him as it could on the way out.

Gasping around his first full breath since the kiss started, 2689 looked up just in time to see the long blue tongue disappear behind Desmodian's lips. It shared the indigo color of his hair, but brighter.

The Dhen'in grinned at him. "That did the trick."

A glance down revealed that 2689 was hard again. The shock of the wet muscle thrusting down his throat had kindled a new flame. He writhed as scaled fingers danced over his heated flesh, but Brog and Xavis held him still.

Desmodian sat up and smiled down at him. "You

weren't expecting that, were you?"

2689 shook his head, craning his neck back against the mattress.

"You won't be expecting this either."

A jingle of buckles caught 2689's attention. Desmodian's pants rode low on his hips to accommodate the fringed skin along his sides. He wore a complicated crisscrossing of belts to keep them in place which took some effort to remove.

Once the clothes lay in a heap on the floor, 2689 got a look at his next surprise.

Desmodian's cock had two fully formed shafts extending from a single root. Curving upward toward his stomach, they stood as a proud pair.

2689's already abused hole clenched at the thought of how the dual cock would feel inside him.

Brog hitched the leg he held higher and opened 2689 wider. "Told you he's eager. Look at 'im. His cock's already weepin', he wants it so bad."

"I shouldn't make him wait then." Desmodian delicately traced the head of 2689's cock.

The feather-light touch made him keen. Feeling pressure against his hole was still not familiar and became even more bizarre when two shafts pushed inside him at the same time. Neither was too large on their own, but together they created an irregular stretch. Smooth scales covered Desmodian even on this part of his body, and the cool texture slid deep inside 2689 until he was tightly filled again.

2689's legs strained as Desmodian grasped his ankles and pulled his legs out straight to the sides. The dual cocks moved independently of each other, able to hit multiple spots at the same time, like a pair of extra-large fingers scissoring him open as they plunged in deeply.

While Desmodian dominated the lower half of his body, Brog and Xavis took control of his upper half. They pinned his arms to the mattress and mouthed paths along his chest and neck. Xavis spent several minutes lapping at his nipples, obviously relishing the pebbled texture, and Brog's sharp teeth scraped the hollow of his throat.

Each new ravishment made 2689 cry out. He could only throw his head back and let them do what they wanted as his third orgasm approached much slower than the first two. Arousal tightened his stomach again, but the edge he needed remained just out of reach. Frustrated tears gathered in his eyes. A hand wiped them away, but he couldn't tell whose.

Desperate to find release, his hips rolled in search of more stimulation.

"God." Desmodian hunched over and lost his rhythm. "You sly little whore. Rolling your hips like that. Trying to drive me crazy." Regaining his composure, he sat up straight and looked down at 2689 with dark promises. "I'm going to fuck you into oblivion, and you're going to love every moment of it. Because you asked for it."

His long tail swayed back and forth behind him like a snake about to strike as its six spines flexed and contracted.

The next thrust hit so hard it shoved 2689 up the bed. He squeaked and clung to Brog and Xavis for leverage, but Desmodian shooed them away.

They let go and hung back to watch as Desmodian turned 2689 on his side. He straddled one of 2689's legs while bracing the other over his shoulder.

The position stopped 2689's hips from moving. He could only lie there, hands tangled in the sheets, as Desmodian pounded into him. The sound of slapping skin echoed around the room.

Desmodian hugged 2689's leg to his chest, using it to keep him in place as he fucked him harder and faster.

It was even more than Brog had dared, and 2689 sobbed at the overwhelming pace. His hole clenched and fluttered as it adjusted to the double penetration.

Desmodian groaned against his thigh. "Fuck. You're so tight. How are you still so tight?"

He didn't relent for a moment, and the constant abuse of 2689's inner pleasure spot pushed him closer and closer to release.

The chamber filled with 2689's babbled begging. He needed to reach that edge and his mouth ran away from him without permission. Embarrassed by his words, he buried his face into the sheets, yet he couldn't stop.

This was apparently the opposite of what Desmodian intended.

"Look at me. I want to see your eyes when you come. Show me the moment you break."

2689 didn't know where to look. Desmodian had no visible eyes. Instead he fixed his gaze on the bone mask covering his face. This seemed to be enough, because Desmodian didn't repeat his order.

A gray calm washed over 2689 as his orgasm approached. He lay back against the mattress, watching as the Dhen'in neared his own completion. The surrender felt good, like his body finally had a purpose he could understand. When his climax hit, it came not with a sharp fall like the others had been, but a gentle drifting. Indescribable pleasure washed over him in waves. He had no words, but he didn't need them as Desmodian came at almost the same time, flooding him with a dual rush of heat.

For as long as it took him to come, it took an equally long time to end. The pleasure just refused to stop. He could barely breathe through it and lacked the strength to even writhe. His muscles pulled tighter and tighter until finally, all at once, they released. By the time it ended, he was openly sobbing, and his tears stained the sheet beneath his head.

Hands stroked his body, soothing him, as someone spoke into his ear. He felt their touch and their breath but couldn't identify them. His eyes closed as what little energy he retained went into calming his racing heartbeat. More hands repositioned him on the bed, laying him out flat. Then a damp cloth wiped down his skin.

His last thought before he fell asleep was a silent appreciation for their care. While he liked the mess they made of him, he was glad they were willing to clean up what they created. They hadn't done that with the dining table. It gave the illusion they valued him as more than an object, even after they got what they wanted.

# Chapter Seven

*Now*

With one arm around his shoulder, Desmodian led Pet from the control room. His hands lingered but remained unusually casual until they reached the bedroom.

The moment the door closed behind them, however, Desmodian grabbed him by the hair and forced his head up, exposing his throat. He buried his face against Pet's pulse point so Pet could feel the displeased rumble in his voice.

"You smell. Too many people have had hands on you today. Their scent's all over you."

He bit at Pet's throat right over the pounding pulse and pulled harder at his hair, making Pet's knees collapse like a reverse marionette.

"I really don't like you obeying other people. The sight of you standing there, like a good little object, mouth open and waiting. I could have killed them right then."

Pet thought he'd left the object mindset behind him. Yet, the moment those agents stepped into the club, he slowly reverted into familiar silence.

Scaled fingers with short but pointed nails brushed over his lips. "Nothing to say?"

Unable to find his words, Pet tried to bury his face

in Desmodian's chest, but the Dhen'in held him at arm's length.

"So that's all it takes to make you a pretty little object again? A couple of sophisticated landowners show up, and you're eager to submit."

Pet trembled under the onslaught of accusations. He only obeyed the agents to make things easier for his trio, but the explanation stuck in his throat. Memories surged up in his mind of a dark chamber filled halfway with water and halfway with silence.

Desmodian let him go with a heavy sigh to run a hand through his own hair instead. "If that's what you want, we'll pull over at the next inhabited asteroid. You can get off with the agents. They'll be glad to take you to auction and find you a real owner again."

"No." Tears dripped from Pet's eyes and he buried himself against green scales. "I don't want that. I want to be here, with you. I like it here."

Hands threaded into his hair again, soothing instead of pulling this time.

"If that's what you want, then say so. Those agents may not listen, but they definitely won't listen if you don't speak." The perfect shape of Desmodian's mouth more than made up for his lack of other facial features, especially when he gave Pet a soft smile.

The tears stopped, and Pet wiped away their ghosts from his cheeks. "I will."

"Good." Desmodian carefully removed the headpiece with the kaleidoscope pearl from Pet's disheveled hair. "I intend to spend the rest of the night reminding you how loud you can be. But first, you still stink of other people."

The adjacent bathroom looked empty at first

glance. Bathroom features hid within the smooth metal walls, out of the way until needed. It kept the room safer for anyone inside if the ship hit turbulence. Panels along the floor slid back to reveal a square pit filled with water, already heated and ready for use.

They stepped into the hot water. Steam turned the sterile environment warm and inviting as Pet leaned back against Desmodian. Soap-slicked hands immediately ran over his hair and skin. The hot water and gentle care were a baptism washing him clean.

"Don't get quiet again." Desmodian kissed his cheek. "Tell me what you want."

Pet turned to straddle Desmodian's lap.

"I want you."

His fingers danced down the scaled abdomen until they found their way between strong legs where the dual-shafted cock eagerly waited for him. "I want this." He grasped the shafts, needing two hands to handle both.

With a growl, Desmodian pulled Pet into a kiss that nearly swallowed him. The long tongue gave no quarter as it pushed into his mouth and down his throat.

Hot water sloshed as they clung together, but arousal scalded Pet more than the bath ever could as he rutted against Desmodian's stomach. The rippled muscles and smooth scales added extra stimulation that dragged a needy whimper from his occupied mouth.

Desmodian's hands groped his ass. Greedy fingers pushed inside, bringing water with them as Desmodian opened him.

The stimulation was good, but it could be so much better.

Pet pulled away and held tight to the short horns on

his lover's shoulders. They provided a perfect grip. "More."

Desmodian laughed and kissed him again, tongue filling his mouth before their lips even made contact.

They kissed until Desmodian's prodding fingers turned Pet into a writhing mess that could do nothing but beg. The echo off the bathroom walls turned his voice into a choir.

Eventually, Desmodian grew tired of their game and lifted Pet out of the tub. The panels snapped closed, sealing off the water so it could be filtered and cleaned for later use. Keeping Pet's legs wrapped around his waist, Desmodian carried him back to the bedroom and deposited him onto the sunken bed.

He stood at the edge of the bed, surveying Pet like a king deciding which country to conquer next.

The sense of Desmodian's unseen gaze mapping his body made Pet squirm. He spread his legs and arched his hips to coax the Dhen'in into joining him amongst the pillows.

His bait worked, and Desmodian descended on him, flipping him onto his stomach and kissing a path down Pet's back.

"Let's see how loud you can be."

Lips on his skin brought satisfaction. He had won. His trio couldn't resist him. Pet tucked his head and spread his legs, letting Desmodian settle between them. However, what he felt next wasn't the dual shafted cock he expected, but the hot wet slide of a tongue.

The slick muscle slithered inside him.

They had done this before, but not often. Desmodian made the most sinful sounds, sending vibrations over Pet's skin as his tongue pushed deeper.

It didn't spread him open as much as a cock, but it twisted into delicious shapes that made him cry out in pleasure.

The torment continued until Pet sobbed into the sheets. Desmodian's tongue touched all the best spots, except for that one pleasure spot that made him see stars. His own cock wept as well, desperate for release that didn't seem to be coming any time soon. He moaned and arched his back in desperation. "Please, Des. More. I need more."

The long tongue slid in and out of him. Desmodian's mouth worked over the rim of his hole as if trying to consume him.

His pleas went ignored, and he writhed like he'd been hooked to an electrical current. Strong hands pinned his hips in place, leaving him helpless to do anything but wail. Slick sounds that he could hear but not see played havoc on his imagination.

When Pet thought his pleasure could reach no greater height, that sinful tongue finally hit home. He choked on his moans, panting so hard saliva dripped from the corner of his mouth. Desmodian tormented that same spot over and over, and pleasure twisted tighter in his stomach. He trembled in his own skin and clenched down on the invading tongue.

In response, Desmodian slid it farther in so the whole length of his tongue ran along Pet's pleasure spot in one relentless motion.

Every muscle in Pet's body tensed, so close to coming.

Then Desmodian pulled out and did it again.

Pet came hard, covering the mattress below him with his orgasm. White lights danced behind his eyes, and every nerve burned. Through it all, Desmodian's tongue continued pushing the pleasure higher until Pet collapsed, spent and exhausted.

That wicked tongue finally left. He tried to turn over, but Desmodian stretched over his back and pinned his wrists to the bed.

"No. Just like this." He pushed Pet's legs farther apart with his knees and thrust inside.

Pet was overstimulated from his orgasm, but something still didn't feel right. The stretch of Desmodian's cock felt good, but not as much as he expected. "Not...not enough." Oh, Desmodian had only thrust one shaft inside him. The second one brushed along his rim, distinctly outside his body.

Desmodian taunted him, giving a hard thrust with just one shaft. "What? You want both? You'll need to beg for both." He started a rough pace, using only half of what he could give.

"I...I... Please, Des. Please." Each thrust forced out another desperate plea for more. Face buried against the mattress, he clenched internal muscles to goad Desmodian into giving him what he really wanted.

Desmodian grunted but kept the same pace, his voice gruff and hot against the back of Pet's neck. "Oh, you little whore. Trying to make me fuck you harder. That what you want? You have to ask for it."

The words couldn't escape Pet fast enough. As Desmodian continued to fuck him, his begging turned to incoherent babbling. "I want it. Need it. Need both. More. Please."

Desmodian gripped his wrists tighter and growled right in his ear. "Say you're a little slut that wants to get fucked."

He did, without hesitation.

"Say you only belong to us."

These words felt more important than the usual meaningless prattle during sex. Pet twisted to look over his shoulder. Even without visible eyes, Desmodian's stare scorched him. "I only belong to you."

"Good Pet." Desmodian pulled out. He thrust back in a moment later with both shafts.

The stretch of their combined girth burned in the best way. The dual shafts moved in opposite directions at the same time, stimulating multiple spots at once. Pet buried his keening into the mattress as Desmodian thrust hard and fast, already pushing him toward another orgasm.

One of Desmodian's hands fisted in his hair and pulled his head away from the mattress.

"Don't silence yourself."

Pet cried out as he approached his edge, but little sound escaped his convulsing throat.

Another devastating hit to his pleasure spot proved to be too much. The coiling tension in his gut snapped, and Pet tumbled into his second orgasm, sobbing at the ecstatic waves crashing over him. His body clenched hard around the dual cocks still thrusting inside.

A moment later, the Dhen'in found his own peak and buried his face against Pet's neck as he came.

They stayed locked together, trembling against one another as they rode their passions to the end. Finally, they collapsed, although Desmodian was courteous enough to fall to the side so he didn't crush Pet beneath him.

Their panting duet filled the otherwise silent room. Eventually Pet found enough strength to turn on his side and face Desmodian. The Dhen'in looked limp and comfortable, and possibly asleep. It was hard to tell.

With a careful touch, Pet traced the edge of Desmodian's mask. He had never examined it very closely before, too scared of what it might mean. Its edges perfectly followed the contours of Desmodian's face, leaving only his jaw exposed. The mask reached up to his hairline, ending in a rim of small knobby horns. Two sets of similarly colored horns extended from his temple, but only the downturned pair came from his skin. The upturned pair came from the mask, with a perfect cutout for the two to fit together. At the very corners of the mask, thin bony ridges followed the upper edges of his fin-like ears.

"You have questions."

Startled by Desmodian's words, Pet pulled away. The dread swirling in his chest brought flashbacks of a time he accidentally bumped a painting in his previous owner's home. No one had noticed, but he felt guilty for weeks.

Before he could retreat too far, Desmodian caught his hand and returned his fingers to their exploration. "It's all right. You can ask. I'm surprised you haven't asked before."

"I just… I can't tell. Is it a mask, or part of your face?" Even with permission he merely let his touch rest quietly on the bony surface.

Desmodian laughed.

They lay close enough together that the sound resonated in Pet's bones. He liked Desmodian's laugh. It cascaded like an avalanche, slowly at first but gaining strength even as it fell from its heights.

"And if I claimed it was both?"

Pet pursed his lips. "That's not an answer."

Desmodian laughed again. "It is. I wasn't born with it. But it's part of me now. There's no taking it off."

"Why?" Even as the question left his mouth, another one immediately took its place. "And how do you see? It covers your eyes."

His head bobbed with Desmodian's sigh.

"Why I have this is a long story. I'll tell you eventually, but it's not a tale for pleasant moments like this. As for how I see, it doesn't cover my eyes. I never had eyes there to begin with."

From his position, Pet could only see the underside of Desmodian's jaw, so his fingers blindly mapped the place where eyes should have been on a human.

The unspoken concern was quickly soothed as Desmodian guided his touch to other parts of the mask. "Don't worry, I'm not blind. Most species have one organ for one sense. Ears to hear, tongue to taste, etcetera. Dhen'in senses are cross wired. For example, I can smell a scent, but I can also taste it." His tongue flicked out to lick the tip of Pet's nose, making him giggle. "Instead of eyes like yours, my people have distributed sight. Every scale on my body carries its own lens. Your two eyes let you see in one direction at a time. My entire body is an eye, and I see in all directions at once."

His knee tucked between Pet's legs. Smooth scales slid against skin. What must it be like to indulge such an intimate sight of someone? Oh, even Desmodian's dual cocks had scales—might be better not to pursue that line of thought further.

The abundance of blood rushing to his face must

have given away his thoughts, because the curve of Desmodian's smile spelled pure lechery.

"Don't worry, I know how to close my eyes. Though you have nothing to be embarrassed about. It's a very pleasant view."

More questions wouldn't be worth the headache. Pet cuddled up to Desmodian's side and closed his unimpressive number of eyes.

It didn't take long for the two of them to fall asleep. The bedroom lights dimmed automatically, and with the last of his awareness, Pet pulled over a blanket to keep them warm. It had been a strange day, but at least it ended pleasantly, as had most of his days over the last year.

\*\*\*\*

Sometime while they slept, Xavis joined them in bed. Pet woke to find his head still pillowed on Desmodian's chest, with the feathery Scaacax pressed against his back. A pair of arms embraced him from either side. Forest green crisscrossed pale yellow, creating an inescapable prison of flesh.

Careful not to wake either of his sleeping companions, Pet tickled a fold of the fringe running along Desmodian's sides. Starting near the arm where the skin was the same dark green as his scales, he moved down toward the edge where it turned a bright aqua color.

Desmodian's arm tucked against his side to protect the sensitive fringe, getting Pet halfway to freedom.

Xavis, in contrast, had little feeling in his arms below the elbow. Soft yellow skin turned dark brown, with a similar texture to a bird's leg and bits of brightly colored down sticking out around the joints. Pet could easily grasp one sharp talon and move Xavis's arm out of the way, so long as it didn't disturb the rest of his body.

Freedom achieved, he escaped from the sunken bed. Stiff muscles protested, and it took him a couple tries to climb over the edge. His first objective lay within the bathroom. Unlike their mattress, which had already cleaned itself of the previous night's activities, Pet had to take care of his own cleanup. A glass wall extended across a corner of the bathroom, turning it into a small triangular shower. Pet spent more time than necessary basking under the warm water. He loved nights with his trio, but their enthusiasm left its mark.

Back in the bedroom, he dried off, then pulled out a collection of lotions and ointments. The first one, a thin opaque liquid, he applied everywhere. It finished what the hot water started, leaving his muscles loose and relaxed. Then he applied a thick yellow ointment to his bruises. The memory of Desmodian's fingers decorated his hips and wrists.

The ointment instantly dissolved any discomfort from the bruises, but it would take a few hours for the discoloration to vanish. Once clean and refreshed, he slipped into his most casual pair of clothes—an overlarge T-shirt cut off just below his chest, and a pair of clingy black shorts that could be classified as underwear. It still showed a lot of skin but lacked the flashy colors of his usual outfits.

He left his sleeping companions behind and headed for the kitchen, located in a different arm of the ship. A year ago, when he first imagined the *Vanguard*'s kitchen, he pictured a wasteland of barely functioning equipment and shelves of dehydrated rations. Instead, he found a range of state-of-the-art appliances and a huge walk-in pantry filled with fresh ingredients from all three of his trio's native cultures. That morning, he decided to make a dish for Brog called jaacht. It would be a good reward for the Ocan after being stuck at the controls all night.

Of all the needed ingredients, yabbie was the most important. The creature resembled a lobster, though it lived in trees. Pet shucked the meat from its shell and dumped it into a pan. The dark purple flesh looked weird to his human sensibilities.

Footsteps approached from behind as he added the last of the meat to the pan. He could recognize each of his trio by the sound of their walk. Brog's steps echoed since his feet struck flat and didn't rock as he moved. Xavis's talons scritch-scratched against the metal floor. Desmodian walked with a soft heel-toe metronome.

The footsteps drawing nearer matched none of these.

As casually as he could, he glanced over his shoulder. The female agent stood in the doorway, scanning the room. When she didn't find whatever she was looking for, she huffed and crossed her arms.

"It's as I feared. Décor should never be in the kitchen. There're too many ways it can be damaged. Proper owners would know better."

She came closer and reached for his pan.

On instinct he jerked away, sending hot oil spilling onto the burner. How could he have no problem telling the handsy stranger to leave him alone in the neon light of the Gravity Well, yet struggle to defend himself in the comforting light of the *Vanguard*?

He moved the pan farther away, but this only drew

her attention to his wrists.

"What is this? This wasn't here before." She grabbed his wrist and rubbed at the bruise as if it were a stain, and then she clicked in disapproval when it didn't disappear.

With her grip still strong on his wrist, she pulled him away from the stove, knocking a bag of flour to the floor. White powder tracked their footprints as she marched him toward the door.

"Ship-dwellers. Irresponsible, the lot of them."

After his pleasant night, the strange touch bothered him more than usual. He could practically feel her invading through his pores.

With the memory of his time with Desmodian firmly in his mind, Pet planted himself in the doorway. "Don't touch me. I don't like it."

She gaped at him as he ripped out of her grip and brushed past her out of the kitchen.

Neither day nor night existed out in the vacuum of space, but the *Vanguard* maintained the illusion through its lighting. The ship's early-morning settings had the lights down low with a warm yellow hue. It cast everything in a cozy glow, like dawn. He stepped through the soft shadows, bare feet silent on the metal floors, and headed to the control room. Nauzeia would eventually get over the shock of his outburst, and when she did, she would come after him.

He walked faster.

Brog's music greeted him long before the control room came into view. Most would probably mistake the heavy banging sounds for construction noise. Even now Pet wasn't sure it could be classified as music.

Inside the control room, Brog leaned back in his

chair with his feet kicked up on the controls. His hands smashed the air in time to the music, playing invisible instruments that Pet could only guess at.

"Hey, Pet." His casual greeting quickly turned tense when he saw the look on Pet's face. "What's wrong?"

Pet pressed himself against Brog. "That agent approached me in the kitchen."

A hand wrapped around his waist and another threaded through his unbrushed hair. This still left Brog two hands for the controls.

"Nausea, or the other one?"

Brog's continued mispronunciation of the agent's name took the edge off Pet's agitation. "Nausea. I told her not to touch me. Don't know if she'll listen."

"Oh, she'll listen. One way or another. They'll both listen."

Taking it from a shelf near the control chair, Brog returned Pet's music box.

It couldn't be heard over Brog's music, but Pet turned the key just to see the galaxy spin. "Why did you choose me?"

That wasn't the question he expected to ask. He hadn't even known the question existed in his head until his mouth gave it life. However, once he did, he wanted an answer.

"Back at that Vunqril's place?"

The Ocan stared at him, but Pet continued to watch his mechanical galaxy. "My previous owner had a dozen décor, but you approached me. I laughed at you, but that doesn't seem like a good reason. Did you just meet me by chance? Could I have been anyone?"

The music box slowed, though Brog's own music

kept playing while he considered the question. "No one in that place even looked at us. You did. When you met my eye, I knew you were interested. Yes, I ran into you again by chance, and maybe I was a bit eager. But it had to be you. No one else wanted us like you did."

The galaxy in his hands stopped, but the one out the window kept spinning. Even without their attention, the ship stayed its course, rushing forward without heed for the obstacles in its way.

Sometimes Pet felt like the ship, always two seconds away from crashing without someone's help. Other days he felt like the music box, just a fake galaxy that needed someone else's hand to come alive. He hadn't been awake long enough to decide if it would be an almost-crashing day, or a barely moving day.

"You could have left me there. It would've been easier, but you chose to keep me. Everywhere we stop, people are always interested in you. You never keep them, but you kept me."

Brog sighed with enough force to shift Pet's entire body where he lay against the Ocan's chest. "I'm not the one you should be askin' this kind 'a stuff. I'm not the deepest thinker. You should ask Xavis or Des. They're better at emotions and shit."

"I already know their answers. Xavis kept me because I needed to be kept. Desmodian kept me because I belonged here. I want to know your answer."

For a moment it looked like Brog's eyes glowed with their own internal light. They showed no whites. The eye socket covered right up to the iris, leaving only the orange visible. He also never blinked. A transparent lid kept the eye protected.

Many people struggled to meet Brog's gaze, but

Pet found it comforting. When Brog looked at him, the Ocan never looked away, not even to blink.

"I'll admit, when I first approached you, I was just lookin' for a fun distraction while stuck planetside. Afterward, I wouldn't 'a thought about keepin' you, but you fought for us. You knew you'd get hurt, but you still protected us. At least for me, that's why I kept you. And I have no interest in keepin' anyone else we come across, 'cause they're also fun, but they wouldn't fight for us. Not like you did, without any concern for your own sacrifice. The only people I've ever met willin' to do that are my mates."

There was that word again. Mate. Sometimes the term slipped out of his trio when talking about each other, especially in emotionally charged situations. It sounded closer than friends or brothers. Not even married couples shared the way his trio did.

Brog leaned farther back in his chair, bringing Pet with him. "To be honest, we've needed a fourth for a while. I love those two idiots, but the physical stuff just don't work between us. We've tried bringin' other people in, but it's never lasted. Wasn't sure you'd work, either, but now that you have, not givin' that up for nothin'."

There was a lot to unpack in Brog's declaration. Pet had never been good at reading between the lines, partly because he lacked reading skills in general. Better to focus on the part of Brog's admission that mattered most.

"I'm your fourth?" He liked the sound of that title. It felt more permanent than décor.

Two sets of shoulders shrugged. "Yeah, 'cause, like three is great, but four is better. Right, Des?"

Off to the side, Desmodian leaned against the doorframe, a bowl in one hand and his tail curling around his leg.

"Having a fourth keeps us balanced. Take a break, Brog. Breakfast is ready."

A flick of a switch and the three control chairs swapped places along their tracks. Brog's chair carried them away as Desmodian's chair took their place at the main console. Unlike Brog's chair, which had been reinforced to support the Ocan's size, Desmodian's chair had low armrests to accommodate his side fringe. The backrest was held aloft by curving support poles looping over the top to leave an open space for his tail.

With a pat to Pet's head as he passed, Desmodian took command of the ship. Like Brog, he also kicked up his feet on the console while balancing a bowl of half-eaten jaacht in one hand.

"By the way, the agents will be joining you for breakfast. Make sure they mind their manners."

"Oh, they'll be mindin' somethin'." Brog led Pet from the control room.

The ship's lighting adjusted as early morning aged into true morning. The halls grew brighter, but still not the equivalent of full daylight. Most of the *Vanguard*'s main body consisted of a large cargo bay intersected with railed catwalks. Personal spaces, like the bedroom and kitchen, resided along one of four arms branching from the center sphere. It was important to know what rooms resided in which arm. His first weeks on the ship, Pet often reached the end of one arm, only to realize he had chosen wrong. Then he had to march all the way back.

A very awkward atmosphere met them in the

kitchen.

Xavis sat at the table, focused on his food as he ignored the two agents a few feet away. As usual, he disregarded utensils and ate directly with his hands.

The agents watched him out of the corner of their eyes, struggling to hide their disgust, with empty bowls in front of them.

Pet considered ignoring their expectations of being served, but they were at least trying to be polite. Once Brog descended on the food, there would be nothing left.

On his way to the seat nearest Xavis, he grabbed the agents' bowls. Brog took the seat between him and the agents, so Pet filled the dishes from the pot, then he slid the bowls back to the agents across the table.

Their shock over his uncouth serving style nearly let the bowls slide right over the edge. It would have been hilarious. Yet they reacted just quick enough to avoid a mess. Though not everything stayed in the bowls.

Once everyone had a serving, Brog pulled the whole pot of jaacht to himself and ate directly from it with the serving spoon.

Shared meals would forever be awkward when one of them couldn't eat. Even when Xavis passed him a bowl of nutriment, it wasn't the same as food. Bright colors made the thin mush look more appealing, but it had no smell. Plus, with only one flavor at a time, it lacked the nuanced enjoyment people got out of real food.

Today it was the bright flavor of citrus.

Beside him, Xavis casually licked his talons clean.

They clacked against each other, adding extra

punctuation to his words when he spoke. "How much longer 'til we're out of the Penumbra Belt?"

Brog's version of table manners meant speaking around a mouth full of food. It gave everyone, especially the agents, a good view of his teeth. "At the rate we're goin', another two days. Assumin' we don't run into any problems."

Simultaneously, Brog and Xavis both traced a circle on the tabletop with one finger, then slammed their fist in the middle to ward off the will of the universe. No ship-dweller worth the bolts of their ship would underestimate the universe's ability to turn lethal on a whim.

"If I may." Nauzeia set down her spoon despite barely touching her meal. Apparently Ocan food didn't appeal to Yce. "Where exactly are we going? We bustled off so quick, we never got to ask what this job of yours entails."

Brog and Xavis looked to each other, and Brog pulled out a single die from one of his many pockets. Each called a number and Brog tossed it on the table.

It landed on five, closer to Xavis's six than Brog's two.

Brog grumbled as he put the die away. "We're lookin' for a lost colony ship. The CS *Trailblazer* set out from Oculi 5 to build a new colony out in the Stardust, but it disappeared. No one can find it. No signal. Nothin'. That's what we've been hired for."

At the mention of the Stardust, Irih's red skin dulled a few shades. "And do you have a plan to find it?"

Nauzeia looked no better than her partner. Traveling to space's version of a third-world country visibly unnerved the pair.

Pet pitied them. His first time traveling so far had come with the assurance that his trio would take care of him. These agents, who had likely spent their lives in atmosphere-controlled rooms studying fragile works of art behind glass, had no one's protection but their own.

Four shoulders shrugged, and Brog returned to his meal. "The Oculi system neighbors the Partition system, so the *Trailblazer* had to take a longer route to avoid the warzone. Made it harder to track, but we managed as far as the Penumbra Belt. Heard it was headin' from there toward the Iota Cloud. We'll try to track it from there."

The male agent's face dropped, as much as a face with its nose pinched higher than its eyes could drop. "Wait, but we're not going into the Iota Cloud, right? It's dangerous even for large ships to cross. For a smaller ship like this, it's suicide."

Brog's fist hit the table and sent the dishware rattling. "What part of 'we fly where no one else does' did you not understand?"

"But…but…"

Xavis pulled Pet away from the encroaching argument into his own chair. Rough legs straddled either side of Pet's hips, and taloned feet tangled with his.

This not only distanced Pet from the conflict but put Xavis in the perfect position to groom Pet's unbrushed hair. It had grown out over the year and now tickled the back of his neck.

The male agent made the wise choice to give up arguing with an Ocan, but he made the very unwise choice to challenge Pet instead. "I thought you didn't like to be touched?"

Despite it being a question, the agent apparently didn't expect a response, for he startled at the sound of Pet's voice.

"I don't like to be touched by other people."

"And we're going to respect that." Nauzeia gave her partner a pointed look. "If two-six-eight-nine doesn't want to be touched, it's no hardship to comply."

Xavis leaned in so only Pet could hear him. "Well, as long as it's no hardship."

Pet laughed but schooled his expression back to neutral when Nauzeia tracked their interaction.

"But I must question your decision to take this patchwork ship into the Iota Cloud. Poachers fly ships made from scavenged parts because they have to. You do it by choice. Yet your décor has already been bruised after one day of safe flying. That does not bode well for how it will fare in a dangerous place like the Iota Cloud."

Finishing his meal, Brog pushed the empty pot away and wiped his mouth with the back of one hand. "We ain't no damn poachers. This ship is safe. It's made from different parts 'cause no existin' ship had everythin' we needed. The *Vanguard* is the safest place for Pet."

Whatever Nauzeia meant to say was cut off by her colleague.

"Pet? That's what you call it?"

Brog pounded the table again. "Better than callin' him by a damn number. There's somethin' wrong with people that can call another livin' person 'it'. Like he's no better than the chair you're sittin' on."

The look that flashed over Nauzeia's face made Pet

nervous. That kind of creased expression couldn't mean anything good.

She carefully folded her hands on the table as if attending a religious ceremony and she was about to start praying. "So, you admit you consider décor a living person. Yet you also claim ownership of…him. That is slavery, and illegal."

At his back Xavis grew tense and arms wrapped tighter around his shoulders. "There's no law against giving him a name, or what pronoun to use. We aren't slavers, but we can't just ignore the mind that comes with the body."

Although Pet agreed with everything Xavis said, he was reluctant to say so out loud when Nauzeia stood up so quickly her chair tipped and crashed to the floor.

"Décor have the opinions you train them to express. Proper owners know it is best to keep them blank slates. To encourage décor to have opinions, only to turn around and claim ownership of them, is cruel."

Her partner stood and placed a hand on her shoulder. "I think we've seen enough here, Nauzeia. They don't understand how to care for décor. Added to the fact that their job routinely drags them out to dangerous parts of space, it's obvious this is no environment for décor. We need to call the authorities and remove two-six-eight-nine before it's damaged beyond repair."

"No, you can't." Pet meant to shut the conversation down, but he only gave the agents more confidence.

Nauzeia gestured toward Pet like a tour guide at a museum. "See. It's upset. This wouldn't happen if you cared for it properly."

Brog reminded everyone that he was still the tallest

in the room when he stood and stared down the agents. "You're the ones upsettin' him. You're either too blind or too stupid to realize he doesn't want to be sold to someone else."

The challenge made Nauzeia fall silent, while Irih grew louder.

"It hates being resold because you've made it think that way. This is what happens when décor are encouraged to have opinions. It makes being resold that much harder for them."

Brog puffed up like he was about to jump across the table. "You're assumin' he's goin' to be resold."

"Of course it is. After what we've seen here, we can't leave it with you. That décor needs to be taken to auction and have its mind wiped clean of you. Then it can be sold to a real owner."

Out of everything Irih said, the threat of losing all memory of his trio scared Pet more than anything.

Brog didn't lash out like Pet expected. Instead, he nodded Xavis toward the door.

Taking the cue, Xavis pulled Pet out of the room. This left Brog alone with the agents.

Pet couldn't call it an improvement. "What's going on? Why are we leaving?"

The door to the kitchen slammed shut, though who did the slamming remained unclear.

Pet tried to go back and ensure Brog was okay, but Xavis's grip on his arm kept him walking the other direction.

The smile he gave Pet lacked its usual easy comfort. "Don't worry. Brog's just going to have a few words with our guests."

## Chapter Eight

*Then*

The only thing more shocking to 2689 than his first night of intimacy was the morning after. A nest of limbs surrounded him on all sides.

When they finished, the trio had fallen asleep piled together on the makeshift bed. It explained why they put so many mattresses on the floor. Even Owner's lavish guest beds wouldn't have held them all.

They resembled puppies snuggled together in a basket. Not something 2689 would ever tell them. As part of the pile, he could only move his head enough to look at the nearby clock. His fellow décor had woken up hours ago and already received their outfits and postings for the day. If they hadn't noticed him missing last night, they would now.

2689 could detangle himself from the pile, seek out Curator and try to make his case. Owner had invited their guests to make themselves at home. Surely, he couldn't be blamed for attending to them.

Or he could forget about leaving, put Curator, Owner, and his fellow décor out of his mind, and stay put. That seemed like the more comfortable option. Plus, if he were already in trouble, staying longer wouldn't make it any worse.

An arm around his waist pulled him back against a

hard body. Thick dark-brown skin meant Xavis was behind him kissing his neck. Blue-gray in front of him meant Brog currently acted as 2689's pillow. The feel of smooth scales against his legs put the Dhen'in near the bottom of the mattress.

Xavis's kissing turned to muttering against his skin.

"This would be a great way to start the morning, but there's work to do. Maybe later." With one last squeeze to 2689's ass, Xavis pulled away from the group.

Cool morning air rushed into the void he left and 2689 shivered.

Desmodian propped himself up on an elbow. "Hold on, Xavis. You're testing the shields this morning, right?"

2689 sniggered. The half-awake Dhen'in's mane of indigo hair stuck out in every direction as if he had been electrocuted.

"Yeah." Xavis pulled on shorts which looked to have seen the wrong end of his talons many times. "I have an idea for a shield against electronegative pulse weapons. It'll be a one-off, but a shield that works once is better than no shield at all."

One of Desmodian's hands fought to tame his wild bedhead while the other blearily reached for his clothes. "Give me a minute. I'll come with you."

"You may as well wake up the lazy ass. Then we can replace the outer panels too."

Halfway out of the bed, Desmodian kicked Brog's foot.

2689 flailed within the blue-gray web as Brog wrapped more arms around him and rolled them both over to the other side without waking.

"Hey, get up." Desmodian twisted one of the thick fins on the back of Brog's head.

With a pained howl, Brog sat up faster than a spring-loaded piston, still clutching 2689 like a child's toy. "What the hell, Des?"

2689 hesitantly tapped his arm.

"What?" Brog looked down, confused. "Oh, sorry." He gently placed 2689 back on the mattress and stood, stretching all four arms over his head and showing off long lines of muscle.

"Glad you could join us, Brog." Xavis waited by the door for his companions to finish dressing.

Brog responded to the teasing with a rude gesture. "Fuck off, early bird."

It was 2689's first morning without Curator's orders. He sat cross-legged on the bed, a ship adrift among the sea of used bedding. The trio hadn't dismissed him to leave nor had they invited him to stay.

In fact, as they crowded near the door, it looked like they had completely forgotten him.

That hurt more than it should. Someday he would forget the ship-dwellers. However, if they could at least remember him, then the previous night wouldn't be a complete waste.

Instead, he sat alone on the mattress. Three backs turned toward him, and he sank farther into the mattress. Décor forgot and were forgotten. He couldn't wish for different.

Yet, as he planned out his apologies to Curator, purple eyes found him again.

Xavis hesitated at the door. "What about him? It feels weird to just leave him here."

Brog and Desmodian also looked back, and 2689 lost the thread of his hypothetical groveling. Maybe he wasn't forgotten after all.

"Why?" Brog asked. "We had fun last night. Now it's time to go. No reason to make it more complicated than that."

Xavis's feathers fluffed. "Brog, I consider you a mate, but shut up. You may be a master of one-night stands, but not all of us have your wealth of experience."

Tension hung between the scowling Ocan and the ruffled Scaacax.

2689 drew his knees to his chest to make himself as small as possible. He hadn't known the trio long, but discord didn't seem normal for them. As much as he wanted to be remembered, he didn't want it at the expense of a relationship much more important than their one night together.

Desmodian laid a hand on either of their shoulders. A current passed through them like an electrical circuit being completed.

Nothing visibly changed, but an echo of whatever passed between them danced over 2689's skin as well. It lasted only a moment before the tension popped like an overinflated bubble.

"Why don't we just ask him?" Desmodian faced 2689. "Do you want to come with us, or do you need to leave?"

2689's days started with orders, never questions. Did that mean they would change their actions based on his answer? The trio barely listened to Owner, the person who held ultimate authority in 2689's life. Yet they gave 2689 authority over them. Even if it was only this one decision, the shift in power left him lightheaded. "I...I want to come with you. If I can."

No matter what they were doing, it had to be more appealing than facing Curator. She might order him back into deprivation since he skipped out the night before. Going with the trio could at least put that off for a while.

He waited to be told "no" but was instead prompted to get dressed and join them. 2689 scrambled for his clothes. A few strategically placed knots held the white silk together, and he didn't bother with the headdress. Not only were some of the crystals broken but also it was heavy. Owner would be horrified at the sight of him if they happened to cross paths, but it was all 2689 had to wear until he returned to the other décor. Twelve cots waiting in a perfect line held little appeal after a night spent in such a huge crowded bed.

Out in the hallway, they found the usual bustle of morning activity. Staff averted their eyes so quickly from the trio 2689 doubted anyone noticed him. He had worried about being seen with their guests, but at this rate, it wouldn't be an issue.

Xavis gave him an odd look. "Why're you back there?"

2689 glanced behind, but the hallway showed no one else.

"Why are you walking behind us?"

"It's..." 2689 trailed off, measuring the space between himself and the trio. He shrugged, having no answer to give. It was where décor always walked, so it was where he always walked.

Brog pulled him forward. "It's weird. Stop it."

Being positioned at the middle of the group

immediately made 2689 feel uncomfortable. Décor walked single file in order of item number. 2689 never had to question where to stand because he always came between 2397 and 3155.

The trio didn't stick to any order. They stood where they wanted, walked where they wanted, and often shifted places with each other as they moved.

How did they decide who stood where or who walked in front of who? Even with Brog holding his wrist, he felt lost, like a mouse trying desperately to swim in the middle of the ocean.

Desmodian noticed first and came to his rescue, twisting Brog's head fin and slapping his hand away. "You look like you're kidnapping him. Don't drag him around. Show some gentility."

Brog yanked Desmodian's tail in turn, which earned him a swipe from its spines.

Xavis sounded like a hissing snake that sprung a leak when he laughed. "Don't use big words, Des. Brog doesn't know what they mean."

Rather than get offended, Brog puffed with pride. "Damn straight."

The spiny tail swiped at Brog again, and Desmodian huffed when it missed. "Remind me again why I put up with you."

The response came from both Brog and Xavis, in unison. " 'Cause we're the only ones who could put up with you."

Desmodian sighed again, though there was a smile on his face. He offered 2689 his elbow the same way previous guests to the estate would escort their dates. "Don't let my mates scare you. We're not completely uncivilized."

Brog amended Desmodian's claim. "Just mostly uncivilized."

Then Xavis amended Brog's amendment. "Particularly around people we don't like."

Listening to the trio was like standing at the center of an echo chamber with a single conversation coming at him from three different directions at once. After only a day of knowing them, 2689 had already given up trying to keep track of who was talking. The three voices were a single unit.

The cutout patches along Desmodian's clothes resided only on outer areas.

When 2689 placed his hand in the crook of the offered elbow, his fingers met cloth rather than scales. The shirt had an unusual weave, with fibers going in seemingly random directions instead of straight across. He absently traced their edges, looking for a pattern while at the same time lengthening his stride to keep up with Desmodian's taller legs.

The staff continued avoiding them until the group reached a set of outer doors where they were stopped by the guards.

"You'll have to leave Mister Stiril's property where it belongs." Estate guards rarely interfered with guests, but even they knew décor never went outside.

Under the guard's scrutiny, 2689 tried to pull away, but Desmodian gripped his hand and kept it trapped within his elbow.

"We're not taking him off the grounds. Just to our ship docked at the landing pad."

The guards didn't budge. "Décor don't go outside."

Feathers brushed 2689's arms as Xavis bristled.

"Wait, like…ever?"

The guards' silent frowns were answer enough, and none of the trio looked happy.

The familiar clicking of Curator's heels announced her arrival. A Vunqril's feet always made sounds due to the stiletto shape, yet her steps carried more impact than others.

Suspicion buzzed among the décor, claiming she filed her heels to make her legs look longer.

She rounded the corner and the clicking grew louder. "What's going on?" A glance between the trio, the guards, and 2689 told her everything she needed to know, and her face twisted into a frightening grimace.

Even the guards looked cowed. "These guests wanted to take the décor outside."

Desmodian tried his explanation again. "We're just going to our ship and thought he would enjoy coming along."

"Why?"

The question was a simple one, but 2689 already knew the trio would never be able to answer in a way that made sense to Curator, or anyone else within the estate.

Desmodian must have realized this as well because he didn't even try. "Why not?" He tipped his head so that, if he had visible eyes, he would be looking down at her. "We've enjoyed his company so far and would continue to do so while completing the work you've hired us to do."

Curator's grimace turned into a disgusted sneer. "Yes, I've heard how much you enjoyed Mister Stiril's décor. He's glad to provide for all his guests' needs. But the décor can't go outside. It could get damaged or sullied."

The "more than it already is" went unsaid, but 2689 heard it. Did the trio know how much trouble he could get in for their actions? Based on their nonchalance, probably not.

Curator glanced at him, briefly, and the curl of her lip amended his thoughts. He was already in trouble. The smart thing to do would be to excuse himself from their guests, return to décor quarters, and avoid the trio until they left.

Except, he didn't want to. He would likely never meet people like them again and wanted to soak up as much of them as he could. Not just sex but conversation, emotions, and even learning trivial things like how to walk within a group.

Desmodian's smile might have seemed charming to any other audience, but landowners would never respect him enough to see him as anything other than rude.

"He won't really be outside. He'll be in the *Vanguard*. Getting our ship ready for the kind of voyage your boss wants is tedious work. Good company can make it go faster. Without it, who knows how long preparation could take."

Violent waves of anger rolled off Curator. She didn't like being given orders by ship-dwellers, not even orders phrased in such a disarming way. The tension boiled until it snapped, but she didn't respond the way 2689 expected.

"Fine. If having it with you means you'll be able to leave sooner, then by all means. Do whatever you want."

Brog elbowed Xavis twice. "Whatever we want? That's a dangerous promise."

"Visiting our ship is enough for now." Desmodian turned expectantly to the guards.

They stood steadfast in front of the door. "But ma'am, we can't let ship-dwellers take décor on their ship. What if they steal it?"

However, Curator was already walking away. A strike of her heel on the floor marked each word she tossed over her shoulder. "Don't worry. There's a magnetic lock on the landing pad. They won't be going anywhere without our permission."

Finally, the doors opened, and 2689 crossed the threshold for the first time in years.

It wasn't a far walk from the estate to the landing pad, but 2689 reveled in every inch. A breeze not generated by air-conditioning blew against his skin. Rays of sunlight struck his face, fading between warm and cool every time a cloud passed. The flowers of the garden let off a spicy scent that hung heavy in the humid morning. The cloying smell clogged his nose, but it was a refreshing change from the dry, conditioned air that surrounded him every day inside.

Yet, out of everything, it was the sky that drew his eyes. It felt so much larger when not viewed through a window with a ceiling above. Ceilings had a solidity that kept everything inside. The sky had no limitations.

"Hey, Des." Brog leaned close and whispered to Desmodian in a way that stirred 2689's notice. "A magnetic lock could be a problem. We don't do so hot with magnets."

"If Mister Stiril wants his goods delivered, then he must let us leave. He tries to hide it, but he's desperate, and there's no one else he can hire."

Rows of cultivated flowers lined either side of the

gravel path. Gardeners and landscapers looked up from their work, but no one stopped them. Compared to the rest of the staff, the groundskeepers didn't sneer or look away when the trio passed.

The trio, in turn, were happy to ignore them.

This changed, however, when one worker shot them a sour look and muttered something to another worker nearby. The two snickered under their breath, as if doing so quietly could disguise their actions.

2689 didn't need to hear what they said to know it was derogatory. He could see it in the trio's faces.

When they passed, Xavis stopped, ignored the bundle of nicely pruned flowers available on the ground, and tore a handful off the bush. His rough skin protected him from the thorns, but the workers had to jump back to avoid injury. As he walked away, Xavis plucked the blossoms bare, leaving a mess of petals along the path.

Just before it hit the ground, 2689 caught one of the petals. "Why did you do that? It was the same in the dining hall. You know they won't like it, but you make a mess anyway."

Xavis cast the empty twigs aside. "Because they won't like it."

The bare thorns crunched under Brog's boot. "And angerin' people we don't like is fun."

"More importantly, it leaves a message." Desmodian gave 2689's hand a squeeze, assuring him that Brog and Xavis spoke half in jest. "In this universe, landowners hold most of the power. Ship-dwellers are forced to accept the will of landowners, fair or not. We're in a unique position to remind them we're not doormats."

Doormat was an odd term to use. It was an object, like décor, though not as pretty. He wondered whether the trio protested the idea of being considered objects or being considered less beautiful than other objects. Neither option seemed right.

2689 couldn't remember if the estate even had a doormat. He never walked through the front entrance. However, the staff kitchen had an old rug outside the door. 2689 saw it on the rare occasion he passed through the kitchen at the same time someone stepped outside. It was a dusty, threadbare old thing no one bothered to replace. Years of stomping feet had pounded it flat until it almost merged with the dirt.

He couldn't imagine any of the trio being used in such a way. They would never lie down as people wore them into the ground.

However, he realized with a growing horror, décor would do exactly that. If Owner ordered his décor to lie in front of the door and let every passing person step on them, they would do it. Some would be more enthusiastic about it than others, but all would comply.

2689 decided right then and there he didn't want to be a doormat either.

As big as the *Vanguard* looked from the estate's windows, it looked even bigger from the landing pad. Four triangular legs stretched along the ground like miniature mountain ranges, each made from different materials. 2689 ran a hand over the outer hull. What looked like one solid surface turned out to be small panels layered like roof shingles. It also had a strange texture that felt nothing like metal.

"What is this?"

Next to him Desmodian rapped his knuckles

against the hull so 2689 could hear the difference in the sound. "The ship is coated in a special type of plastic. It blocks space radiation, so we don't die from cancer. All ships that spend time in deep space have something like it."

The *Vanguard*'s body rested on its landing gear, hovering a few feet off the ground.

By the time 2689 and Desmodian reached the main hatch, Brog had already pulled down a ladder. It looked new compared to the rest of the ship, so it obviously didn't get much use, which meant they brought it out only for 2689's convenience.

Xavis helped him up the ladder. "Careful when you enter. Artificial gravity is on. It'll feel like falling sideways."

An entire dissertation's worth of warnings wouldn't have prepared 2689. He climbed the ladder and stepped through the hatch, only to be immediately pulled to the side. It felt like the wall sucked him in. No, he wasn't lying against a wall. He was on the floor. A network of catwalks crossed a large open chamber. The edge of one catwalk rested only inches from his face, beyond which was a long fall to the bottom. Or was it the side? The change in gravitational direction made everything very confusing.

"It's never easy the first time." Desmodian hoisted himself through the hatch and swung his legs to catch himself on the floor ninety degrees from where he started.

As Desmodian helped 2689 off the floor, the other two joined them inside.

Xavis perched on the catwalk's railing like a bird on a twig. "I'm going to the engine room. See if I can divert more power to the shields. They'll need everything we got if we're hit by an electronegative pulse weapon, and I'm not eager to stall out in the middle of a warzone."

He jumped off the railing and opened his wings to glide into the abyss below.

2689 ran to the edge of the catwalk, but Xavis had already disappeared. Without wings, Desmodian had to use a ladder, which looked much less fun.

"I need to check that hitch in the venting we noticed earlier. Brog, Xavis will need someone to watch the main systems while he runs engine checks."

Brog saluted as Desmodian also descended out of sight. "Aye-aye. Come with me, Pet. You'll enjoy the view."

2689 kept one hand on the guardrail as he followed Brog along the catwalk to the main control room. It held more screens, buttons, and blinking lights than he had ever seen in one place, but none of it compared to the observation windows. With the *Vanguard* sitting on its tail end, its front faced directly into the sky. The windows showed no horizon. Just an endless expanse of orange, as if the ship couldn't wait to take flight.

The glass felt cool against his hands and too thin. "What's it like, flying through space?"

He watched Brog in the window's reflection, tapping at something on a control panel.

"Mostly lots 'a the same. Occasional excitement between big stretches 'a nothin'. You've been on a ship before when they brought you here from Earth. Imagine that but for longer periods 'a time."

2689 shook his head. "I was sold at an auction house on this planet."

Any landowner or décor would have understood, but through the reflection in the window, he saw no sign of understanding from Brog. "Décor have their memories wiped before we're sold. I was brought here on a ship, but I don't remember it."

The sound of tapping stopped, and Brog gave him his full attention. "Wait. You mean you don't remember anythin'?"

"I remember my time here. But nothing before the auction house."

"Why?"

The word hung in the air, echoing off the many screens. 2689 turned his back to the window. The vastness of the open sky felt so large compared to his little life. What had been awe-inspiring at first now looked overwhelming.

"It's done to make us blank canvases for our owners and keep us as close to inanimate objects as possible. That's the way of décor. When I'm resold, I'll be made blank again, like my time here never happened."

"That's…" Whatever Brog meant to say faded into nothing.

Until two days ago, 2689 hadn't given it much thought. It only mattered now that he had memories worth keeping. Nothing changed except to introduce him to the emotion called regret.

The feel of a hand against his cheek startled him. Despite the alien's size, he hadn't heard Brog approach.

"They can't do that."

2689 didn't want sympathy and removed the hand from his face. "Yes, they can. I signed up for this. To become décor, we have to willingly sign away our rights as living beings."

Brog refused to be moved and clung to 2689's wrist. "But if you can't remember anythin' before your auction, how do you know you agreed? They could be lyin'."

The last few days had given 2689 a lot of new thoughts. This was an unwanted addition. "I agreed. I must have. I don't want to think differently."

"Sounds to me like you haven't been able to think much at all."

2689 couldn't deny the accusation. The more he thought, the more he realized how little he thought before. It hadn't been a happy existence, but neither had it been unhappy. It had been nothing at all.

Purple light pulsed through the floor, interrupting their conversation to zap 2689's feet. He danced from foot to foot, trying to escape the stinging sensation, but there was nowhere to go. It covered the entire floor.

With one arm, Brog picked him up and slung him over his shoulder. He stomped through the hazardous light unharmed, muttering curses under his breath and some over his breath. At the side of the room, he slammed a fist on the ship's intercom.

"Xavis, what the hell?"

"Sorry." Xavis's voice sounded muffled as if he were far away from the speaker. "Tried something new with the engine. Didn't work, but it won't affect you."

"That would be great if we were the only ones on the ship."

The intercom crackled with silence. When Xavis responded, he sounded closer to the speaker this time.

"Oh, shit. Is he all right?"

"I'm carryin' him right now, but he gets zapped if

he touches any part of the ship."

"Hmmmmm." Xavis's thoughtful hum sounded like a badly tuned instrument. "I'll fix it, but it'll take a few minutes."

"Well hurry up. I'm not carryin' him around all day like a damn purse."

"Oh, like it's such a hardship. Poor Brog, forced to keep his hands on the pretty Pet."

"Fuck off."

"Love you too."

The intercom shut off with a disproportionately soft click, and Brog shifted 2689 to cradle him more comfortably in two arms.

They left the room, but 2689 didn't ask where they were going as he clung to Brog's neck. The Ocan's low head and tall double shoulders meant he had almost no neck to speak of. Whenever Brog moved too fast, 2689 feared pitching over his back.

"What is Xavis doing?" He had never heard of a malfunction that electrified some passengers on a ship and not others.

"Hell if I know. That technical stuff is Xavis's area. This kind 'a thing happens a lot. He made the ship's systems from scratch. Mostly through trial and error, emphasis on error. We've never flown through the Partition system before, so he's tryin' to make sure we can withstand gettin' caught in the crossfire."

"Because they're at war?" Repeating facts he knew was better than focusing on the long drop below the catwalk Brog crossed. Walking over them himself had been intimidating enough. Being carried across was much scarier.

"They are. Have been for a long time." Keeping

two arms around 2689, Brog used his other two to climb down a ladder from the catwalk to the bottom of the ship.

2689 tucked his head against Brog's nonexistent neck and tried to ignore how much empty air lay below them. "Why? I know Earth had war. They say it was part of the reason our planet died. Shouldn't that warn other planets not to do it?"

He felt more than heard Brog's sigh.

"War ain't that simple. There's lots 'a reasons for it. For the Partition system, it's because the two habitable planets are circumbinary."

That was a new word. Ugh. He hated having to ask for a definition.

"Means the two planets orbit each other. There's one moon that orbits both, and the two planets war over who owns the moon since it would add a significant amount of livable space."

Desmodian's voice echoed up from the bottom of the ladder. "They're in a constant cycle. They fight over space until enough people die that space isn't a problem anymore. Then after a couple generations, the population increases and they're back to fighting."

2689 dared to look up from his hiding spot against Brog's neck. Desmodian's presence below the ladder didn't lessen the distance to the floor, but now someone could catch him if he fell.

Brog finally reached the bottom and followed Desmodian into the main cargo hold. The pair discussed how to ensure the organic materials didn't spoil before they reached their destination.

2689 couldn't follow the conversation with his head full of war. A lull in their conversation provided him an opportunity to exercise his thoughts. "No one stops the Partition system from fighting?"

Desmodian shook his head as he opened a sealed door to deeper parts of the cargo hold.

A cold breeze rushed from the opening, bringing with it the sharp smell of frozen metal.

"If the intergalactic government cared about people, they would, but war is too profitable to stop. A lot of planets use the Partition system's consistent warring to supplement their economy. The Chandra system sells them metal, and the Oculi system provides military vehicles and transport. Your Owner as well. Normally Mister Stiril would have an Oculi ship transport his goods, but recent conflict has grown too hot even for them. That leaves him stuck with us."

As Brog bent to inspect the frosted pipes, he had to switch his hold on 2689, "accidentally" grabbing his ass in the process. "Serves the bastard right. Relyin' on someone else's war to make money is not good business strategy. Des, we haven't used these in a while. We'll hafta defrost 'em first."

Normally 2689 was skilled at keeping his thoughts to himself, but Brog's wandering hands distracted him. "You also profit off war."

Only after he spoke did he remember that insulting the people keeping him safe wasn't a smart idea. His hands trembled against Brog's shoulders, waiting for the Ocan to abandon him in anger.

The pair paused their inspection of the pipes, sharing a look 2689 had no hope of interpreting. However, instead of dropping him, Brog shrugged both sets of shoulders and went back to adjusting valves.

"Not our problem."

Metal protested as Desmodian opened a hidden panel to inspect the insulation inside the wall. "If they can't figure out how to share the moon, they deserve to kill themselves fighting over it. We'll take care of ourselves and leave them to their conflict. Other people's issues aren't our responsibility."

Their conversation returned to pipes, cargo, and the shelf life of food rations, but 2689 couldn't move on so easily. Their comment was a blunt reminder that, for as well as they treated him, he wasn't their responsibility either. It was easy to forget he was only a momentary entertainment for them.

Talons scratched against metal when Xavis landed in the cargo hold. "Why wasn't I invited to the party?" His feathers barely made a sound against the air as he folded them against his back.

"The refrigerated room is frosting over, but we can't get it to stop." Desmodian adjusted valves with increasing frustration when they had no effect.

"Let me take a look." Xavis brushed past, only to stop and turn toward 2689. "Oh, Brog, you can put him down now. I fixed the problem."

" 'Bout time." Brog set 2689 back on his feet.

Without the advantage of Brog's height, the world looked much bigger. Except for Xavis, who looked smaller as he nervously withdrew his wings as far as they would go.

"Sorry about that, Pet. I hope you weren't hurt."

He was fine, and he said so. Yet, at the same time, his feet shuffled against the memory of pain lancing up through his soles into his body.

Purple eyes tracked the movement as Xavis held something out to him. "It's not much, but consider it my apology."

2689 took the object with numb hands. It was his first gift. For all the fancy clothes and jewelry he wore every day, he owned nothing.

The trio were deep in their inspection of the pipes before 2689 remembered to look at what he had been given. A circular pendant sat atop its coiled chain in his palm. It had a simple design with a purple stone at the center. When he rubbed a thumb over the stone, it glowed just like Xavis's eyes.

A frustrated sigh caught his attention.

Xavis hit his fist against the wall next to the pipes, feathers fluffed in agitation. "Search the cargo hold next door. Maybe there's a leak over there affecting this one."

Brog did just that.

2689 barely noticed him leave. The words 'search the cargo' caught on something in his memory. He had heard those words recently. Décor didn't need to recall things often. An occasional order carried over more than one day, but otherwise they had no use for retaining information. It took him a few minutes to entice his memory into cooperating.

Just before the trio showed up, Owner had been talking with Assistant about the shipment. Owner didn't want the trio searching the cargo. It hadn't mattered then, but now it seemed suspicious and dangerous. If the cargo contained something bad, the trio transporting it could get into trouble.

The pendant glowed again. Pain in his hand made him look down in confusion. Oh, he had been gripping it so tight the edges pressed lines into his palm. He didn't want the trio to get in trouble, but telling the trio his suspicions about the cargo could get Owner in trouble if he hid something bad.

2689 added another unpleasant addition to the list of new things he understood.

The feeling of confliction.

## Chapter Nine

*Now*

Pet followed Xavis away from the conflict in the kitchen. Anywhere that put distance between them and the agents would be preferable. Even better, they headed toward one of his favorite areas. An indoor garden took up an entire arm of the ship. The plants grew wild and spilled out over their beds. More plants, and even some trees, climbed the walls and draped over support beams as they reached for the clear honeycombed roof.

A branching path bisected the garden from end to end. It stood out as the only inorganic thing in the garden. The dark metal had purple lines running through it like a circuit board. The plants grew over the path, doing their best to disguise it, but the straight lines and right angles would never look natural.

Despite the living wonderland around him, Pet's thoughts strayed from the garden. "Are you sure we should leave Brog alone with the DPS agents?"

Xavis's voice came from farther into the garden, hidden by the greenery. "In these situations, it's best to let Brog throw his weight around. Come here and hold this panel up for me."

For someone the color of fire, Xavis could be hard to find. Pet picked his way between thorny bushes heavy with berries and tall grasses with cottony puffs on their ends that smelled like lemon. Eventually he found Xavis behind a curtain of hanging flowers. "But what if he upsets them? They could take me away just out of spite."

Crouched in the grotto created by the flower curtain, Xavis opened one of the floor panels. The purple circuit board lines glowed brighter wherever he touched them. He motioned for Pet to hold the panel open while he rooted through the wires underneath.

"We spend so much time around him, we forget how terrifying he can be. I learned that for myself the day we met. If they want to take you away, they'll need a reason worth challenging an angry Ocan."

The panel was heavier than Pet expected, and he shifted its weight to both hands as he watched Xavis work.

Long talons handled delicate wires with astonishing precision. They also acted as tools and easily sliced away any wires that looked worn out. The cut wires lost their purple glow, and the rest of the panel went dark. Yet the light persisted, hovering around Xavis's hands as if emanating from his skin.

Pet leaned in as far as he could without dropping the panel. He had seen Xavis manipulate the purple light before but never from such a close perspective. It couldn't be a Scaacax talent. Their species was part of civilized space and had been meticulously documented. There was no record of any Scaacax wielding such an ability.

As far as Pet could tell, no one did. There was so much he still didn't know about his trio. "How did you meet?" Asking about the light seemed too intrusive, but learning how his trio became a trio should be innocent enough.

Xavis looked up from his inspection of the damaged wires, equally purple eyes wide and startled. "Oh, right, you don't know about that. I met Brog when I was part of Unit 22."

He said this as if it should mean something. To the rest of the universe, it probably did.

The light from Xavis's hands soaked into the cut wire. He twisted them together as if spinning thread, and the damaged pieces merged into a single pristine wire. Then he pulled the ends to lengthen the single piece until it was as long as the many pieces combined.

Pet watched, fascinated, while also listening to Xavis's explanation.

"You don't know about the Unit, either. Not surprising, honestly. Let me clarify something first. Different countries and planets have their own military, but there is also an intergalactic branch of military, called the Gantry. For a planet to be considered *civilized*, they have to host at least one Gantry base."

The newly refurbished wire was inserted in place of the old one, and the purple glow returned to that area of the panel. Xavis repeated the process on another damaged area, his hands moving quicker and with more certainty than before.

Oh, this was a test. The panel nearly slipped from Pet's numb fingers, but he held on tighter. Xavis had shown him the strange ability to judge his reaction. Luckily, it seemed he had passed, based on the way Xavis grew increasingly more relaxed.

Definitely not going to ask about the light now. "I think I've heard of the Gantry. My previous owner shipped goods intergalactically, so he had to deal with them a few times. He hated them."

"Again, not surprised. Anyway, the Gantry has a special unit, called Unit 22. It's supplemented with criminals. Not people who have committed big crimes, but crimes small enough to be forgiven through service."

Pet nearly dropped the panel again. He caught it, but this time the slip was too obvious to go unnoticed.

Xavis sighed. "You can put it down. I'm done here."

The panel returned to its place on the floor, the purple lines bright and even once again, yet Pet felt like he stood on unstable ground.

Petals cascaded to the floor as Xavis brushed through the hanging flowers, stirring up a scent as delicate as rain. It seemed like he would leave the garden all together, but he stopped at the widest part of the path.

Still halfway concealed in the grotto, Pet hovered at the edge of the hanging flowers. Then Xavis turned back to him and offered out a hand. Ah, he could breathe again. He stumbled through the plants to accept the hand.

They pressed close enough for their chests to touch. Xavis held up his other hand at eye level, carefully watching Pet as it began to glow. When Pet showed no reaction, he flicked his talons in a motion that turned the light into a ball hovering inches above his open palm.

The ball of light flew off on its own, disappearing into the depths of the garden, and moments later, music rolled through the air. Xavis's choice in music usually featured vocals with very few instruments. A sweet, upbeat song filled the garden with singing voices, some providing words and others creating the tune.

They danced. Xavis turned them in simple circles, giving their feet an easy pattern to follow so they didn't step on each other. Considering the wicked nature of Xavis's feet and Pet's own lack of shoes, the simplicity was appreciated.

With each step Xavis took, the lines glowed brighter beneath him. "You can ask. I'll answer."

"What…" Pet's voice failed him, and he tried again. "What did you do?"

The smile that came to Xavis's face was the kind Pet hated most. It was an expression that should have meant joy but held no trace of humor.

"I was arrested on drug charges. Possession and intent to deal, although that last one was a damn lie. They didn't find nearly enough on me to think I was selling."

That one answer brought so many more questions. Should he ask? No, not a good idea. He was already demanding too much.

Xavis led Pet through a spin before bringing them back together. "I used to be a cage fighter. I know, I don't look it. I'm too skinny, but I'm scrappy, and these talons are good for something other than looking cool. It was a way to make money, but I found out pretty quick that I'm horrible with money. Ended up in more debt than I started. I got desperate to win, so I turned to performance enhancers. Everything became about the drugs after that. I would do anything, hurt anyone, to get the next fix. Eventually my sponsors had enough. They turned me in, and I was arrested. The local prisons were full at the time, so I was shipped off to Unit 22."

"That's where you met Brog?"

"Yep. You'll have to ask him about how he ended up there. Now, normally I can take care of myself, but withdrawal hit me hard. Plus, I didn't have this at the time."

He let several spheres of light spin before Pet's eyes like galaxies.

"I was easy prey. Not for the other serving criminals, but for the Commanders in charge. One in particular took delight in harassing me. He thought since we were criminals, he could get away with doing whatever he wanted. Wasn't wrong either. It escalated, and one day I was badly injured. Brog found me hiding in a cupboard, my arm broken in three places. I barely knew him then, but he got me to a medic, then disappeared to 'have words' with the Commander. The man resigned immediately, and we got a new Commander. That's how we met Desmodian."

The music fell into a quicker tempo. Xavis picked Pet up and twirled him. "But that's another story for later. I'm more concerned about the here and now. Out of all the arguments those agents made against us, they've never mentioned our criminal records."

Coming out of the twirl, Xavis then dipped Pet and held him parallel to the ground. Despite supporting all of Pet's weight, he showed no sign of strain.

Pet ran his hands through Xavis's crest of hair. "Would a criminal record be enough for them to take me away?"

"Possibly. If they bothered to do any research, they would have brought up our pasts by now. The fact they haven't means they never did a background check.

Probably assumed ship-dwellers would bow to landowner authority. They'll regret that."

With his weight supported, Pet wrapped a leg around Xavis's waist and hooked their bodies close together. "Why's that?" Through their minimal clothes, he felt the Scaacax's growing arousal. He ground his hips forward.

Xavis gasped. "Because…because we're heading out to the Stardust. Once we leave the Penumbra Belt, they're ours."

Pet thrust forward again, and Xavis hoisted him up to press him against one of the support pillars. His head was still spinning from the sudden change when Xavis kissed him. It was a surprisingly gentle press of lips, despite the rough start, that trailed from his lips down to his neck. "They're…ours?"

"They. Will. Be." Xavis punctuated each word with another kiss. "They've never been outside civilized space before, so they don't realize there's no communication relays out in the Stardust. Unless they brought their own communication system, which I doubt, they'll have no way of contacting anyone. Space is dangerous. No one would know if something happened to them. Their attitude will change when our mercy is the only thing keeping them alive."

A shiver ran up Pet's spine, and he placed both feet on the floor. "You'll threaten them?"

"We'd prefer to do things legally, but if we have to, we'll remind them how the universe really works. Their authority means nothing out here." He drew back as a concerned look appeared on his face. "That's okay with you, right?"

Heat flushed through Pet's veins. Demonstrating

his opinion would work better than any words. He dropped to his knees, pulled open Xavis's pants, and wrapped his lips around the still-aroused cock.

"Fuck." Xavis braced against the pillar to keep himself standing. "I'll take that as a yes."

Pet hummed in agreement, which made Xavis's legs tremble. Unlike Brog or Desmodian, Xavis fit perfectly in his mouth. Just enough to strain his throat without causing pain.

The Scaacax's natural lubricant provided an extra bonus. Not only in easing the way in and out of his throat but also providing an aphrodisiac that heightened Pet's pleasure. The taste alone could make him come, and he wanted more. Gripping Xavis's hips with both hands, he forced the Scaacax to press as far down his throat as possible. Breathing through his nose kept the gag reflex at bay, and he swallowed around the hard shaft.

Xavis sighed and stroked his hair. "Ah, Pet. Such a talented mouth." His touch was gentle at first, but then he tightened his grip in Pet's hair.

Pet kept his mouth and throat relaxed as Xavis held his head still and started thrusting, chasing his own pleasure.

"Greedy little thing. You gonna drink all of me?" Xavis sounded composed, but his pace faltered into an erratic rhythm.

Since Pet could neither speak nor nod, he instead rolled his tongue the way Xavis enjoyed most. The fingers in his hair tightened hard enough to make his scalp sting.

Broad wings expanded, blocking out the light as Xavis reached his peak. "Ah. Good Pet."

He came down Pet's throat, fast and hot.

Each of his trio had their own taste. Pet could recognize them by it alone if he had to. While he enjoyed each, Xavis's was the sweetest and easiest to swallow. No matter how he tried, though, some always escaped. It spilled from his lips onto his chest, and a few hot drops landed on his legs.

He waited until Xavis finished before pulling off. While he was still gasping for air, Xavis yanked him up and switched their positions. Pet found Xavis kneeling at his feet, swallowing his throbbing cock whole. Where had his shorts gone? The slick tongue and lips on his flesh forced him to grasp the pillar behind him for support.

When he came, he could feel Xavis smirking as he swallowed every drop of Pet's pleasure. His legs refused to support him by the end, and he collapsed.

Luckily Xavis was ready to catch him, and lowered Pet to the floor.

"We should threaten government agents more often if that's the response we get."

Pet scoffed and tapped his shoulder, the biggest action he could muster until he recovered. "You're going to end up in jail."

"Again."

It meant a lot to Pet that Xavis already felt comfortable joking with him about such a personal subject. "Never again."

They sat in silence, Xavis stroking Pet's head as they both calmed. Pet was on the verge of falling asleep when Xavis suddenly sat up, accidentally knocking Pet aside.

"What?" Pet rubbed his hip which had collided

with the floor.

"Sorry. Thought I heard something."

They cleaned up and left the garden.

Pet heard nothing, but Xavis's ears led them out to the ship's open main area.

One catwalk below them, Nauzeia and Irih argued with a combination of soft words and strong gestures. Both looked incredibly pink. On another race, this would have suggested embarrassment or exertion, but compared to their natural tones, pink was their version of pale.

Pet and Xavis stayed low, lying on the floor to peer through the grate from above as they listened in on the agents' conversation.

Irih ran hands over both swollen cheek tubules, soothing his rough breathing. "There's something weird here."

"And there's nothing we can do without proof." Nauzeia also looked flustered, but not as much as her partner. "We may not like it, but they've done nothing illegal."

"Keeping décor in a rusty flying tin can like this should be illegal. But this crew is not what I expected. They don't take our authority seriously at all."

A shiver passed through both and they turned even paler. Whatever Brog had done, neither showed signs of injury, yet they acted like they just escaped with their lives.

Nauzeia clasped her hands in front of her to still their shaking. "I'll admit they don't act how I expected. Either they don't care if we take the décor, or there's something else going on."

The catwalk offered little room for pacing, but Irih

tried anyway. "They must be up to something. Only criminal ships are crewed by more than one species like this."

"The *Vanguard* is legally registered. I checked. All licensing is in order."

His pacing stopped. "That just means they're better at hiding it."

The distance between the catwalks made it hard for Pet to listen as Nauzeia walked away with her partner. He crept after them, bare feet keeping his steps silent on the metal floor. Just before they left the catwalk, he caught one last comment from Nauzeia.

"We need more information. I'll call headquarters and see what else they can find about the *Vanguard* and its crew."

The agents disappeared, and Pet turned back to Xavis in a panic. "We can't let them talk to other people. You said they'd use your criminal records against you."

"Obstructing their communication would look suspicious. We'll be past the Penumbra Belt soon. We must stay calm until then. Remember, we haven't done anything illegal yet."

As if the universe took Xavis's claim as a challenge, the warning alarms chose that moment to come alive. They flashed red and filled the halls with wailing that would wake even the deepest sleeper.

Wings allowed Xavis to bypass the catwalks and head directly for the control room, while Pet had to take the longer path on foot.

By the time he reached the control room, his trio were busy at their stations as the warning alarms still flashed. He stayed out of the way, standing quietly to the side.

Brog's muttered "This is gonna be a ride" felt more like a promise than a warning.

Right on Pet's heels, Nauzeia and Irih stormed into the room, demanding to know what was going on. Despite the emergency unfolding around them, Pet breathed a sigh of relief. The alarms had at least distracted the agents from contacting their headquarters.

From the main control panel, Desmodian gave a frightening announcement. "There's a gravity wave approaching."

Pet's knowledge of gravity waves was limited to what he had read about them. When two bodies large enough to generate their own gravitational pull drifted too close together, the clashing forces threw out waves of squashed and stretched gravity. They didn't happen often but were incredibly dangerous.

The agents didn't take this news well. Nauzeia started demanding they leave immediately, while Irih repeated over and over how he didn't want to die on some filthy ship.

Momentarily abandoning the controls, Desmodian snapped at them. "There's no outrunning a gravity wave. We have to ride it out, and that means shutting everything down. So, sit down and strap in."

Past experience said the agents would argue. They always had before. Yet, this time the agents complied, though not silently.

"Why turn everything off?" Nauzeia's hands slipped three times before she managed to secure her safety straps.

"You ever gone divin'?" Brog asked, seemingly out of nowhere. "You know, like down in deep water?

The biggest risk is the pressure difference between outside your body and inside. You need to decompress as you go, or you'll get injured. It's the same. Turnin' everything off is like decompressin' the ship."

There wasn't enough water left on Earth for diving. The Ocans' homeworld, however, was mostly covered by a large ocean. Their species could even breathe under water, and Brog had gills along his neck that were invisible when closed.

The warning alarms shut off, then the lights followed.

Pet headed for his antigravity bubble, but Brog grabbed him.

"Not this time, Pet. In a gravity wave, an antigravity bubble would only make it worse. You'll stay with me." He placed Pet in his lap and locked two arms around him, while the other two stayed on the controls.

From Brog's section of the control room, Pet couldn't see the agents very well, but he could hear Nauzeia protest. "That's not safe. Décor need to be secured properly."

"Safer than a seatbelt." Desmodian had a smirk on his face despite the situation. "No force in the universe can make Brog let go of something he doesn't want to."

Pet stroked the arms holding him, feeling the strength of muscle and bone. Brog's inner set of arms didn't bear spines like the outer arms and shoulders did. They felt safer.

The engines cycled one last time before Xavis announced all systems were offline.

Moments later, their gravity abruptly disappeared.

Straps creaked as they kept people in their seats

against the sudden weightlessness.

Brog's arms tightened around him. It would be so much more enjoyable to float freely. He loved bouncing around in his antigravity bubble, and it was even more fun on a larger scale. The lurking sense of danger sucked the joy out of this idea, however, and Pet pressed farther into Brog's arms.

Without functioning systems, they couldn't monitor the gravity wave's proximity. Their only choice was to sit in the dark and wait.

A tense minute passed with the ship dead around them. No one spoke, and the windows showed only the usual debris of the Penumbra Belt.

The stars outside the windows shifted like a heatwave, followed by a groan of straining metal.

The wave hit with an uncomfortable squashing and stretching of Pet's organs. It grew more and more intense until he was clawing at his skin to alleviate the pressure. Brog's breath warmed his ear as the Ocan whispered words of comfort, but they went unheard. The changing gravity affected him right down to his eardrums, and all he could hear was the wet, static sound of rain on an umbrella.

A sudden shifting brought him out of his misery, and he lurched in Brog's hold.

The gravity wave pushed the ship like a piece of driftwood right into the surrounding debris. An asteroid crashed against their flank and threw up chunks of broken rock. The hull of an abandoned ship floated by the window, casting sparks of metal against metal.

Pet had never feared space before. It was uncomfortable and confusing at times, but his trio handled it with such efficiency he never knew fear until now. The universe could tear them apart so easily if it wanted. Even his years as décor hadn't left him so powerless.

Unlike the agents who had practically fainted in their seats, his trio sat calmly, waiting for the chaos to pass.

Desmodian even laced his fingers in front of him the same way he did when watching a mildly interesting show.

The silent display of confidence eased Pet's fears, especially when Xavis passed him a wink over his wing. If his trio were fine, then everything would be fine.

As quickly as the wave started, it stopped, with just as little ceremony to mark its passing. The *Vanguard* drifted under its own momentum until collision with an asteroid brought it to a halt.

The static left Pet's ears just in time to hear Desmodian asking about damages to their ship. Uh-oh. They still weren't in the clear.

Xavis unbuckled from his seat and pushed off toward the ceiling. No gravity meant he floated effortlessly, and his wings gave him some control in the air. He pulled various panels from the ceiling, studying the blinking lights as he clung by his talons like a bat.

"A few cosmetic things. The coolant system in the cargo hold sprang a leak again, and the atmosphere generator has turned the linen closet into a steam room. Let's leave the artificial gravity off for a few hours while the ship readjusts, but everything else is good to go."

The lights came back on, and a tremble ran through the floor as the engine warmed up.

Pet tapped Brog's arms and asked to be released. Once free of the Ocan's hold, he kicked off into the air. Despite the careful hand he kept on the chair, his legs drifted higher. It startled him and he accidentally let go, which left him turning helpless circles in the middle of the room.

His trio laughed at his flailing.

"Need a hand?" Desmodian reached up to catch him as he floated past.

Pet took the offered arm but stayed airborne. If only the pleasant weightlessness were easier to control. "It's different than the bubble."

Xavis's wing brushed him just hard enough to send him into a slow spin. "Moving around isn't so hard once you're used to it. Let's get going. We've delayed enough."

"Wait, just like that?" Nauzeia also stood from her seat and floated at an odd angle as she clutched to the safety straps. "You're not going to do any repairs?"

"Don't need any. Ship's fine." With all four arms free, Brog's hands flew much faster over the controls. The *Vanguard* had a lot of systems to monitor as everything reengaged.

Irih joined in his partner's skepticism, though he didn't remove his safety straps. "I don't believe you. No ship gets through a collision like that undamaged. You're just grandstanding."

Desmodian sighed, his tail striking a spark against the floor as Pet hovered over his head like a kite. "What'd you want us to say? Whether you believe it or not, the ship is fine."

"And I say you're lying. If you move this ship without making the necessary repairs, I'll contact the

Bureau of Spacecraft Vehicles for reckless endangerment. Knowingly flying a damaged ship is illegal and grounds for losing your license as captain."

Another sigh, this time from the entire trio.

The *Vanguard* wouldn't be going anywhere any time soon.

**\*\*\*\***

It took over two hours to convince the agents the ship could fly. His trio carefully explained each system, which showed nothing but "go ahead" lights. In the end, the agents insisted on seeing the engine for themselves.

His trio resisted at first, until Pet admitted to being curious as well. Despite his year onboard, he had never seen the engine.

Getting to the engine room with the gravity deactivated turned out to be a journey all on its own. The engine lay directly below the control room, but it could only be accessed from a separate hatch.

Since he couldn't maneuver very well in zero gravity, Pet hitched a ride clinging to Desmodian's shoulders.

The Dhen'in expertly kicked off walls and propelled himself from target to target. Catwalks became valuable handholds they followed like stepping-stones to the bottom of the ship.

Things didn't work out so well for the agents. They managed the jump-and-catch method of travel at first, but a particularly out-of-the-way catwalk proved too difficult. Nauzeia barely caught a railing with one hand, while her partner missed by a good foot. When she tried to help, she lost her own grip and they both drifted into open air.

Watching them fail to swim their way back to safety proved entertaining for about two minutes. Then it grew tedious.

Brog pushed off from a catwalk above and slammed into them, propelling them to the opposite side of the cavernous cargo hold where they barely avoided crashing into the wall.

The agents protested until they were reminded what would happen if they were still floating when the gravity returned. After that they quietly let themselves be dragged along by their clothes until they reached the engine room.

A few maintenance lights lined the walls of the engine room, turning Nauzeia into a silhouette of herself when she floated inside the door.

"What is this?"

Pet peered past her into the room.

A metal cylinder ran from floor to ceiling. It was too tall for anyone to reach the top without stairs, which the room didn't have. What it did have were perches sticking out of the wall like tree branches, making it plainly obvious who had designed the space.

"It's the engine." Xavis fiddled with the various tubes and pipes looping along the bottom of the cylinder.

Nauzeia watched over Xavis's shoulder. "This is not an engine. I don't know what it is, but it's nothing like an engine. Is this even legal?" She opened a flap on the side of the cylinder. Bright purple light emanated from inside, bathing the whole room in its glow.

Xavis squawked and slammed the flap down, nearly catching her hand.

"Don't mess with things you don't understand.

This is, by definition, the thing that makes the ship go. Therefore, it's the engine. We built it ourselves, so I'm not surprised you don't recognize it. Now, I'm telling you, everything is running fine."

The agents relented, and by then, enough time had passed to reinstate the artificial gravity.

Rather than haul everyone back to the control room, Xavis left for the control room while the rest of them stayed put. A few minutes later gravity returned.

Weight descended on them gradually so they could find their footing, though Pet stayed in Desmodian's arms until gravity reached normal levels. They would have to experiment with sex in zero gravity once they weren't so busy. Assuming they could find a way to make it work.

The ship could fly, but some minor damage remained.

Desmodian and Brog set themselves to fixing the secondary issues as well as scanning for nearby distress signals in case another ship had been caught in the wave.

Neither of these tasks required Pet, leaving him nothing to do. According to the ship's inner lighting, it was almost midday, so he might as well prepare an early lunch. Everyone would need the extra fuel after such a hectic morning.

However, a nightmare waited for him in the kitchen. When he and Xavis fled earlier, he left his music box behind. The poor thing must have been sitting on the table, waiting to be retrieved. Now it lay on the floor in pieces.

Pet screamed and dropped to his knees. There seemed like more pieces than the little music box could hold. Sharp edges nicked his fingers as he scraped the fragments to himself.

"Hey." Nauzeia startled him as she knelt at his side. "Um, it's going to be okay."

He moaned and hunched over the pieces. "No, no, no. I let it get broken."

"Don't worry." Her hands hovered as if to touch him but never crossed that line. "It doesn't matter. It's just a trinket."

Tears reached the bottom of his cheeks and dripped onto the broken cogs. "I'm just a trinket." He glared at her, human eyes against Yce. His anger burned hot. As much as she claimed to be concerned for him, she was useless when he needed help.

"What's goin' on?" Brog stormed into the room. He took one look at Pet's tears and rounded on Nauzeia. "What'd you do?"

"N-nothing. It's…He's…" She struggled to explain, probably because she had never dealt with décor showing emotion before.

"I broke it." Pet hung his head so he wouldn't have to see Brog's disappointment. "The music box. You gave it to me, and I let it get broken. I'm sorry. Please don't be mad."

Knees hit the ground right in front of his downturned eyes, and broad hands rubbed soothing circles over his back.

"Hey, Pet, it's okay. Not mad. It'll be fine. We'll fix it."

Still sniffling, Pet looked up. "Fix it? How? It's in pieces."

Brog continued to rub his back while simultaneously collecting missed cogs. "Everythin's made 'a pieces. If those pieces can be put together once, they can be put together again."

He picked up the key, and after a moment of searching, selected a cog that fit on the rod behind the key. "See? Do that enough times and it'll be good as new."

Pet's tears stopped, but his head felt stuffy. The soothing hands on his back pulled him forward until he was captured in Brog's strong embrace, basking in the reassurance.

"What're you doing here?"

Brog wasn't talking to him. Over his head, Brog stared at Nauzeia, who still knelt awkwardly off to the side.

She had no answer.

## Chapter Ten

*Then*

His time with the trio couldn't last. During the day, he joined them in their ship while they completed preparations, and at night, he discovered new pleasures with them. But the best two days 2689 ever experienced eventually came to an end.

On their third morning together, they enjoyed the early sunlight out on the lawn. The humidity had lowered overnight, so the spice of the garden wasn't as overpowering as before. 2689 fretted over grass stains on his clothes, but it was a lost cause. The ripped silk he had worn over the last two days was already beyond repair. Grass stains would make no difference.

"Is the new shield working?" Desmodian sat against the base of a tree, looking as comfortable among the roots as he would in a proper chair.

Above them, Xavis perched on a low tree branch. "It's working, but we still can't use it more than once. Let's try to avoid any shootouts." With each word, Xavis plucked petals from the flowering tree and cast them into the air so they fell like rain. It could have been intentional or a coincidence of the wind, but the petals kept drifting in Brog's direction.

"Radiation panels are fixed as well." Brog lay on the grass, all four arms stretched to their full length. A petal landed on his face, making him sneeze when he nearly inhaled it. "Would you stop that?"

Xavis snickered and pelted him with whole flowers.

2689 chuckled under his breath. It was more than he would have been able to do a few days ago.

Desmodian, on the other hand, was immune to his companions' antics. "Then we just need to load the cargo and we're good to go."

Two people approached them from across the lawn. The number of spires on their heads identified them as Assistant and Curator.

2689 curled closer to the tree at the sight of them. While the tree's flowers gave no scent, its bark had a distinct spicy smell like cinnamon. It permeated the grounds of the estate, but before meeting the trio, he had only caught brief whiffs of the scent clinging to other people's clothes. He loved being able to indulge in it for himself.

However, that ended with a chipper clap of Assistant's hands.

"Excellent news. The cargo is ready to be loaded. You can be on your way by evening."

Neither Xavis nor Brog looked away from their floral exchange, and only Desmodian was willing to address Assistant. "That sounds fine. Though if you want the loading finished by tonight, we'll need to borrow some of your staff. The three of us alone can't move that fast."

"Of course. Anything to make the job easier."

Just behind Assistant, Curator stood silently watching. Her countenance was naturally unfriendly, but she looked particularly hostile holding the broken crystal headdress. It had spent the last few days sitting forgotten in a corner of the guest room. For her to have it now meant she stopped there first.

It had been his hope to put off reporting to her until the trio left, but apparently that hope had been in vain.

The conversation with Assistant stopped when 2689 stood. Curator said nothing. She didn't need to. His respite was over. He had orders to follow and needed to leave the ship-dwellers behind.

"Pet?" Brog managed to put a lot of concern into one word.

2689 turned back to them. With hands clasped and posture stiff, he kept his gaze averted to the grass. "It was lovely meeting you. I hope everything goes well."

Décor were never expected to give proper goodbyes, but he wanted to extend the courtesy. The trio's eyes bore holes into him as he walked away, but he didn't look back. It would make following Curator that much harder.

Silence greeted them in the hallway when they returned to the estate. Any staff that made the mistake of wandering too close immediately fled at the sight of Curator muttering to herself. "Ship-rats. Can't be happy with the hospitality we provide. No. They have to break the décor as well."

2689 started to explain, but her glare cut him off.

After only two days, he had already lost the habit of silence. As he walked a few steps behind Curator, the role of décor settled over him like an ill-fitting helmet. It squeezed his brain and made him want to rip it off. For the first time, he understood why décor had their memories wiped. Memories made them people, and people couldn't be objects.

1834 stood at her typical post in the main foyer. She remained perfectly still while in Curator's view, but as 2689 drew near, her hand clenched into a fist. Most would never notice the slight movement, but for décor, 1834 may as well have been screaming.

Her reaction played in his head over and over until they stepped through the door of Owner's office.

The too-large room held only a single desk, making it look comically empty. This provided plenty of space for 2689 and Curator to wait for Owner to notice them as he stood staring out the window.

"We're loading the cargo today. I'm finally getting these ship-dwellers off my estate, so this interruption better be worth it."

Curator began by placing the broken headdress on the desk like a peace offering, or maybe a ritualistic sacrifice. "About the décor our guests…borrowed. What should I do with it?"

The outside light created a highlight around the edge of Owner's face when he looked at them. His head spires struck across the window, framing the *Vanguard* like prison bars.

Who lay on the inside and who lay on the outside?

Attention went to the broken headdress first, and Owner scoffed over the cost of repairs. Consideration of 2689 came second after that. "I don't want something defiled by ship-rats in my home. Take it to auction. Tarnished décor won't sell for much, but it's better than nothing."

Resale had crossed 2689's mind, but it never felt real. He expected reprimand and correction, but décor were too expensive to be resold so casually.

"We could try to fix it."

Curator cast a discerning eye over 2689, taking in more details than he was comfortable with her seeing.

"A few blemishes can easily be erased."

His hands stayed clasped behind his back. They had already seen the bruises on his wrists but hadn't seen the pendant cupped within his palm. He intended to keep it that way.

Owner never gave him a second glance. "Fixing it won't erase the memory. Every time I look at it, I'll be reminded of those ship-rats' debauchery. No, remove it from my home."

2689 nearly laughed. It sounded like a bad joke. Owner complained about unwanted memories when 2689 wanted nothing more than to hang on to the ones he had.

"They came to me." His declaration startled Owner, causing him to knock the broken headdress from the table. "You said they should make themselves at home. I was only keeping the guests happy." He was keeping himself happy too, but they didn't need to know that. They only needed to understand that his actions helped their goals. There was no reason to resell him. Punishment he would accept, but not resale.

Worse than falling on deaf ears, Owner and Curator heard, but his words meant nothing.

"See." Owner dismissed him with a wave. "Ruined. It's already making a disturbance. Best to resell it quickly as possible. I have to get this shipment settled first, but then we're going to the auction house. Hopefully they'll have new merchandise to replace it. Put it in the sensory deprivation chamber until then. Get it cleaned up as much as possible."

Curator bowed out of the room, but 2689 didn't

follow. His feet felt rooted to the floor. There had to be a way to stop his memories from being taken. Yet, nothing inspired him while he stood frozen in the middle of Owner's office.

When Curator realized he wasn't following, she tried to command him under her breath. "Two-six-eight-nine. Item number two-six-eight-nine." Then she grabbed him by his already-ruined outfit and dragged him out the door, ripping the silk further.

He tripped over his own feet as she pulled him along, unable to keep up with Curator's longer stride. Down the hall and around the corner, they passed more gossiping staff and horrified décor.

A pair of cleaners made the mistake of not immediately leaving when Curator approached. The punishment for their mistake was having Curator toss 2689 in their direction so he fell at their feet.

"Take this to the sensory deprivation chamber." Then she left with the sound of her tip-tapping footsteps marking her departure.

The stunned staff didn't know what to do with him. Too afraid to touch an item belonging to their employer, they used a broom handle to herd him in the right direction.

Just enough light filtered in from the open door to illuminate the dark room and reveal the contraption at the center. It looked like a large covered bathtub, completely enclosed except for a single round hatch on the end.

Still not daring to touch him, the staff ordered him to strip off his destroyed outfit.

He slipped the silk from his shoulders and snuck a glance at the pendant hidden in his clenched hand. If he couldn't keep his memories, maybe he could hold on to this last token.

To do that, however, he needed to keep it out of sight. He pretended to struggle with a knot in the silk. The distraction allowed him to switch the pendant to his other hand, which put it on the other side of his body away from prying eyes.

They were too busy trying to herd him into the deprivation chamber to notice the clandestine jewelry.

Water filled the tank exactly halfway. Neither hot nor cold, he barely felt the liquid as he slipped inside. The hatch closed behind him and shrouded him in darkness.

No sight, no sound, and nothing to feel except still water. The complete lack of sensory input was meant to help people release unwanted thoughts. For décor, this meant any thoughts. 2689 closed his eyes and sank as low in the water as he could without drowning.

The pendant clutched tightly in his hand provided a small but impactful bit of stimulation. It also brought memories. He couldn't see in the darkness, but he remembered the color of the stone, the exact color of Xavis's eyes. Its polished metal reminded him of Desmodian's smooth scales. The pendant's chain scraped along the bottom of the chamber and the sound reverberated through the water. Brog's voice settled into the depths of his chest the same way when they lay close together.

He would lose those memories when they erased him, so only his body remained. To most people, it was the only valuable part of him. This he could accept. His memories had been taken once before and he survived. He could do it again. Yet, he hated the idea that he would leave nothing behind to mark his existence. 2689 may be only an object, but he existed.

As he lost himself in memories, his thumb stroked the stone at the center of the pendant. It glowed at his touch. The chamber felt huge and crushing in the dark, but the pendant's light reflected off the sides, revealing it wasn't as big as he had built in his mind. If he stretched out his arms, he could almost reach from one side to the other. The light also showed a vague outline of the hatch at the front of the chamber. A handle stuck out on the inside. It was probably a safety feature no one bothered to remove since décor never left if told to stay.

2689 would accept his fate, but that didn't mean he had to accept it passively. Before he was erased, he could leave a mark no one would forget. Then, in a way, 2689 would continue to exist even after he became a new number.

He felt along the metal wall toward the hatch, using the pendant's light to guide his way.

## Chapter Eleven

*Now*

The days following the gravity wave were some of the slowest since Pet joined the *Vanguard*. Usually, his trio exceled at finding things to do on long trips. Namely him. They had passed many days in the depths of space taking Pet against every surface in the ship.

Unfortunately, after Nauzeia threw a fit over a few bruises, they decided it was best to avoid sex until they left the Penumbra Belt. Once in the Stardust, the agents could complain all they wanted. Without a communication channel they would be screaming into the void.

After going his whole remembered life barely knowing about sex, one would think two days of abstinence should be easy. This assumption would be wrong. A year spent having sex on an almost daily basis meant the loss of intimate contact left an expansive hole in his life.

Their third day traveling the Penumbra Belt found him running on a treadmill, working off excess energy. Upbeat music with a heavy bass played in his ears through a pair of headphones as his legs pounded against the treadmill's belt. It drowned out all other sound, but what he really needed was a way to block his eyes.

On a bench in front of him, Brog lay on his back and pumped weights with both sets of arms. The sight of so much straining muscle made Pet wish it were possible to run blindfolded.

He called it quits at the five-mile mark. Not his best pace, but he had nearly fallen off the machine three times. He couldn't work out with distractions, and Brog's physical abilities were a definite distraction.

Removing his headphones, Pet set the treadmill to a brisk walking pace as a cooldown.

Off to the side, Brog slammed the weights to the floor with an angry clang.

Pet slowed his pace more. "Problem?"

"It's too easy. I need heavier."

This didn't seem like a problem, and Pet waited for the other metaphorical shoe to drop.

Brog gestured at the weights in frustration. "These are the heaviest set of gravity weights they make."

Gravity weights worked by increasing their gravitational attraction. It was a good solution for ships with limited storage but restricted the weight to how much strain the mechanics could bear.

The treadmill came to a stop. "I have an idea." Pet's hungry smile got Brog's attention. He instructed Brog to lie back on the bench and pick the weights up again. The Ocan did, and once he held the bars over his chest, Pet perched on the weights as well.

He gazed down at Brog between his knees. "Now try."

"How am I supposed to concentrate with this kind 'a view." Brog dropped both bars until they almost touched his chest, bringing Pet's legs to either side of his head, then pushed back up.

It became a game. Pet stubbornly held to the bars, as Brog moved them in more erratic ways trying to make him fall.

By the end of the fourth set both panted heavily. Pet climbed off the bars to straddle Brog's stomach.

With one pair of hands, Brog turned the gravity distorter off and tossed the bars aside, while he used his other pair to pull Pet into a kiss.

Their difference in height meant their hips didn't line up, but Pet enjoyed the feel of grinding against Brog's well-defined stomach just as much.

Brog pulled away and let his head fall back against the bench. "Fuck this."

"It's a lack of fucking this that's the problem."

"Damn. Little Pet cursed. It must be serious."

Pet draped himself over Brog's massive chest, idly tracing the lines of the Ocan's neck. His double set of trapezius muscles connected near the top of his head, much higher than they would on a human. Details like this emphasized his trio's alien origins. He loved exploring the differences between them.

A hand slapped his ass, but his scowl only earned a laugh from Brog.

"Get up. You're too temptin' like this."

They left the gym, both sweaty from exertion, though not the kind Pet wanted.

In the bedroom, Desmodian lounged in the sunken bed. Deep, haunting music trickled from the speakers, the kind that should be played on an organ late at night during a thunderstorm. Desmodian barely paid it any attention as he read one of his books.

The wonderful artwork that decorated the cover fascinated Pet. Modern digital text rarely came with so much decoration. On paper, even the worst writing, filled with mistakes and horrible imagery, received the same grandiose presentation.

Maybe he'd skip the shower and sate his curiosity instead. "What're you reading?" He peered over Desmodian's shoulder, leaning around the war hammer perched at the edge of the bed. Oh, it was in an unfamiliar language. Each letter looked like a sun, with a different number of light rays and dots in the center.

Desmodian flipped to a picture Pet could appreciate.

"It's an old Echoid folktale."

The person on the page resembled Vige, with a clear cranial dome and toothy smile on prominent display. The man or woman stood alone, surrounded by a barren wasteland and the bodies of dead fish.

"What's it about?" Pet traced the lines of the picture. The ink had been pressed so hard into the paper it left divots.

"It's about a man who falls in love with a water maiden. She can't leave her pond, so he diverts the water into a nearby stream. Unfortunately, this doesn't free her, but kills her instead. He spends the rest of his life alone, guarding the meadow that grew in the place of her pond."

A drawer in Brog's alcove slammed shut. "Yeesh, Des. Could you have picked a more depressin' story?"

Paper slapped against paper as Desmodian flipped to a new page in the book. "They're not all like that. Many Echoid folktales have happier endings, but this one has been translated into different languages, so it's perfect for Pet to practice with." He held the book open to a page with recognizable letters.

Pet groaned and buried his face in Desmodian's shoulder. "Do I have to?"

Desmodian shifted, and a moment later, the music quieted to a ghostly waltz of background noise. "Yes, you need to practice. When they erased your memories, they also erased skills like reading. You need to relearn those skills if you're going to travel with us."

The letters swam before his eyes as Pet glared at the page. He wanted to do as Desmodian asked, but by the time he finished sounding out each word in a sentence, he forgot how they connected. Then he would have to start the sentence over again.

At some point during the arduous task, Brog ruffled Pet's hair and wandered off. A moment later the shower turned on in the bathroom.

It distracted Pet from his work mid-sentence. He looked up to see how far he had read, only to find he was still on the first paragraph. In a fit of frustration, he grabbed the book and threw it across the room. The moment the book left his hand he regretted it but could do nothing as he watched it fly.

The hard cover made a disproportionately loud sound when it hit the floor.

"I'm sorry." The words felt meager against the silence that followed, like the world's smallest knight jousting the world's largest dragon. Earth fairy tales were no easier to read than Echoid ones, but the analogy fit. He waited for Desmodian to speak.

The Dhen'in sighed as he stood to retrieve the book. "I know it's hard, but you need to keep at it. The words will come easer with practice."

Sitting in their sunken bed, staring up at Desmodian, Pet barely came up to the Dhen'in's knees.

He felt smaller than ever, and yet his thoughts felt much too large. "It's not the words. I understand the words. It's the sentences. They're all long and confusing. I keep getting lost. And the pictures don't help. They're pretty, and they show the story, but they don't tell me what the story means."

His outburst ended as quickly as it began. He slumped against the pillows, hiding from Desmodian's considering stare. Now that he knew Desmodian watched him with his entire body, it was like being judged a thousand different ways at once.

"The sentences are too long?"

Looking up from his pillow, Pet nodded.

Desmodian tapped the book against his bottom lip.

Hmm, did his crossed senses allow him to glean more information from the book's taste?

"Maybe we should try something less…artsy. I have an idea." He replaced the book in his alcove and returned to the bed with a new, even bigger book.

The size of it and the many words it must contain nearly sent Pet running from the room. Then he saw inside. Desmodian had abandoned the stories to instead present him with a science textbook.

"I've been meaning to talk to you about this anyway. We can make a stellar collision out of two stars. This book is old, but the information inside is still mostly accurate."

A bold word greeted Pet at the top of the page Desmodian showed him. Without a sentence around it, he read the title much easier. "Plasma?"

Pointed nails tapped at the page to draw attention to a picture of a simple atomic structure. "Also known as ionized gas. You've probably heard about the other three states of matter. Solid, liquid, and gas. However, there is a fourth state of matter called plasma, and in space, it's the fourth state that's the most important. The first three create the planets, while the fourth one creates everything in between. For example, the Iota Cloud, where we're headed, is a giant cloud of concentrated plasma. It can be dangerous, and you should know how it works before we get there. Plus, the sentences in science books tend to be straightforward. At least the introductory ones."

The sentences may have been simpler, but the words were more complicated. However, Pet found he preferred sounding out a hard word than trying to keep track of a long sentence. With Desmodian's help, he read through the section concerning Plasma. The concept of gas becoming ionized was difficult to understand at first. However, diagrams showed the process step by step. A gas could become energized to the point that some of its electrons would break free. This created an imbalance in the atom, which it fixed by bonding with other ionized atoms, turning the gas into a whole new type of matter.

The interactions described on the page made more sense than the social interactions Pet read about in stories. Atoms followed rules, and even when they broke those rules, they then switched to a new set of rules. Pet had broken his own rules once before when he chose to defy his old owner, but that didn't mean he wanted a life devoid of rules entirely. He just wanted more comfortable rules to follow.

Unlike the Echoid tale, Pet read the textbook much quicker. By the time Brog returned from the shower, he had already managed to work his way through several pages.

Desmodian let him go, promising to come back to it later, and Pet took Brog's place in the bathroom. He hurried through his shower and washed off the dried sweat from his run. Four people sharing one bathroom meant they had to monitor their time.

The guest bunks held a secondary bathroom, but right now no one wanted to go near the agents staying there.

After drying his hair, Pet stepped back into the bedroom fully naked. Nudity couldn't embarrass him when his trio had seen every part of his body.

While Pet showered, Desmodian had abandoned books altogether to, instead, discuss their schedule with Brog. "I'm surprised we haven't reached the end of the Penumbra Belt by now."

Brog had forgotten about dressing halfway through the act. His pants hung from his hips unbuttoned, and only one glove had made it to his hands. "The gravity wave may have knocked us farther off course than we thought. Plus, it took so long to get started again. Damn meddlers."

Desmodian's tail betrayed his agitation. "Not much longer. Once we're out of the belt, we'll make a hyperspace jump. Then we'll be too far out for the agents to do anything."

Everyone was growing tense the longer they had to censor themselves.

Pet made his own protest by selecting the most revealing outfit in his wardrobe. Sheer black silk connected to a collar around his throat and did little to disguise his body. Only a matching belt kept the silk in place. Similarly dark leggings reached up to mid thigh, with bold stripes adding the only bit of color. The outfit also came with a headpiece draped in the same shadowy fabric. He never said it out loud, but it made him feel like some sort of dark bride. Except, instead of a ring, around one biceps he wore a gold band with a spiral design and a loop of black pearls .

He knew the moment Desmodian and Brog noticed his outfit, because their conversation abruptly stopped.

"Now you're just not playing fair." Desmodian tipped his head back against the edge of the bed with a groan.

Brog said nothing. His eyes spoke for him, briefly flashing orange before he turned away to search through his alcove for gloves that matched the one he was wearing.

"It's a promise." Pet edged closer to Brog. "Once the agents aren't a problem, we'll celebrate, and you can take this off me." He would have said more, made more promises for what they could do later, but a flash of familiar colors in one of Brog's drawers caught his eye. "My music box."

Brog hesitated with his hand over the drawer, ready to slam it closed, but stopped and let Pet look inside. The music box nestled on a bed of black cloth, partially reassembled with the remaining pieces organized in neat piles.

"You're fixing it?"

"Um…" Brog shrugged and turned away to tug on his gloves.

Desmodian kept his head tipped back, laughing as he watched them upside down. "Oh, Brog, did you really never tell him? Our big oaf hates to admit it, but he's a bit of an artist. He made that music box."

Picking up the reassembled half of his music box, Pet looked at Brog with a threat of new tears. "You said you bought it. You made it for me? And I broke it? I'm sorry." It was a rare moment when Brog looked sheepish.

The Ocan tried to hide the expression as he took back the half-finished mechanism. "Don't worry 'bout it. Gives me a chance to make it better. I wanted it to play more than one song but was too impatient."

Now that he knew the truth, Pet could picture Brog's large hands tinkering with the small cogs, getting frustrated as it took longer to make than planned. When he first joined the *Vanguard*, Pet had been a nervous wreck. Not only was the ship a completely new environment, but he had no idea what his new owners wanted from him. Brog had given him this gift to make him feel welcome.

He stepped back and let Brog stow the half-finished project in its drawer. "Take as long as you need. I'll wait."

It was a good time to leave the room and let Brog maintain his gruff persona, though not before pressing a kiss to his and Desmodian's cheeks on the way out.

He headed for the control room to join Xavis for his shift at the controls. The Scaacax would appreciate a distraction, and Pet was in the mood to tease. He would pay for it later when their sex ban lifted, but for now, he enjoyed riling up his trio.

Stepping into the room as quietly as he could, he found Xavis draped over the controls, idly directing spheres of purple light to twirl circles over his head. Pet crept up behind him and reached out to cover his eyes. Before he could make contact, two spheres morphed into cuffs around his wrists and pulled him into the air. More light wrapped around his mouth to silence him, oddly insubstantial yet solid as iron at the same time.

"Sneaking up on me, Pet?"

The light laid Pet over the control panel, open and helpless to Xavis's perusal. He couldn't see it, but he felt Xavis snap the band of his legging against his thigh.

"Such a naughty thing. Making yourself so tempting when you know we're trying to behave. This kind of behavior needs to be punished."

Talons traced down Pet's stomach, catching over ribs and hipbones. They pushed his legs apart, exposing more of him. He moaned against the solid light still covering his mouth, leaning his head back and thrusting his hips forward for more contact.

"This really does nothing to cover your body." Xavis tugged at the trailing ends of sheer cloth. "You may as well be naked. Enjoy it for now. Once you're free game, you won't be wearing clothes for a long time."

He tugged the cloth again, threatening to pull it from its belt and expose Pet completely.

With vindictive glee, Pet snapped his legs closed and shook his head.

"Oh, that's how it's gonna be? Making me work for it. What if I keep you tied up right here, nice and ready for us? We'll take you one after the other, over and over, until you can't even beg for it anymore. That sound like fun?"

Pet couldn't nod fast enough. Forget behaving. He wanted to feel his trio inside him, and he wanted them now.

Xavis leaned over him, wings spread wide like

their own private tent. "I'm afraid, Pet, you're gonna have to wait."

Not one to be rejected, Pet rubbed his leg up Xavis's hip, hoping to incite him into action. Their teasing continued back and forth. Pet made no more headway toward his goal while Xavis kept him restrained. They had been at their game for a while when Pet saw movement through a gap in Xavis's feathers. He shouted, but the gag muddled his warning.

Just as Xavis looked over his shoulder, he was hit with an electrical current and collapsed.

The lights holding Pet disappeared. He climbed down from the control console, but the DPS agents got there first.

They rolled Xavis over.

A sliver of purple could be seen as Xavis struggled to open his eyes, head lolling on his shoulders. His limbs twitched as whatever the agents hit him with continued coursing through his nervous system.

Nauzeia checked Xavis's pulse. "Restrain him while I disable the ship. If we barricade ourselves in this room, we should be able to keep the other two at bay until backup arrives." She moved to the controls and Irih pulled Xavis's hands behind his back.

Flapping wings struck Irih in the face. The agent brandished a prod and jabbed Xavis with it, making him screech as another electrical jolt shot through him.

When it ended, Xavis lay deathly still.

"You're under arrest." Irih clamped cuffs on Xavis's wrists. "Stay still, you damn junkie."

Pet watched it happen, filled with a bitter rush of horror, fury, and helplessness. They paid him no attention. Didn't even consider décor a threat to their plans.

They would regret ignoring him.

While Nauzeia hesitated over the ship's controls, Pet charged her and knocked her to the floor. He hit the intercom system and opened a ship-wide channel.

Then he lunged for Irih.

"Get away from him." He shoved Irih away and threw himself over Xavis's unconscious body.

Red hands reached for him and he lashed out. His flailing hit one of Nauzeia's facial tubules.

She collapsed, sputtering like a drowning victim while clutching the back of her head where the tubules connected.

More hands grabbed Pet's shoulders and tried to pull him away. He clung to Xavis and blindly kicked out behind him. His foot connected with something, though unfortunately nothing sensitive like he managed with Nauzeia. Irih grunted but grabbed Pet by the hair and yanked back hard enough to make him let go.

"What is wrong with this thing?" Irih sounded winded, but otherwise fine.

Pet desperately searched for help. Desmodian and Brog should be barging through the door any moment, unless they were unfortunate enough to be caught at the opposite end of the ship. He needed to stall until they arrived.

Slumping in the agent's hold, he pretended to surrender. Both agents had guns holstered at their hips, small single-handed things that a human could wield. Even better, the male agent had grabbed more of Pet's headpiece than actual hair. With enough force he should be able to slip free.

"We're refurbishing this thing as soon as we get

back." Irih gave Pet a shake for emphasis. "No one will want it with this kind of personality."

Pet gritted his teeth and stayed slumped in faux-defeat.

"Careful with the décor." Nauzeia stilled her partner's hand. "And help me seal these doors. The control room should have an emergency barricade."

She returned to the controls, and Pet took his opportunity. Throwing himself forward, he caused Irih's hand to slip over the fabric of his headpiece and allow escape. Pet grabbed the agent's gun, fumbling over the holster's strap but managing to get the weapon in hand.

He dropped to his knees and leaned protectively over Xavis's body, pointing the gun first at Irih, then at Nauzeia when she stepped toward him. "Get away from the controls and stay away from us."

Neither moved as they shared a bewildered look. A gun pointed at them by décor must hold the same absurdity as being threatened by a toaster.

"Get away. Now."

Nauzeia raised her hands and stepped from the controls. They may not take him seriously as a threat, but a gun was still a gun. Even an object could pull a trigger.

"Two-six-eight-nine." Nauzeia kept her voice soft as if calming a spooked animal. "Listen, you don't know what you're doing. I don't know what these people have told you, but you can't interfere with police work."

"You're not police."

"But police are on their way to arrest this criminal." Irih had enough sense to back off when the gun swung his way.

Brog charged into the room. "What the hell is goin' on?"

Desmodian followed a moment later, overcoming his shock faster than Brog and pointing the business end of his war hammer toward the agents. "Back up. Both of you."

Outnumbered, or at least equally numbered since they wouldn't count Pet, the two agents retreated until their backs hit the wall.

Brog placed himself before the agents.

Desmodian knelt to check on Pet and Xavis. "Pet, give me the gun and tell me what happened."

It was a chore just to pass over the weapon. Relief hit Pet so hard his hands shook, bringing his voice with it. No one would be able to understand his explanation when his words couldn't stand in a straight line. "They said Xavis was a criminal. But he's not. Xavis hasn't done anything wrong."

"I know." Desmodian pulled him close. "We'll sort it out. Look after Xavis while we do." He then stood at Brog's side and faced down the agents.

"You've attacked two members of our ship, and I want to know why." He sounded calm but gripped his weapon like he would start swinging any moment.

Nauzeia looked to her partner first, but he offered no help, so she stepped forward. "Your friend is under arrest. We've contacted authorities to pick him up."

"Like hell." Brog's shouting frightened the agents enough for Nauzeia to draw her gun. It looked harmless compared Brog's overall size, but even a small gun posed a threat.

Her hands shook almost as much as Pet's had. "Sir,

please step back. We're just doing our job."

"What part of your job includes attacking innocent people?"

The presence of a gun pointed for their side resurrected some of Irih's indignation. "Innocent people don't get arrested, and junkies aren't innocent."

Brog protested, but Desmodian silenced him with a hand on his arm. "I think I know what this is about." He turned to the ship's controls and, even with the mask, his face looked uncharacteristically resigned.

Nauzeia lowered her gun. "If you cooperate and turn the ship around, it will help everything go smoother."

With a heavy sigh Desmodian nodded, then started tapping at the controls.

"Des, you're not seriously giving in to their demands?"

Brog sounded as shocked as Pet felt watching him.

Desmodian hit a few more buttons, setting off a series of lights on the control panel. "Haven't you noticed? We're past the Penumbra Belt."

One more tap to the controls sent the ship lurching forward.

Pet gripped Xavis tighter, bracing him against the sudden shift in momentum.

Brog and Desmodian managed to stay on their feet, but the agents had no hope. Irih nearly landed on his face while Nauzeia dropped to one knee to keep her balance. In their precarious positions, neither could stop Brog from swiping Nauzeia's gun.

The ship fell quiet as if it had stopped moving, yet the stars outside the window passed by faster and faster.

Hyperspace left a telltale tingle along Pet's skin. It

was a very pleasant sensation to play with. An hour ago, that would have been the only thing on his mind.

The agents struggled to their feet, demanding an explanation for Desmodian's actions and threatening to have him arrested as well.

Before Pet could panic, Desmodian braced one cocky hip against the control panel and crossed his arms. "Go ahead. Try it."

Irih unclipped his communicator from his belt. "Dispatch, we're going to need more reinforcements sent to our location. We've got two more criminals to bring in."

The communicator replied with static.

"Dispatch?" No matter what he did, the communicator gave him no response.

The voiceless noise ended when Desmodian grabbed the communicator and dropped it to the floor. "We're in hyperspace, which means we're moving too fast for communication. Now, explain what the hell you're thinking, attacking my mate."

"Mate?" Nauzeia repeated the word once out loud, and once to herself. "That's a strange term for someone not your species."

The handle of Desmodian's hammer crushed the communicator at his feet. "You wouldn't understand. Now talk."

Realization descended over them like the fragments of a collapsing roof. They'd lost their illusion of protection. Nauzeia smoothed her hands down her long robe and collected herself. "We had our people do some more research into your crew. Two of you have criminal records. Xavis of Xylanthia is a known drug user."

The agent spoke so starkly, hurling words like weapons.

Pet wrapped his arms tighter around Xavis to shield him from their accusations. Xavis never denied his past or tried to make himself look better, but he told the story in a way that painted a whole picture. Ugly details and all. The agents ignored everything leading up to Xavis's original arrest and skipped right to the end result, making it sound like he had been labeled a criminal by choice.

More pieces of the communicator crunched under Desmodian's boot. "Former. He served his time. You can't punish him for it again."

"Not for previous crimes. But he was seen at the Gravity Well with a man named Maddax. Records show Maddax has been arrested for multiple counts of drug dealing and was your…mate's main supplier in the past."

Memories surfaced like air bubbles. Xavis *had been* up in the rafters of the Gravity Well speaking with a man neither Desmodian nor Brog seemed to like. Running his fingers through Xavis's dark red hair, Pet shook the memory away. It couldn't be true. Xavis talked about his past with too much contempt to repeat the same mistakes.

Four arms lifted Xavis from the floor as Brog took Xavis from Pet. "Des, you explain it to them. I'm taking Xavis to medical."

Pet stayed with Brog, leaving Desmodian to deal with the agents. Ahead of him, Xavis's wings draped over Brog's arms, low enough to brush the floor. It was difficult to linger at Xavis's side without stepping on feathers. He had never seen Xavis so sedate. Even in sleep, the Scaacax twitched and moved, too full of energy to ever lay still.

During his year on the *Vanguard*, Pet had walked its halls hundreds of times. Never in all those days had the familiar setting looked so threatening. Each step that lay between them and the medical room became a new villain to defeat. He couldn't live without his trio, and he doubted the trio could last without all three.

The agents had never seemed like a threat compared to his trio's bravado. Yet with the thrust of a single weapon, the pair had punched a hole right through the foundation of his life.

They eventually reached the medical room, though not as quickly as Pet would have liked. It occupied a seldom-used corner in one of the *Vanguard*'s arms that mostly housed maintenance equipment. Not once in the last year had Pet or any of the trio needed to step through its doors. Pet christened a new threshold into an unexpectedly small room, bare except for storage shelves and a glass window on one wall.

"Stay here." Brog brought Xavis through another door into the room beyond the window, where Pet could only watch from the other side of the glass.

A round bed at the center of the room took up most of the space. In many ways it resembled their bedroom, but with the bed hovering in the air instead of sunken into the floor.

Xavis never even twitched as Brog laid him over the flat surface.

Rings detached from the edge of the bed to spin concentric circles around it, scanning Xavis with different colored lights.

An equally round screen dropped from the ceiling

to show the results from the scans, a series of numbers, graphs, and words that Pet couldn't read from the other side of the window.

Bright orange at his feet caught his eye. A feather lay on the otherwise sterile floor, one of the covert feathers from the middle joint of Xavis's wing. It wasn't as important as the flight feathers, but it had no place on the floor, just like Xavis had no place on the medical bed.

Muffled shouting preceded Desmodian through the door. A strap held his hammer to his back, leaving both hands free to deal with the agents. He gripped each at the nape of the neck, right where their breathing tubules connected.

Pet snatched the feather before it could be crushed underfoot.

Irih tugged against Desmodian's grip with little result, but Nauzeia held both hands out in front of her in a universal show of nonresistance.

The door closed behind them after Desmodian shoved them the rest of the way into the room. "You caused the damage. Now you can see the result."

Free of Desmodian's hand on her neck, Nauzeia turned quickly enough that her robes brushed Pet's leg. "Damage? There's no need to exaggerate. We only used a neural disruptor. A few minutes of muscle paralysis and he'll be fine."

Desmodian's only response was to point at the window.

Xavis's yellow skin looked ashen white in the fluorescent lights, and more fallen feathers wreathed him on the table.

The feather in Pet's hand barely tickled against his

palm. It was as light as the beeping of the machines telling him Xavis was still alive.

Brog turned one of the screens for the rest of them to see. "These readin's are erratic. I'm gonna try wakin' him up, but no tellin' what'll happen."

"He shouldn't even be unconscious." To her credit, Nauzeia didn't flinch when Brog glared at her, though that could have been because of the glass that separated them.

Out of all the different weapons Brog had wielded in the past, the Ocan never appeared more threatening than he did holding medical equipment. The way he grasped the syringe looked like he was planning to stab someone in the neck.

"We don't live in a universe of 'should.' "

The beeping of the machines around Xavis slowly sped up.

Pet counted them. Their rhythm must hold good meanings. With eyes locked on Xavis's unconscious face, he drifted from the window to stand closer to Desmodian, ignoring the way this put him closer to the agents as well.

Xavis twitched, at first just the tips of his feathers, but then both wings shot out to the side. They filled the room and knocked Brog into the wall. At the same time, a new screeching overtook the beeping of the machines.

Xavis was screaming.

How could such a tortured sound could come from one of Pet's trio?

Desmodian's fist hit the glass. "Put him back under."

Xavis started thrashing, and Brog needed two arms just to hold him down while his other two readied another syringe. "I can't give him heavier drugs, and the sedative I can give him isn't fast."

Amongst the flurry of feathers and limbs Pet never saw the syringe find its mark but assumed it must have when Brog threw it aside, empty.

Xavis continued to scream.

Scales slid against Pet's arm as Desmodian brushed past him, grabbing both agents by the backs of their necks again and pressing them up against the window.

Their startled shouts joined Xavis's screams.

Pet retreated to the far side of the room to avoid Desmodian's lashing tail. The six spines were extended to their full length. While Desmodian would never hurt him on purpose, his trio weren't immune to accidents.

"Xavis spoke to Maddax about rumors of the *Trailblazer*'s location." Desmodian shoved the agents a little harder against the glass, forcing them to watch as Brog struggled and Xavis screamed. "We couldn't go running off into the Iota Cloud without being sure. Maddax is a source of information, and you've done this to my mate just for doing his job."

It was Irih who spoke instead of Nauzeia. He hadn't said a word since entering the medical room but filled the gap when his partner failed to respond.

"That explanation will never hold up in court. Surely there are other informants he could have gone to other than his old drug dealer."

Pet's heart rate climbed to match the beeping medical machines. They had been completely deafened by Xavis's screaming a moment ago. The fact that he could hear them at all meant Xavis had calmed a little, but it hardly felt like a win.

Desmodian's tail fell still and poised stiffly in the

air. "So you plan to blackmail us? Hand over the décor or you'll have Xavis arrested?"

In that moment, Pet saw two possible outcomes stretching before them like a diverting river. White water waited for them with both options, but on one they had a hope of reaching calmer waters eventually, while the other would inevitably bash them against the rocks. It all depended on which words the agents chose.

It wasn't Irih but Nauzeia who made the choice for them.

"We're not trying to blackmail you. As DPS agents, we're mandatory reporters, and a known drug user communicating with a drug dealer looks suspicious. Add to it your other companion's previous charges of prostitution, and it paints a bleak image of the character of your crew. We're asking you to turn the ship around and hand the décor over willingly. If we report that you cooperated, a judge will give you leniency. You might be innocent, but you've chosen to surround yourself with criminals. If you continue to defend them, you'll be one too."

Desmodian laughed.

Pet flinched. That laughter, combined with Xavis's distress, sounded like breaking mirrors and sharp edges.

The laughing ended abruptly and Desmodian spun the agents around to face him. He unstrapped the hammer from his back and braced it on the floor in front of him. It stood only inches from the agents' faces, and he crossed his arms over the head.

"I'm curious. When you contacted your people, what did they tell you about me? Or did they even bother looking into me?"

From his position, Pet couldn't see Desmodian's

expression, but his posture said more than his masked face ever could. He looked like an executioner just before the blade fell.

Both agents remained with their backs pressed to the glass while Nauzeia spoke as if reading directly from a report. "Desmodian of Gonthorn. Born to an affluent family. You voluntarily joined the Gantry shortly after coming of age and ended up Commander of Unit 22. On your last mission, you and your team were MIA for six months. When you returned, you were honorably discharged. Within a year of returning home, you were disowned from your family, then registered the *Vanguard* with yourself listed as captain."

At each item on the list of his life, Desmodian gave a little nod and waited for her to finish. "You're missing a lot of details, but I'm not surprised. My people aren't considered part of *civilized* space since we refuse to host a Gantry base, so we don't share much information with the intergalactic government."

Nauzeia couldn't seem to decide between watching Desmodian's face or his weapon. "How does this relate to your shipmates' crimes?"

With the scrape of metal against metal, Desmodian dragged the end of his hammer against the floor. "You keep prattling on about their crimes. You should be more concerned with mine."

In the other room, Xavis's screaming finally fell to a more bearable level. Pet inched around Desmodian to see through the window. He was glad to find Brog no longer struggling to hold Xavis down, but it was clear the ordeal wasn't over.

Even partially conscious was more conscious than

Xavis needed to be right now.

Against the beeping of the machines, Pet almost missed the sound of Desmodian tapping his mask with one pointed nail.

"If you knew anything about my people, you would recognize this. Your little recitation of my history skips right over the year between my release from Unit 22 and registering the *Vanguard*. Let me fill in your records. After we were released, Brog and Xavis came to stay with me since they had nowhere else to go. My family didn't like this. My biological brother wasn't a nice man. He committed all kinds of crimes, and our family's wealth protected him, but even that has a limit. When I brought Brog and Xavis home with me, he saw it as an opportunity to dump the blame for his crimes on them. Tried to have them framed using the same reasons you just did. No one would question their guilt. His crimes were serious enough they would've been executed. My brother tried to kill my mates. So I took care of it."

"Took care of it how?" Nauzeia looked like she regretted the question as soon as it came out of her mouth.

Desmodian hesitated, tracing the edges of the mask that perfectly fit his face. "In Dhen'in culture, murder is such a heinous crime, even prison isn't good enough. Murderers are banished from the planet after being forced to wear the face of their victim." He tapped the mask again. "My brother and I looked alike, so it was a perfect fit."

Something slimy squirmed in Pet's stomach. So many times he had casually remarked that the mask looked like bone. He could never have predicted how right that observation was or that it once belonged to Desmodian's own brother.

Xavis grew quieter as his gradual sedation took effect, but the silence was shattered when Irih started screaming in his place.

"Murderer! This whole ship is full of junkies and prostitutes and murderers. Forget jail, it needs to be purged."

Pet blinked, and suddenly, Desmodian had Irih pinned to the window by his throat.

"You really should watch your mouth."

"Let him go. You can't do this." Nauzeia moved as if to defend Irih but backed off when Desmodian pointed his hammer at her.

She backed right into Pet, who quickly shoved her away. If asked, he would say it was because he didn't want her touching him, but just for a moment, with Nauzeia standing so close, it had looked like Desmodian was pointing the weapon at him.

Desmodian kept Irih pinned while addressing Nauzeia. "This isn't how I wanted things to play out, but here we are. You don't realize the position you're in. This is the Stardust. Your authority means nothing out here, and we're past communication range. Even when we leave hyperspace, you won't be able to reach anyone. You're alone, and if you don't return, no one will ever know what happened to you."

"You wouldn't."

"I killed my own blood to protect my true family. Compared to that, killing you would mean nothing."

Xavis finally fell completely silent.

A moment ago, this would have brought relief, but when Irih pushed Desmodian's hammer to truly point in

Pet's direction, it became a footnote in his mind. He tried not to react. Logic insisted the threat wasn't meant for him, but he couldn't stop himself from flinching.

Desmodian quickly pulled the hammer away.

Despite the hand around his throat, Irih turned his grimace into a grin. "Killing us might mean nothing to you, but what will it mean to him?"

It was time to speak. He needed to reassure Desmodian and show a face of confidence. He did neither of these things, not by choice, but simply because he was incapable. An emotion had to be identified to be controlled, and Pet couldn't understand his own twist of fear and confusion enough to keep it off his face.

When Pet remained silent, Desmodian drew back, bringing the agents with him. They left the room, chased by Pet's silence.

At the door, Desmodian hesitated.

For a moment Pet thought he would offer some clever solution to the situation like he usually did. However, this time he left without a word, marching the agents away and leaving Pet alone in the little outer room.

The sounds of the medical machines provided the only mark of time as Pet stood indecisive. Should he run after Desmodian? No, he still had no idea what to say. Xavis's past with drugs was exactly that, the past. Pet had been happy to ignore it.

Murder, on the other hand, felt much more present. Even after the incident with his previous owner, it was a level of crime Pet had never considered before.

Looking down, he still held Xavis's feather, which had been crushed during his moment of fear.

The door behind him opened, and Brog leaned out without leaving the medical room. "Des lock the agents up somewhere?"

Pet shrugged but kept looking at the crumpled feather, smoothing the barbs back into place.

If Brog saw, he didn't comment. "You can come in now."

The main medical room brought a new series of sounds. The steady rhythm of Xavis's heart, the rise and fall of his respiratory rate and other complex readings all beeped in mechanical symphony. Pet sat in a chair near the bed, feather clutched in his lap, and matched his breathing to the machines until he throbbed with the rhythm of Xavis's life.

Across the bed, Brog threw himself into another chair designed to handle his weight. "I've got Xavis stable for now, but we'll have to keep him sedated for a while. His nervous system's in overdrive. That's why he was in pain."

It almost looked like Xavis was just asleep, except for the pallor of his skin and a burn mark just under his ribs.

Pet reached out, and when Brog didn't stop him, lightly touched around the wound. He could have covered the damage with his thumbprint. "This isn't how people are supposed to react to a neural disruptor. Something went wrong, didn't it?" He paused, waiting for Brog to either agree or correct him. All he got was a noncommittal nod. "Does it have to do with that purple light he controls? I've never seen anyone with that kind of ability, or even heard of it."

The legs of Brog's chair screeched horribly against the floor as he shifted. "Well, uh, yeah. With Xavis, it's a…special situation. But, uh, it'll be fine. Don't worry. More importantly, I should explain somethin' those agents said about me."

Pet recognized the change of topic as a diversionary tactic but didn't have the energy to care. It was enough work searching his memory for the agents' only mention of Brog. "They called you a prostitute. Is that how you ended up in Unit 22?"

Brog shifted again, and the chair scraped in the other direction. "Right, Xavis told you about the unit. Heh. I can't even deny it. That's exactly what I was. It seemed like a simple equation to me. I didn't have any money but had people who wanted to sleep with me. Ocans usually stay with their family units, so a lone Ocan tends to draw people in. Everyone was happy until I took the wrong client. His father was some xenophobic politician who didn't like the idea of their son sleepin' with an alien. The man reported me to the authorities and bribed someone to ship me off to Unit 22 just to make sure I was as far from his son as possible."

"Jerk." It was the best support Pet could offer at the moment.

"Yeah, but I'm not unhappy about it. Would prefer not to have a criminal record, but it brought me to Xavis, and later Desmodian. You know, when Des first came to Unit 22, I didn't like him much. He seemed the same as all the other commanders. Just some rich boy usin' the military to skive off from family duties. Didn't take me long to realize I was wrong. Unlike the others, he was a good guy. And he is, you know. He's a good guy. I know hearin' about his past may sound scary, but you don't have to be afraid of him."

"I'm not afraid of him."

"Yeah, but—"

"I said, I'm not afraid of him."

Brog's silence felt as unnatural as Xavis's stillness. Unlike Xavis, however, Brog's unnatural state was fleeting.

"All right, you're not afraid. But you've had a lot thrown at you today. No one would hold it against you if you're feelin' unsettled."

The words of understanding should have brought him comfort, but the slimy thing in his stomach that had found life at the first mention of murder renewed its efforts to crawl up his throat. He couldn't hold Brog's gaze and stared down at his own lap instead.

A final screech sounded from the chair as Brog stood.

Pet still didn't move. He counted Brog's footsteps as the Ocan rounded the table and approached him. If given the choice, he would have been happy to watch nothing but the floor for the rest of his life, but strong fingers hooked under his chin and forced him to look up.

"It'll be okay." Brog never looked away from him, not even to blink. "I know this is probably more than you signed up for when you joined our ship, but we've faced far worse dangers than a couple o' overzealous agents. We always come out fine. Just have a little faith."

He didn't say what Pet should have faith in. Them? The ship? The universe in general? Wherever the faith should be placed, Pet certainly had none in himself.

# Chapter Twelve

*Then*

2689 felt smooth metal walls on all sides, even under the water, until he found the edge of the circular hatch. If he could count on one thing, it was the arrogance of landowners. So expectant that décor would always do as told, they hadn't bothered to lock the hatch door.

Even with the light of Xavis's pendant, opening the hatch proved difficult. The handle was stiff and refused to move. 2689 threw all his weight against it, fingers growing numb, as he convinced the handle to turn little by little. Eventually the hatch swung open. Climbing out of the tank with the grace of a newborn, he clung to the side of the chamber as he regained his balance while dripping water everywhere.

Luckily, a set of robes hung on the wall. He hadn't looked forward to sneaking around the estate naked. Outside the deprivation room, the few people he passed were too busy to pay him any attention. He had to move quickly. Someone would inevitably notice 2689's escape, but the staff's habit of ignoring décor bought him a little time.

His first real obstacle came at the door. The guards had grown used to letting 2689 outside over the last few days, but never unescorted. 2689 insisted their guests had asked for him and stuck to the story until the guards gave up and let him out. They would undoubtedly report him, shrinking 2689's already limited time even further.

An abnormally high number of guards lined the path between the estate and the landing pad. A good bluff may have gotten him out the door, but it wouldn't get him near the ship while Owner's cargo was being loaded.

2689 hid behind an unused cargo transporter as he weighed his options. From this angle, he could just see the top of the *Vanguard* over the wall. If he couldn't reach his goal, his goal would have to come to him.

Fiery feathers caught the sun. Xavis knelt on top of the ship, messing with one of the panels.

Pendant in hand, 2689 ran his thumb over the jewel so it glowed and pointed it toward the ship. The light which looked so bright in the deprivation chamber barely showed under sun.

Hope blossomed and died in almost the same moment as Xavis looked up then disappeared inside the ship. 2689 clutched the pendant, letting the jewel dig into his palm. He couldn't wait for another of the trio to emerge. He would be dragged away soon, and he would lose his one chance to do something worthy of being remembered.

Movement appeared on top of the ship again, and Desmodian stepped from the upper hatch in place of Xavis. He stood haloed in sunlight, as bold as a lighthouse beacon.

Then he leapt off the top of the ship and disappeared from 2689's view. Voices shouted words too far away to distinguish.

A moment later Desmodian reappeared on top of the surrounding wall, more than twenty feet up in the air.

It was quite a show of strength and agility. Even the guards looked unnerved as Desmodian jumped from the wall to land in front of him.

"What're you doing out here, Pet? Were you lonely? Sorry we got separated so quickly, but the job has to come first."

Scaled fingers twisted around a lock of his short hair, making him blush. He tucked the hair behind his ear, simultaneously pulling it out of Desmodian's grasp. "It's fine."

Behind the Dhen'in, several guards talked over their radios while glancing his way. Whatever they heard made them look increasingly more concerned. His time limit had almost run out.

Desmodian didn't let him go, abandoning his hair to run a thumb over his lips instead. "You say that, yet you look upset. Don't be. These last few days were fun. I'm looking forward to taking another job on this planet so we can see you again."

2689 pulled away, his arms wrapped protectively around himself. "If you do see me again, I'm sorry. I won't mean to ignore you. In fact, you should probably stay away."

"What do you mean?" Desmodian pursued him as he retreated.

A pair of guards left their position by the wall and headed toward them. They didn't run, but they walked with purpose.

His time was up.

"Owner is going to resell me. I won't remember

you. But that's not what I'm here for. You need to check the cargo. Some of it may not be what Owner said it was. I don't want you to get in trouble."

"What?"

The guards reached them.

"Is this décor bothering you? We're deeply sorry, sir. We'll take it back inside where it belongs."

While one addressed Desmodian, the other grabbed 2689's arm and dragged him away.

2689 didn't fight. He'd done what he meant to do. The trio had a chance now.

Desmodian protested, but the guard pulled 2689 away and out of sight.

Then he was back inside the estate, behind walls and under ceiling where décor belonged. No more open sky or fresh grass. No more nights of pleasure or days of companionship. That was gone and soon would be forgotten.

Guards deposited him at the feet of Curator, who looked like she wanted to hit him but restrained herself. They stripped him of everything, even Xavis's pendant, then dumped him back inside the sensory deprivation chamber.

This time they learned from their mistake and locked the hatch. He had no choice but to float aimlessly in the water and wait. Nothingness pressed around him, invading his mind and turning his thoughts equally blank. His memories still existed, but they felt distant, like watching a recording on a small screen very far away.

The harder he fought to hold on to his thoughts, however, the further they drifted away. He could only admire them distantly, like little stars in the night sky.

The pleasures he recently discovered became the most intangible. Such intense feelings seemed impossible while all his senses were damped. Had he only imagined them?

Like a crack in an already struggling dam, that single thought brought waves of nothing flooding into his mind.

Time no longer existed. A distant thought said he would be there for a long time, but he struggled to understand what *a long time* meant. He would be there until he was not. That was as far as his thoughts could go.

Unable to worry about anything else, he floated.

## Chapter Thirteen

*Now*

They spent eight hours in hyperspace, the maximum limit a ship could safely spend in such a state without hurting its crew. This didn't get them to the Iota Cloud, but another hyperspace jump would be too risky so soon after the first. They would have to cover the remaining distance the long way.

A clear path lay between them and the Iota Cloud, but sometimes in space, a clear path was the worst. Distant star after distant star passed slowly by the windows, each the same as the next. Xavis remained asleep, and the strained atmosphere between Pet and the conscious two of his trio made the days awfully long.

Pet spent most of the time hiding in their bedroom. His attempts at reading didn't go well since all the books technically belonged to Desmodian. He tried watching movies, but everything programmed into the holographic tablet was something he had either watched or planned to watch with his trio.

His efforts to write music lasted a little longer. Music had a proper writing system, but that was a much later lesson. Instead he made up his own symbols to represent the music in his head. It would look like mindless scribbles to anyone else, but it made sense to him.

He needed a change of scenery. The bedroom felt stale after days spent soaking up his discontent. For the sake of the ship, if nothing else, he decided to relocate his ill mood.

Leaving the bedroom and his attempted music behind, Pet headed for the garden instead. It looked the same as when he'd helped Xavis fix the floor panels. The same path cut through the same plants and trees, all under the same honeycombed glass ceiling. This brought comfort, while mocking him at the same time. Something should have changed without Xavis.

At the center of the garden, he found the first change, or, more accurately, an addition.

Desmodian rarely ventured into the garden. It had always been Xavis's designated space.

Pet peered through the greenery at Desmodian sitting under a flowering tree, hammer strapped to his back. Leave? No. He'd developed a sudden comradery with the surrounding plants and become rooted to the ground.

Desmodian shifted, giving the impression of opening his eyes without eyes to open. "I just heard from Brog we've reached the Iota Cloud. Entry will be rough, so we all need to strap in."

"All right." Pet traced one of the purple lines of the path with his toe. Did the glow look darker than normal? It was hard to tell without a comparison.

Desmodian slowly stood and approached Pet from between the plants.

His scales camouflaged him among the leaves, green on green. Wherever his feet touched the path, purple lines changed to another shade of green. The bright aqua color outshone the dull purple, but it faded when he passed, leaving afterimages of his footsteps behind. "I...have something for you. It got a little ripped up, but nothing that couldn't be fixed." From a pocket, he pulled out the headpiece Pet lost in the scuffle with the agents, whole and unbroken once again.

Pet grimaced at it. "I don't want it."

Desmodian pulled away. "Oh. I'll just hold on to it then. If you want it later." He turned to leave.

Pet grabbed his arm. "Wait. I'm...I'm sorry. It's all my fault."

Cool hands cupped his face and Desmodian pulled him closer.

"What'd you mean? What's your fault?"

His touch felt so good Pet shuddered. "Everything. I put on that outfit because I wanted to be a tease. I went to the control room to distract Xavis, and because of me, the agents were able to sneak up on him."

"Oh, Pet, that's not your fault. I'm sure Xavis isn't mad."

"He should be." Pet's composure crumbled. His spine curved over itself until he needed Desmodian's help to stand. "And you should be. You...you didn't want to."

Desmodian tipped his head up, forcing Pet to look at him. This earned a broken laugh. Desmodian saw through every scale in his body. No matter where Pet looked, he always met Desmodian's gaze. Making Pet *look* at him was done solely for Pet's benefit.

Although useless, the gesture did help him calm down and explain. "You didn't want things to 'play out that way.' That's what you said. But because I made myself a distraction, they were able to attack Xavis. If they hadn't hurt him, you wouldn't have had to threaten them like that. I forced you to do something you didn't want. It's my fault, and I'm sorry."

Desmodian stroked Pet's cheeks, wiping away tears that never fell. "I feared you hated me after learning what I'd done to my brother. It's not your fault, Pet. The moment those agents chose violence, they made violence inevitable. Plus, no matter what you wear or do, you're always distracting. We're used to it."

The wet sound that came out of Pet didn't sound like any recognizable emotion, which was appropriate since he couldn't classify what he was feeling. He leaned in to Desmodian's hands, and the Dhen'in met him halfway so their foreheads touched. The hard mask pressing against his skin reminded him of the core of their misunderstanding. With a tentative hand, he traced the line where foreign bone turned to familiar scales. He was touching something that had once been part of another person's body. It should have horrified him. Murder was a serious crime, yet it also showed how far Desmodian would go for those he cared about.

The Dhen'in people thought they shackled Desmodian with the mask of his victim. Instead, they provided a visual reminder of his dedication.

Pet may not be Desmodian's mate, but he knew in some small way, that dedication extended to him as well.

They breathed in each other's air and Desmodian's arms locked tightly around him. "We need to talk about this. All four of us. But that discussion will have to wait. Right now, we need to focus on entering the Iota Cloud. Then we can take time for ourselves."

They left the garden together.

In the control room, they found both agents already

belted into their chairs. The pair looked even more uncomfortable than usual.

Desmodian leaned down to whisper directly into his ear. "Entering the Iota Cloud can be dangerous. So, we brought out some special security straps for their protection that can only be released by a member of the crew."

"Should have left them to bounce around in their bunks." Brog maneuvered his way into the room, cradling Xavis's body in his arms. Even with his wingspan, the Scaacax looked distressingly fragile compared to Brog.

"He's still unconscious?" Nauzeia strained against her straps as if to get closer to Xavis, despite being on the other side of the room. "But…it's been days."

The scathing look Brog sent her made even Pet flinch.

Since it would be dangerous to leave Xavis alone in the medical room, he took Pet's usual place inside the antigravity bubble. He floated limp and weightless. His wings naturally curled around his body, blocking most of him from view.

This also meant Pet would have to take Xavis's usual place. It wasn't a perfect fit. The control chair had been designed for Xavis, and it needed adjusting to line up with Pet's proportions.

"Sorry if this is an uncomfortable ride." Desmodian checked Pet's restraints one last time before joining Brog at the controls.

"You two figure it out?"

"Getting there."

They needed no more than those few words. Then they turned their attention to the latest obstacle looming outside their windows. Apropos of its name, the Iota Cloud looked like a large cloud stretching in every direction. Several solar systems could hide within its borders.

One by one, Brog and Desmodian turned off the navigation equipment. The systems would go haywire as soon as they entered the Iota Cloud, so they would have to navigate by sight. Yet the cloud had almost zero visibility.

Desmodian turned on every external camera the ship owned, filling their screens with images of the *Vanguard*'s hull. "Ready?"

Brog raised a finger asking for one more moment.

Mechanics whirled over their head and the ship went dark. The ionized gases of the Iota Cloud reflected the most miniscule amount of light. It was a counterintuitive idea, but they needed to turn off the lights in order to see.

Sitting in near-total darkness out in the vastness of space was an unnerving experience no matter how necessary, and Pet clung tighter to his safety straps.

Brog's finger lowered. "Good to go."

The ship moved forward, and the cloud embraced them with hungry arms. Windows showed a mass of swirling white that flashed every time it caught the cameras' minimal lights.

Looking at the screens, Pet could barely see the edges of their ship cutting through the fog.

An alarm on one of the still-operating control panels beeped. Not the we're-about-to-crash kind of beep, but the you-need-to-look-at-this-right-now kind. Although insistent, it didn't inspire the same terror as the more urgent alarm.

At least not in Pet.

The agents, however, struggled for composure. "Should we be worried about that?" Nauzeia seemed to be keeping her voice as gracious as possible.

It was enough to get her an explanation from Desmodian. "That's the electrochemical sensor. The cloud is full of hydrogen pockets, which we don't want to hit. The sensor uses carbon monoxide to detect hydrogen."

Of all the *Vanguard*'s sensors, it wasn't very precise. The closer they drew to a hydrogen pocket, the faster the sensor beeped, hinting at which directions were safe and which to avoid.

The scene outside the window never changed.

It looked like they weren't moving, but the safety straps pressed against Pet every time the ship's momentum shifted. First digging into his left shoulder, then pressing against his right hip. He wished for the comfort of his antigravity bubble, but he wouldn't deny Xavis the extra protection.

Had the CS *Trailblazer* really tried to cut through this? From what his trio told him about colony ships, they moved slowly, so most of the passengers stayed in cryosleep for the voyage. Only the captain and a basic skeleton crew remained awake to maintain the ship. The decision to cross the Iota Cloud would have been made by a couple dozen people and had put hundreds at risk.

Pet hoped his trio found them, not only for the sake of saving so many lives but also because he wanted to see a colony ship for himself. Colonizing other planets was the human race's only hope for survival, but it required resources their planet didn't have. Funding colonization was the whole point of selling décor. By giving up his rights as a living being, he made it possible for other humans to live. From that angle, it seemed like a worthy trade.

Beeping kicked up again as the sensors warned them of another hydrogen pocket. The *Vanguard* changed course, only to activate a second alarm.

"Shit." Brog pounded furiously at the controls.

Desmodian slid his chair along the tracks to check a screen in front of Pet. "Can we get around?"

Brog didn't need to look up to answer. "No. They're too close together. Watch out."

The ship lurched. One side tipped up and the other down, spinning them like a top.

Pet curled as small as possible and clung to his safety restraints, waiting for it to stop.

They hit another pocket and went spinning in the opposite direction.

It felt like someone shoved Pet's brain to the back of his skull.

"Fuckin' hell." Brog had all four arms braced against the control console. "Perfect time for Xavis to be asleep."

They spun so fast Pet could barely turn his head to look over at the antigravity bubble.

Xavis floated like an eddy of peace among the chaos as his wings gently bumped against the sides of his protection.

His trio worked so seamlessly together, yet with one piece missing they came unraveled. Pet regretted that he couldn't fill the role. He couldn't be Xavis for them. He could only be Pet.

The ship flipped in another direction.

Pet lost track of whether they were going up, down, or sideways. In space, concepts like up and down didn't matter, yet his stomach still seemed to be going a different direction than the rest of his body.

Desmodian shoved his chair back to the center of the room closer to Brog. "Hold on."

"What'd you think I'm doin'?"

Pet and Brog both shouted in alarm as Desmodian unbuckled his safety straps and pushed out of his chair.

The centripetal force of the ship threw him into the observation windows.

From Pet's perspective he looked suspended in the middle of the swirling fog.

Rather than try to stand, Desmodian crawled to the edge of the window and dragged himself along the wall until he reached the ceiling. There he clung to the various pipes and pulled out one of the panels Xavis often tinkered with.

Green light surged through the panel and out to the rest of the ship. External cameras showed the light passing along the hull from bow to stern.

The ship came to a sudden and jarring stop. Everything froze as if a cosmic hand reached down to momentarily halt time.

Pet rocked against his straps and slammed back into the chair. Winded and dazed, he looked around for the others.

The agents were in a state similar to his.

Brog remained cognizant but panted as he braced against the control panel.

Desmodian dropped to the floor on soft feet. He stumbled with an unusual lack of grace but regained his balance before he fell.

"You couldn't have done that earlier?" Brog flopped back in his chair hard enough to make the poor thing groan. It may need to be replaced soon.

"I didn't see you trying anything." Desmodian reclaimed his own seat with equal exhaustion. "You okay, Pet?"

Bruises ached along Pet's chest and shoulders. "Let's not do that again."

They all took a moment to catch their breath, silently questioning what to do next.

Pet had completely forgotten about the agents until Nauzeia disrupted their pause.

"Are you sure the ship you're looking for came here? Colony ships carry a lot of people and equipment. This seems like a big risk for them to take."

Metal jingled against metal as Pet struggled with his safety straps. The restraints had done their job and kept him in place. Now he wanted out.

Desmodian slid along the tracks back to Pet's side of the room, answering Nauzeia while simultaneously helping him escape.

"That's the word among other ship-dwellers. To avoid the conflict in the Partition system, their path would have led them right toward the Iota Cloud. They wouldn't be the first large ship that tried cutting through the cloud instead of going around."

Brog took Desmodian's place at the center console. "Idiots think their size will protect 'em. Not surprised they panicked and tried to hyperspace outta here. At least, that's the best guess. Won't know until we pick up the trail."

Pet's restraints came free. The agent's question rankled his memory. He spun Xavis's chair to face them. "You've never asked about the colony ship. Not if they're okay or if we expect to find them alive. I thought it was because you already understood the situation, but you don't. You just never asked."

Reflections off the swirling cloud provided the only light in the room.

It cast one half of the agents' faces into darkness so Pet could only see one eye on each of them. Together they equaled a whole face, until Irih retreated into his partner's shadow.

Nauzeia pulled forward as far as her straps would allow. "The survival of a lost colony ship is beyond our authority. We're art experts, not scientists or mechanics. There's nothing we can do about the ship. We're here for the preservation of décor."

It was an improvement. At least she answered his questions directly. "There are five hundred people on that ship. Some are rich landowners bringing their possessions with them. There might be décor on that ship. Shouldn't you at least be concerned about that?"

Nauzeia's half of the face also disappeared as she pulled back.

Pet could only see the agents by their silhouettes, two deeper shadows among the dark.

Color interrupted the vast whiteness outside the windows. Creatures swam through the ionized gas, each about half the size of the *Vanguard*. They looked like large fish, if fish were predominantly fin rather than body. Long gossamer appendages trailed behind them like jewel-colored streamers, sweeping paths through the cloud. At least a dozen of the creatures floated near the ship.

Pet took advantage of his freedom to climb out of

his seat and press against the glass. "What are they?"

Brog joined him at the window. "Nimbus glaukos."

The words meant nothing to Pet, but their attachment to such an astonishing sight automatically made them beautiful.

"Live in the Iota Cloud. Best way through the cloud is to follow 'em. Poachers also hunt 'em, so we'll have to be careful."

The *Vanguard* started moving again slowly but with more confidence. Instead of following the beeping of the electrochemical detector, they stayed in the nimbus glaukos's wake. One of the creatures passed so close to the *Vanguard* it brushed the windows. The light reflecting through its fins broke into a dozen different colors.

For that moment, Pet felt like he was the fish swimming in his rainbow bowl as he looked out at the rest of the universe.

"Well. Either I'm upside down, or all of you are."

It was a voice Pet hadn't heard in days. He shouted and ran over to the antigravity bubble. "Xavis."

Xavis was disoriented but blessedly conscious. "Hey, Pet. Hope I didn't worry you."

The smile on Pet's face made his cheeks hurt. It was a good pain. "You're awake. Everything's all right now."

They had a path to follow, and his trio was whole again. Everything would be fine.

****

The nimbus glaukos's path brought them to the center of the Iota Cloud. Yet they found no sign of the CS *Trailblazer*. Without a trail to follow, they would have to send out sensor arrays to look for evidence of a recent hyperspace jump.

Pet sat with Brog and Xavis in the ship's bottommost airlock, preparing the arrays. The devices resembled little people with helmets over their heads. It seemed like abuse to jettison them into the cold vastness of space.

"I really missed all that?" Xavis perched at the top of the airlock, scrolling through a series of pictures on a holographic tablet.

On the floor below, Brog sat amongst a halo of wires and bolts as he fixed a malfunctioning array.

Watching him root around inside the machine was like watching a child's autopsy. Pet flinched every time Brog pulled out another piece.

Brog studied a frayed wire. "It was chaos without you here. We've essentially taken these DPS agents prisoner, and we nearly crashed the damn ship."

Xavis flicked through another image. "Glad you didn't, but I'm never taking my eyes off you again. I've put too much work into this ship for you to break it."

"Don't go away again." Pet poked at various bits of the disassembled array. It looked like chaotic nonsense, so he turned his curiosity to what Xavis was doing instead.

Xavis jumped down from his perch to join Pet on the floor. "You mentioned something earlier. I'm not surprised the agents never asked about the people on the *Trailblazer*. That's not their concern, but it is ours. I'm looking through the ship's passenger manifest."

Another image dragged onto the screen for Pet to see. "Will that help us find them?"

The CS *Trailblazer* originated from Oculi 5, so the entire passenger list consisted of Oculians. They had a very geometric design. Flat planes and hard angles made it look like they were made of folded paper. Each came in a different pattern, but most had long triangular faces and thin limbs. At first glance, they appeared artificial yet were completely organic.

"If our theory about them making a hyperspace jump turns out to be wrong, we'll need to look for other reasons why they disappeared." Xavis turned to the last image on the list, which showed the captain. "I've been focusing on the top-ranked crew. So far everything looks standard. Mostly middle class. No criminal history. No records of domestic trouble."

"Don't bother with the crew." Brog opened the array further to reveal its coiled copper heart. "Keep your eye on the captain. Nothin' happens on a ship without the captain knowin'." The coil sparked. He cursed and yanked it free, resulting in a shower of electricity.

Xavis raised a hand to contain the exposed current within a bubble of purple light. It lasted for a moment but then died.

The distressed warble Xavis made would have broken even the coldest heart.

With a growl of frustration, Brog reached inside the machine, ignoring the zaps to his skin, and turned the whole thing off. "Still havin' trouble?"

Xavis flexed his hands a few times, bringing forth more purple light and watching it fade. "It's better, but I'm still weak."

The coil hit the ground among the other broken parts at Brog's feet. "Damn agents got lucky. Any other weapon and you woulda been fine. But a neural disruptor…that's different."

Xavis closed the holographic tablet with a shake of his head. "Don't get cocky. A bullet would end either of us as quickly as it would anyone else."

All four of Brog's hands raised in supplication. "I'm not sayin' that. I'm just sayin' it's ironic. Neural disruptors are only meant to subdue. Agents were probably tryin' not to hurt you and ended up makin' a mess of it by sheer luck."

Feathers rose along Xavis's shoulders like fur on an angry cat. "You're defending them?"

" 'Course not."

"Then I'm weak for falling to something so harmless."

"Don't be stupid. Desmodian and I wouldn't have done better. Electric. Magnetic. Anythin' that generates its own field is a fuckin' nightmare for us."

Their argument grew more heated.

Pet inched away until he hid behind one of the working arrays. He watched with wide-eyed dismay as Brog's attempt at placation backfired.

Xavis stepped into Brog's space, spreading his wings to challenge the other both physically and verbally. "So now I'm stupid."

Brog threw a piece of the malfunctioning array at the wall. "Damn it, Xavis. Stop puttin' words in my mouth."

Pet kept out of sight, with only his eyes peering around the edge of his hiding spot. The sound of shattering mechanics made him flinch, but not nearly as much as the sour atmosphere brewing between the other two.

"Then you should be clearer about what you're trying to say."

"I'm sayin' I'm sorry."

Xavis's anger deflated. His feathers fell flat, and wings drooped at his sides. "You're what?"

Like an old toy that had been sitting on the shelf too long, Brog slumped onto a storage box, which nearly broke under his weight. "I'm sorry I was such a damn coward."

"A coward?" Xavis repeated the word, incredulous at the very sound of it. "How does any of this translate to you being a coward?"

One set of Brog's arms shrugged, while the other crossed close to his chest. "I warned those agents, but it wasn't good enough. If I'd scared them off properly, they never would have attacked you."

With a bewildered shake of his head, Xavis braced both hands on Brog's shoulders. "You moron. Only you would interpret not scaring someone enough as being a coward."

Affection returned to Xavis's voice, but Pet remained hiding.

With Brog sitting and Xavis standing, the Scaacax was the taller of the two for once. It was rare to see Brog looking up at someone. "I didn't push hard enough. I shouldn't 'ave been afraid of layin' a hand on 'em. I've done it before. When that commander back in our unit was bullyin' you, I made sure he was too scared to ever go near you again. I was already a criminal servin' my time. What'd I have to lose? But now…"

Xavis finished the thought for him. "Now you have something to lose. So, you didn't get physical with the agents, and you think that would have kept them from attacking me."

"It did before. Fuck, Xavis, I still remember the weight 'a you in my arms when I carried you to the medic the day we met. I swore I would never have to pick you up off the floor again."

Taloned hands tugged Brog out of his slump. "It's not your fault."

"I should 'a been able to make a difference." Standing up from the box, Brog managed to avoid stepping on any of the scattered broken pieces.

With a shiver of his feathers, Xavis's wings settled into their usual place on his back. "Everything's been a little off recently. I think we can forgive you for not being up to your usual intimidating standards."

"Now you're just coddlin' me." Brog scoffed at Xavis, but he still seemed pleased. "Sorry about the array."

"It wasn't working anyway. We'll survive without it. But we should send the rest of these out soon or we'll never get this job done."

With their argument finally silenced, they turned their attention back to the sensor arrays.

Xavis noticed Pet's hiding place first. "Oh, Pet, it's okay. It was just a misunderstanding. You don't need to hide."

"Great, now he's gonna be scared 'a us, too."

Pet gripped tighter to the array shielding him. "I'm not scared of you. And I'm not scared of Desmodian either."

Brog held up his hands in double surrender. "All right, you're not scared, but you need to come out so we can finish up here."

Pet held his head high as he stepped into the open. He wasn't scared. His emotions were much more complicated than simple fear.

Together, the three of them gathered Brog's tools and swept away the broken machinery.

When they left the airlock, Pet watched through the window in the door as, one by one, neat rows of sensor arrays dropped through the ejection tubes in the floor.

The metal children would spread in every direction, scan the Iota Cloud, and return with their findings.

"I'll tell Des the arrays have been deployed." Brog closed the window into the now empty airlock. "Nothin' left to do but wait."

"I'll, um, I'll just…" Pet scrambled for something else to do. It was difficult when his job mostly entailed keeping his trio company.

"Come on, Pet." Xavis wrapped an arm around his shoulders to bring him along with Brog. "You can't keep avoiding him."

If Pet had feathers like Xavis, they would have fluffed up with his indignation. "I'm not avoiding him."

Both Brog and Xavis gave him a look. Two sets of inhuman eyes conveyed paragraphs of disbelief without words.

"I'm not. I just don't know what to say. He spent days thinking I was afraid of him, while I was busy wallowing in my own guilt. It sounds so stupid, and I feel like whatever I say will only make it worse."

They crossed a catwalk hanging over the main cargo area. The ship was on its early evening settings, meaning the light lowered to intimate half-shadows.

It made the open bay below them look like a bottomless pit. The kind that, if he fell into it, he would never stop falling.

Xavis refused to let go and casually ensured Pet couldn't run away. "If you don't know what to say, then don't say anything. You should know by now, Pet, you've got assets even better than words."

Brog still bore signs of stress from their fight, and although Xavis seemed nonchalant, there was tension in the arm around Pet's shoulders. They acted as normal as they could, but it was just that. An act. Pet had never been fond of theater. The overdramatization and staging felt manipulative, and he wondered how the audience could buy into something they knew was fake. That opinion hadn't changed since the theater entered his real life.

They diverted into the arm of the ship housing personal rooms like the bedroom and the gym. Neither of these were their destination, however. Instead they headed to the training room at the very end of the ship's arm.

Pet had spent time there before, but it never failed to surprise him with how out of place it seemed. Wood panels and paper screens covered the walls, and those were some of the most difficult textiles to maintain on a ship. It also had no furniture, except for a rack of weapons on one wall. Thin mats covering the floor were soft enough to cushion their steps, but firm enough to provide stable footing.

At the center of the room, Desmodian stood alone. Dressed in loose clothing, he wielded his hammer with an expert hand as if he fought an army of invisible opponents.

Each precise movement was filled with such intent, Pet could almost see the faces of his enemies.

What faces did Desmodian see?

The tall hammer spun so fast it became a metallic blur, yet it was no less accurate for its speed. Twirling the hammer over his head, he slammed it down, stopping only an inch before the weapon hit the mats. He held the pose, breathing hard, knees bent at right angles and tail out straight behind him for balance.

Brog leaned against the doorway. "I think that hammer's gotten slower."

"It's your eyes that have gotten slower." Desmodian came out of his stance and popped the stiffness from his shoulders. "The arrays taken care of?"

"All fired off, except for one…unfortunate piece of trouble. We don't need it though."

"Trouble? I see. I'd ask if you fixed it, but I can already tell." The hammer switched to Desmodian's other hand, so it was half hidden out of sight.

Desmodian watched Pet. It was evident in the way Desmodian angled his body, so that the largest areas of exposed scales pointed Pet's direction.

At the same time Xavis stepped aside to expose Pet a little more, though his arm never left its place around Pet's shoulders.

They were giving him an opportunity to make the first move, but Pet stood on the literal threshold of indecision.

Desmodian sighed and pointed his hammer toward the weapon rack. "Brog, pick something. I need a real opponent to fight."

"You sure?" Brog stepped onto the mats to look over the selection. "Still seems like that hammer's gotten slower. You might not be able to keep up."

"Grab a weapon and I'll prove you wrong."

Desmodian waited at the center of the room, arms crossed and stance defiant.

Brog scoffed at the selection on the rack. "I prefer guns. Or my own fists."

"Shut up and pick something."

From the weapons displayed on the wall, Brog picked a type of handheld blade that formed a perfect circle. A padded handle on one part of the circle provided a safe grip, but the rest wrapped around his fist with the sharp edge pointing outward. Four hung on the rack. More than most people could wield at a time, but the perfect number for Brog.

Light glinted off the metal, emphasizing its sharp edge.

"They're using real blades?" Pet had assumed these were training weapons, not live-edged weapons ready to flay skin from bone.

Xavis led Pet off to the side of the room. "They know what they're doing." He sat against a wall near the paper screens and brought Pet to sit in front of him, nudging him to lean against Xavis's chest.

Brog and Desmodian squared off against each other. Some silent instinct told them when to start, and they lunged at the same time. Desmodian blocked Brog's bladed fists with the shaft of his hammer and the sharp edges slid off without leaving a scratch.

When one blow failed to land, Brog came at him with three more.

Desmodian ducked to avoid a circular blade swinging near his face and the tips of his indigo hair kissed the edge. Never stopping his momentum, he spun and swung at Brog's exposed ribs.

Rather than dodge, Brog stepped inside the

hammer's range and knocked it off course.

Xavis leaned in to speak directly into Pet's ear. "See. They know what they're doing."

Pet was too engrossed in the match to say anything.

The pair heaved against each other as they looked for weak spots. Neither managed to land a strike, but it didn't take away from the impressive display. They pushed each other across the mat, their steps in sync as if dancing instead of fighting.

A hand slipped under Pet's shirt to stroke his stomach. Talons scratched lightly at his skin, making sensitive muscles jump.

"Impressive, aren't they?" Xavis's other hand traced a path up the inside of Pet's leg. "You can hear how hard they're breathing even from here."

Pet would have to take Xavis's word for it. He couldn't hear their breathing over the rush of his own. His blood pumped hot as hands ran over his skin while Brog and Desmodian pitted their strength against each other.

Desmodian struck one of Brog's blades with enough force to rip it from his grip and sent it flying right at Pet and Xavis.

A glint of sharpened metal was all Pet saw before talons snapped out in front of him.

Xavis caught the blade by the handle midair, about a foot from Pet's face, then tossed the blade toward the rack. "A little more care, please."

The weapon landed on a hook.

Neither Desmodian nor Brog gave any indication of hearing him, but their fight gravitated to the far side of the mat.

Two things happened at once. Desmodian caught

Brog's foot with the end of his hammer to tip him off-balance, and Xavis slipped his hand between Pet's legs.

Brog reacted by leaning into his fall. He rolled backwards, putting space between himself and Desmodian and landing on his feet. Another circular blade was lost in the process, but it didn't slow him down. He faced Desmodian with two hands armed and two hands empty.

Pet, on the other hand, arched into the touch, cursing his shorts for blocking skin-on-skin contact. He reached behind him to grip fistfuls of feathers.

Xavis bit his ear. "Who do you think'll win?"

The hand on Pet's stomach slid farther up, drawing his shirt out of the way. Then, finally, the hand between Pet's legs slid inside his shorts. Xavis could be incredibly delicate when he wanted. Talons tearing the cloth of his shorts had to be intentional. Pet helped it along. Clothing could be replaced, and he desperately wanted those hands on him.

The ring of metal against metal cut the haze of lust clouding his mind. He had lost track of the match and looked back up in time to see both Desmodian's hammer and Brog's remaining weapons go flying. They landed far out of reach and the match devolved into a fist fight.

Since he had twice as many fists, Brog should have dominated, but Desmodian's much longer tail provided an advantage. The six spines on the end lashed at Brog's face, forcing the Ocan to back up enough for Desmodian to grapple him to the floor. They became a tangle of green and blue as they strained to subdue each other.

Xavis's hand sped up between Pet's legs, spurring

on his arousal.

"They usually would have stopped by now. Looks like they're trying to impress you."

This made Pet's heart stutter as much as Xavis's stimulations. The stutter turned into a chuckle, which turned into a laugh.

They wanted to impress him? Surely they knew they didn't have to try. He was impressed from the first moment they looked at him as more than a pretty decoration.

Although, from their reactions, it seemed this wasn't known as well as it should be.

His laugher shocked Desmodian and Brog from their fight. They collapsed to the mats, on their backs and panting hard. Both stared at him with equal looks of bewilderment.

Even Xavis fell still behind him.

With his new revelation firmly in mind, Pet left Xavis's lap. No one moved as Pet approached Desmodian and threw a leg over his hips, straddling him.

Desmodian's hands cautiously held his legs. "Something to say, Pet?"

No, Pet didn't have anything to say. Words weren't his best asset.

Fisting his hands in Desmodian's shirt, he leaned down and kissed him. The kiss remained light at first, until Desmodian deepened it by pressing his tongue into Pet's mouth. He welcomed it eagerly. Too much had passed since he felt the familiar muscle twining with his own. A week may not seem like much in the long run, but it was their longest stint of abstinence since Pet arrived on the *Vanguard*.

Pet broke the kiss only long enough to discard both their clothes. Their bodies lay flush together, but Pet was eager for more. He inched down to better align their hips but was stopped when Desmodian grasped the backs of his knees and trapped Pet's legs against his sides.

"I'll take you after. First I want to watch you enjoy it."

More hands roamed his back and gripped his hips. Based on the number, Brog knelt behind him, spreading his ass and moving his hips to a better angle.

Desmodian kissed him again, cupping his face to keep him trapped as Brog pushed one finger inside. It felt bigger than normal, already stretching his muscles to their limit. He squirmed in discomfort.

Brog removed his finger to instead massage at Pet's stinging hole. "Xavis, you go first. It's been a few days, and I don't have any oil on me."

"Oh, I see how it is. Using me as your own personal lube." Xavis sounded exasperated but quickly took Brog's place.

"You like it and you know it."

They needed to quit joking and hurry up. Pet would have scolded them, but his mouth was too full for words.

Desmodian's grip tightened, obviously sensing Pet's impatience and imploring him to stay as his tongue pushed a little deeper.

Finally, Xavis leaned over Pet. The Scaacax's slick cock slid between his ass cheeks, spreading natural lubricant around his hole.

Pet squirmed again, this time from the tingle of Xavis's aphrodisiac soaking into his skin. He wanted to feel something inside him, and he no longer cared if it brought discomfort. His cock throbbed, and he ground his hips down against Desmodian's dual arousal. The friction gave him some relief, but not enough.

Xavis, though, wouldn't be rushed. He took his time getting Pet nice and wet. After what seemed like forever, Xavis deemed him prepared and thrust inside.

Pet's muscles relaxed much easier in response to the intrusion this time. He shuddered as Xavis pushed slowly but steadily into him, filling him the way he had missed so much over the last few days. It was bliss, especially when Xavis teased against his pleasure spot. Pet could have died happy then, with Xavis buried inside him and Desmodian's tongue sliding down his throat. He only regretted the physical limitations that kept Brog from joining as well.

At least the Ocan seemed content to watch, idly stroking his engorged cock as he waited for his turn.

Without warning, Xavis pulled out and slammed back in.

The entire length of his arousal speared Pet open in one quick movement. Pleasure coiled in Pet's stomach and surged through his veins. Milky drops leaked from his weeping cock and landed on Desmodian's scales.

Xavis kept up his quick pace. He molded himself to Pet's back as he thrust in repeatedly, barely leaving Pet a chance to catch his breath.

"I made you a promise before, Pet. Remember. One after the other, over and over, until you can't even beg for it."

He rode hard as Pet braced himself on hands and knees.

Each thrust forced Pet to rut into Desmodian

below, and the drag of those dual cocks provided extra stimulation. Pleasure turned sharp in his belly. Pet pulled away from Desmodian, trying to draw it out, but this only pushed him deeper onto Xavis. He couldn't escape. Against all attempts to hold on longer, he tipped over the edge and came with a muffled scream into Desmodian's kiss.

The Dhen'in stroked Pet's cock, milking him through his climax. He didn't stop until every drop had been coaxed to spill over his stomach and Pet collapsed against him.

Xavis held his hips, continuing to pound inside until he came as well.

Pet lay shuddering against Desmodian's chest as Xavis's heat filled him. It gave him a moment to catch his breath.

Desmodian soothingly stroked his head until Xavis pulled out, but the moment he left, a heavier weight replaced him.

The head of Brog's cock settled against his hole. "You're much looser now."

Pet whimpered, still overstimulated from his orgasm.

Desmodian pressed kisses over his face. "Come on, Pet. Be good and open up. You've taken more than this before."

Brog pushed forward and the head popped inside.

Instead of relaxing as he should, Pet grew tense.

"Fuck, he's tight." Brog groaned and hunched over him like some wild animal. "Wet, but tight. Uh, I could come just from this."

Desmodian ran a featherlight touch down Pet's sides. "What did I say? You need to relax for us, or bad

Pet gets punished."

The sharp crack when Desmodian slapped his ass came as a surprise, but not as much as the flush of arousal that washed through him. His cock grew hard again as the sting resonated long after the initial strike.

"Someone liked that," Xavis said from where he lounged nearby enjoying the display.

Desmodian took a stronger grip on Pet's hips. "Something to play with later. For now…" He gently pushed Pet back toward Brog, spearing him onto the Ocan's shaft one ridge at a time.

Brog groaned as Pet's hole swallowed him. "Oh, fuck. He's squeezing around me."

Pet couldn't keep himself still. His hips jerked in small motions, not sure if he wanted to push forward or pull back. Each ridge that opened him caused a new groan to catch in his throat. When Brog finally hit as deep as he could go, Pet panted so hard a line of spit dripped from his mouth. He ducked his head but forgot there was no hiding from Desmodian's full-body gaze.

"Don't hide, Pet." Desmodian tipped his head up so everyone could see his ruined expression. "You're such a little slut. You love it. We love it. What's the problem?"

Brog grabbed both of Pet's arms just above the elbow. "The problem is you're takin' too damn long." He pulled Pet into him as he began fucking in earnest.

Pet's back arched, and the extreme angle brought a new flood of pleasure every time Brog slammed inside. Desmodian watching from such a close vantage as he was taken apart made it even better.

Scaled hands held his legs just below his ass, keeping him open and pliant.

Pet begged every time Brog hit that perfect spot deep inside him. Two words on repeat. "Please. Please. Yes. Please. Yes." He didn't beg for anything specifically. He just needed to beg, because as good as it felt, he couldn't reach his end.

"Need some help, Pet?" Xavis ran a hand down Pet's stomach.

Before he could reach Pet's throbbing cock, Desmodian stopped him. "No, don't. If he wants to come, he has to work for it."

Pet wept in frustration but couldn't find the air to protest. Brog sped up, hitting harder and deeper than before, and it was all Pet could do to keep breathing. Brog reached his peak, but Pet still couldn't find his own. When the other male came, Pet trembled at the feeling of being filled again but remained unsatisfied.

After Brog pulled out and let him go, Pet tried to catch his breath, but almost immediately, Desmodian's dual cocks took their turn to shove inside him. Pet barely had the strength to moan. He would have collapsed without Brog holding him up.

"You're not done yet. Looks like Desmodian wants you to ride."

Hands on his hips encouraged him to move. No telling whose, but the message was clear. Bracing himself against Desmodian's chest, his legs trembled as he lifted up and down. He clenched against the dual shafts sliding inside him, drawing out the friction.

Desmodian bucked up into him at the same time, nearly throwing him off and encouraging a faster pace.

Pet did his best to keep up, but he felt sloppy and uncoordinated. Someone grabbed him from behind and held him steady. Brog or Xavis, it didn't matter.

Pleasure coiled tight in his gut as the dual shafts hit all his best spots at the same time.

Below him, Desmodian's chest rose and fell rapidly as he gasped.

"You want to come, Pet?"

Pet whined and nodded, but Desmodian didn't oblige. Instead he gripped the base of Pet's cock hard enough to cut through his pleasure.

"That's not how you ask for what you want."

A desperate sob welled up from the depths of Pet's chest. "Please. Please, let me come. I need it. Please." He never stopped riding, grinding down harder on Desmodian with each plea.

"Good Pet." Desmodian released his grip on Pet's cock to stroke him right over the edge of his pleasure.

When he came, Desmodian kept thrusting through his orgasm, pushing it to last as long as possible. Pet barely managed a weak mewl as his pleasure splashed over the Dhen'in's stomach and chest. Only when he finished did Desmodian come as well, adding to the mess dripping down Pet's legs.

He trembled even after the dual cocks slid out, and his trio laid him on the mat.

Xavis curled up against his back, arms secure around his waist and wings acting as a blanket. "You all right?"

Pet nodded against the mats, too tired to open his eyes.

"Look up at me, Pet."

He did, though with great reluctance.

Xavis looked abnormally serious. "Say please."

"Please?"

Xavis grinned at the others. "Guys, we have a

problem. He can still beg."

Oh, they weren't done. Pet groaned, but the noise that came out of him barely reached his own ears.

Desmodian stroked his cheek while Brog ran hands up his legs. "We can fix that."

Pet groaned and let his head fall back against the mat as Brog propped his leg up on his shoulders. It was going to be a long night.

## Chapter Fourteen

*Then*

The hatch opened with a deafening creak. Light spilled into the dark, followed by hands that grabbed him and pulled him from the water. Their touch grated his skin.

Outside the chamber he collapsed.

People spoke around him, their voices buzzing in his ears. "Get up and dry off. Mister Stiril wants this over with. More trouble than it's worth, I swear."

He knew that voice. It was Curator. This meant something, but what? Everything was blank in his head.

"Get up."

His thoughts churned so slowly, he had to translate each of Curator's words individually. Get. To claim something. Up. A direction, usually toward the sky. The sky sounded like something good, but he had no idea how to claim it, or even what it looked like.

More hands grabbed him and hauled him to his feet. He nearly fell again, but weight settling on his legs reminded him how to stand. The hands didn't leave. He hated them. The touch against his bare flesh made him shiver in disgust. A memory of touch that felt good flashed briefly, but this wasn't the touch he wanted.

"What's wrong with it?" This time the voice wasn't Curator's.

Curator answered. "It's been in the deprivation chamber for longer than usual. Plus, we increased the amount of banali root in the water."

"Should we do something?"

Curator shook her head. "No. It'll fetch a higher price at auction this way. Décor are supposed to be blank."

Décor. That was him. An object meant for looking pretty. He didn't need to react, only stand still. So he did exactly that.

It took Curator and not-Curator a few attempts to convince him into a robe. They repeated a number several times. 2689. Did that mean him? It must, but it felt wrong.

They brought him to a room filled with other humans. It reminded him he wasn't Vunqril like Curator. The humans looked strange to him, but so did the Vunqril. There was a species he wanted to see, maybe multiple species, but it was neither of the two beings in front of him.

Curator instructed him to sit on one of the dozen identical cots, told him to sleep, and that she would come for him in the morning. Then she left.

The other humans approached with caution. "Is it true? Did you sleep with them?"

Another décor hissed at the speaking one. "Shh. We aren't supposed to talk about that."

"Yeah, but come on. We all want to know."

"I do not. It's crude and gross. That's why two-six-eight-nine is getting resold."

The rest of their conversation went ignored. He slept with someone? There were twelve beds in the room, so they obviously all slept together as well. Yet they spoke about it like a bad thing. Maybe it wasn't the sleeping, but the person being slept with. He did remember an abnormally large bed.

Thinking about it too much made his head hurt, so he stopped and lay down. Curator told him to sleep. Décor were supposed to follow orders, so he did. The others continued trying to speak with him but gave up when he didn't respond.

The night passed. With his eyes closed, awake and asleep felt the same. Images passed behind his eyes. They seemed like memories, but indistinct, like an image painted on the bottom of a pool. He saw people all around him, hands on him, but not the hands from earlier. He heard laughter, his own and others. Oh, happy images. Hopefully they were memories. His head felt so empty. There had to be room for happiness in there somewhere.

A bell woke him up, if he had slept. It sounded familiar. Other décor rose from their beds and stood in line at the front of the room, so he did too.

Curator arrived and handed out assignments and outfits for the day.

Unlike the crystal and white silk ensemble he remembered wearing, this outfit was made of pale gold chains interwoven like cloth. Most of the decoration lay on the shoulders. The illusion of broad shoulders made the waist look thinner, but it also inspired another memory. Someone else had broad shoulders, two sets of them, with a prominent color of blue.

Curator handed him nothing. He waited in the corner as the others finished their preparations. Once they left, Curator ordered him to follow her. Compared to the other décor, he felt plain dressed in only a basic robe.

At first, he almost walked at her side. He caught himself before she noticed and retreated a few steps. Another memory surfaced, of his hand hooked around someone's arm as he walked at their side. It disappeared before he could remember anything else. It felt like a hole had been carved inside him. Yet, a hole could only be dug if something existed there in the first place.

They arrived at Owner's office. The room looked familiar. Memories of frustration and anger filled the hole in his mind. Owner had been upset with him. He hoped that had changed.

Owner looked up from the paperwork on his desk. At the sight of him, disgust twisted Owner's features.

Anger would have been better. Disgust implied hatred. Whatever had happened was bad enough to make Owner hate him.

Owner walked in a circle to observe him from all angles. "It's better."

He kept still and ignored the feeling of eyes evaluating him.

Curator didn't circle, but she joined Owner's evaluation. "We should be able to get a good price for it. Especially since we don't have to list how it's been used. Only physical or behavioral defects."

A tremor passed through his hands and he clasped them together. He managed to get them under control by the time Owner returned to the desk.

"We may not have to report it, but gossip spreads. We need to sell it before rumors get out of hand. Those ship-rats have finally left, and the cargo is on its way. Once this is taken care of, I can wash my hands of the whole revolting experience."

"You mean to go to the auction house today, sir?" Curator's voice gave away nothing of her opinion.

"We're going immediately. I don't want that reminder in my house any longer. Get it loaded up. We leave in an hour."

During that hour, they stored him in a side room to keep him out of the way. Someone pressed a bowl of bland nutriment into his hands at some point. It was tasteless.

The room had no clock, and no one bothered to inform him of the time. A minute, an hour, or a day, it didn't matter. He stayed until an unnamed Vunqril fetched him. They never looked directly at him. Judging from the number of spires on their head, they had some standing within the estate, but not a lot. The person brought him outside to the garage, passing the manicured gardens on the way. He reached out to pluck a flower and scatter its petals along the ground but was shuffled along too quickly to grab one.

Inside the garage, a transport vehicle waited. More staff loaded him into the vehicle and strapped him to a reclined chair. Décor were always transported this way, in the back of a reinforced vehicle, alone, with small slit vents for air and light.

The vehicle came to life, and he swayed in his restraints. Small slits of sunlight dragged across the floor. Every time the vehicle turned, the sunlight patterns changed. First hiding in one corner, then striking lines across the wall. Since he couldn't move, he imagined the sunlight searching his box for him.

At some point he dozed off, hypnotized by the vibrations and the semidarkness. The next thing he knew, the doors opened and flooded his space with light. The sun hung low in the sky, only minutes from disappearing. They had traveled to another part of the planet, moving against the time zones, so he lost an entire day in only hours.

He was unloaded from the vehicle but never released from the restraints. Instead they wheeled the entire chair into the nearby building.

The auction house sold many valuable things, including décor. Its front catered to the luxurious sensibilities of its clients, but the back of the building maintained a cold sterile design meant to keep the merchandise pristine.

People he couldn't see wheeled his chair through the barren halls and into a processing room. It looked the same as all the other rooms, with white walls and tiled floors, except for the intimidating machine hanging from the ceiling. This room was his very first memory and would be again when they finished.

The few indistinct memories in his head didn't seem worth hanging on to. Losing them would make no difference.

So why did he want to leave?

More people waited for them in the room. Someone spoke with Owner and Curator. A badge marked them as a Processor and the person in charge of removing his memories.

The Processor barely paid attention as 2689 was finally released from the restraint chair. "This is rather last minute. We don't have any auctions scheduled for a few days."

Other people in similar uniforms to Processor's stripped away 2689's clothing. Cold hands poked and prodded him, inspecting each body part. A medical tool slotted into his mouth to take his vital readings, followed by a bright light shining in his eyes to judge pupil reaction.

He stood at the center of the activity, naked and unresponsive.

When the examination ended, he was put back in the restraint chair and wheeled under the hanging machine. The straps didn't let him move, but he could crane his head enough to look up at the looming contraption. His insides squirmed at the sight of it. Something echoed in the back of his hollow head. It felt precious.

Processor lowered part of the machine onto his head.

"Wait."

Unyielding metal clamped around his skull.

"Wait. Wait. Wait."

His words went unheeded, but he repeated himself anyway. He needed to remember whatever lurked at the back of his mind one last time before it was taken. He wouldn't try to stop the memory wipe, if only they would let him remember what felt so very important.

"Wait."

## Chapter Fifteen

*Now*

During the night, they moved from the training room to the bedroom. The mats of the training room were comfortable, but nothing compared to the mattress on their bed. Even then, Pet didn't sleep until it was almost morning. Hours later when he woke, his trio lay around him, limbs tangled together in peaceful slumber.

Attempting to climb from the pile turned out to be a bad idea. Sore muscles protested the night's vigorous exercise, and he curled up on the bed groaning. The noise woke his trio, bleary-eyed until they noticed his discomfort.

Xavis propped him against a mound of pillows. "I think we worked him a little too hard."

From the far side of the bed, Brog handed over more pillows. "You surprised?"

Pet meant to protest but was interrupted when Desmodian lifted his leg and slipped a finger inside him.

"Not damaged. But definitely overstretched. We'll need to recover him."

The trio scattered, but Xavis returned almost immediately with familiar ointments for soothing bruises and stressed muscles. Starting at his hands and feet, he generously applied the various remedies over

Pet's whole body.

Brog returned with a glass of water.

Oh, he *was* thirsty. Pet downed the drink in one go and was left with only an empty glass by the time Desmodian came in carrying a familiar tool, which he set beside the bed.

The tool's main body bore some resemblance to bombs from old movies, especially the display screen on the front and the wires looping along both sides. Its secondary piece looked like a short metal rod with a flared base that connected to the main box by remote signal. More pillows surrounded Pet to support his open legs, and with the help of a little oil, Desmodian slipped the rod inside him.

It went in easy after enjoying his trio so many times. Pet tipped his head back against the pillows, listening for the click and whir sound the tool made when activated. The first electric jolt came as expected. A sharp tingle made his stomach twitch, like the static shock he got if he shuffled his feet and grabbed one of the ship's metal handles.

The strange sensation gave neither pain nor pleasure. If he had to describe it, he would compare it to the moment right before orgasm when he balanced on an edge that could tip either way. It felt like nothing and something all at once, and although he writhed against the pillows, he had no desire to make it stop.

The first time they used it on him, he hadn't been able to relax until they explained the mechanics. Technically labeled as a medical device, it returned elasticity and strength to overworked muscles. Its inventers had intended it for athletes and laborers, but its popularity came when a physical therapist discovered its use for healing the body from the effects of frequent sex. After that, sales spiked drastically.

The process took about two hours. They kept the bedroom lights dim, but judging by the lighting in the hallway, morning had slipped into afternoon.

Brog and Desmodian left to check if the sensor arrays found anything, while Xavis took the first shift watching over Pet. Still tired from the previous night, the two of them curled together for a little more sleep. Xavis's hand draped over his stomach, feeling the rhythmic clenching of his muscles as he dozed.

Xavis left when Desmodian took his place.

"Feeling better?" He rearranged the pillows and tucked Pet under his arm.

Pet gave a languid nod against Desmodian's scales.

"Then it's probably time for more."

A quick adjustment of the settings on the remote, and the tool's electrical pulses increased. They hit harder and lasted longer with little down time between. Pet panted as the repeated throbbing inside him felt like getting fucked again. The internal stimulation conflicted with his otherwise unaffected cock.

Desmodian ran a soothing hand over Pet's back. "Calm down. If you get worked up, it'll take longer. Focus on something else. Let's work on your reading."

"Seriously?" Another pulse hit him, and Pet gasped.

"Yes, seriously." He held out a holographic tablet for Pet to see. "Take a look at this. I'm reviewing information about the *Trailblazer*. Crew logs aren't the most riveting, but the sentences are simple."

Pet tried, he really did, but his concentration lagged as he scrolled through the list of the *Trailblazer*'s officers and crew. Words didn't come easy even under the best of circumstances, never mind while trying to ignore the tool pulsing inside him. "Height, six feet, four inches. W-w-weight, 234 units. Primary color, blue. Pr-pr-previous employment, transportation for Aurora Horizon."

"Good." Desmodian flicked the screen to the next person on the list. "Do it again."

This continued for a few minutes as Desmodian showed him pictures of the *Trailblazer*'s crew.

Oculians looked like folded paper and came in a variety of shapes and colors. It created an interesting collection of personal data below each picture.

Alien names were hard to pronounce, and Desmodian let him skip the ones containing sounds impossible for the human voice, but the repetitive nature of the information made it easier to figure out. "Height, six feet, eight inches. W-weight, 311 units. Primary color, r-red. Previous employment, emergency supply r-runner for Alpha Defense Corp."

"Wait a minute." Desmodian pulled the tablet back to himself.

His fingers blurred through the images, too quick for Pet to read anything on the pages. Probably too quick for Desmodian to read much either. "W-what is it?"

"Aurora Horizon and Alpha Defense Corp are both located in the Partition system."

Pet shifted, causing the tool to press a little harder. He had to catch his breath after the next pulse. "Is…is that important?"

Desmodian didn't need to turn his head to look at him. That full-body vision focused his direction, like the warmth of a hand caressing his skin.

"The Oculi and Partition systems sit next to each other, so sometimes Oculians take jobs in the Partition system. But the Partition system is an active warzone, so it's not common."

Pet looked at the tablet again, searching for whatever connection Desmodian had made. "Is it strange that two members of the *Trailblazer*'s crew used to work in the Partition system?"

"Not just two." Desmodian turned the tablet off and sat thinking, tapping the device against his bottom lip. "There's at least a dozen on the list who used to work in the Partition system. And they're all...fuck. The skeleton crew." He stood and called for Brog over the intercom system.

Pet watched him from the bed. That wasn't a good sign—the aggravated twitching of Desmodian's tail. "So...the *Trailblazer* is in the Partition system?"

Brog appeared before Desmodian could answer him, and the two held a whispered conversation in the doorway.

Their bedroom was small enough that Pet should have heard them talking from the bed. The fact that he couldn't meant they were purposely lowering their voices. The conversation only lasted a minute, and in the end, Desmodian left and Brog joined Pet in the bed.

Pet rolled onto his stomach and hugged the pillows in a futile search for relief. "Do we know where the *Trailblazer* is?"

"We got readin's back from the arrays. They're definitely in the cloud, but it'll take time to narrow down where." He looked as concerned as Desmodian had, but on his already heavy face, the expression carried less weight.

They passed the time discussing the mechanics of their search. Brog did his best to explain the science behind how they tracked the lost ship in a way Pet could understand. When a ship moved faster than light, it cast off superluminal particles that reacted violently to the ionized atoms of the Iota Cloud. Most of the techno-jargon went right over Pet's head, but the sound of Brog's voice soothed him like the rush of deep ocean waves.

The whole thing would have been pleasant if not for the fact that Brog was obviously avoiding something.

During a lull in the tool's pulsing when he could speak without stuttering, Pet tried bringing it up again. "I don't understand. If we can find the ship, why're you so worried?"

Like the first hints of a storm rolling across the horizon, Brog's sigh whistled with a hollow resonance. "Over two dozen members 'a the *Trailblazer*'s crew used to work in the Partition system. They were at a bunch 'a different companies doin' different jobs, but that's a lot. Desmodian's double-checkin', but looks like they're all on the *Trailblazer*'s skeleton crew."

"That's the crew in charge of the ship while everyone else is in cryosleep, right?" Pet had no experience with cryosleep. The *Vanguard* was small, and only three people could fly her, so they had no need for a skeleton crew. They did things the old-fashioned way and stayed awake for the whole trip.

"Yep." Brog popped the word in a show of annoyance. "And that means they were in control 'a the ship when it went missin'. Active warzones like the

Partition system have a lot 'a corruption. Long trip like this would be perfect to hide a smugglin' run, and the Iota Cloud attracts a lot 'a poachers."

Pet sighed. "That doesn't sound good." The resonance of the tool inside him changed, pulsing harder in a sign it was almost done. He buried deep in the pillows to stifle his voice.

Brog lifted the corner of one pillow to peer down at him. "You keep moanin' like that and you're gonna need to recover again."

Pet smiled from within his fortress. The Ocan was only half kidding.

Finally, after two hours of stimulation, the tool finished its job and fell quiet. Pet slumped over the bed, gasping as he caught his breath.

The rod slid out, only to be replaced by Brog's fingers. "Like our first time."

Those fingers teased him just long enough to get him riled up, then pulled out and left him empty. His whine of disappointment turned to a yelp when Brog pinched his ass.

"Maybe later, Pet. For now, get up. We need to figure out what to do next, and we're not leavin' you alone. Not with those damn agents still on the ship."

Pet's legs trembled under his weight, but otherwise he felt great. His body had been rejuvenated, like the strain of the last day never happened.

If only their entire voyage could be erased so easily. From the moment they left the Gravity Well, things seemed to keep getting worse. No matter how much effort his trio put forth, after what happened to Xavis, their confidence rang hollow. They never traveled alone or left their backs exposed to a room. It was all wrong. Their ship should have been safe.

After a quick trip to the bathroom to clean up, Pet dressed in the same outfit he wore to the Gravity Well. The short vest, long arm gloves, and translucent harem pants cheered him up. Its orange-to-purple gradient made him think of sunsets. That was exactly what they needed, the end of one day so they could start another.

For the final touch, he also added the simple headpiece with the kaleidoscope pearl. He didn't need the reminder of his trio's generosity, but he suspected they did.

Brog stayed with him, never straying more than an arm's length away. He even insisted on stepping through any doorway first. When Brog suddenly stopped at the entrance to the control room, Pet slammed into his back.

"Why're they out?"

His width filled the entire doorway, blocking Pet from seeing into the room.

Desmodian answered from somewhere beyond Brog. "Apparently there is a long list of laws dictating the accommodation of government agents on private vessels. We can restrain them for their own safety, but not ours. And even that has a time limit."

Fed up with staring at a wall of flesh, Pet crouched to peer between Brog's legs.

In the farthest chair, Xavis hunched over a screen at the controls. He was preoccupied with something but occasionally threw a glance toward Desmodian.

At first Desmodian looked relaxed, slouched in his own chair with one leg thrown over the armrest. Yet, it was only an act. The position angled a significant portion of his scales toward one corner of the room.

Leaning forward until his shoulders pressed against the backs of Brog's knees, Pet saw the agents standing in a corner of the control room. Judging by their stiff postures, the agents knew they were being watched.

"So what?" Brog still refused to move from the doorway. "No point worryin' about their damn laws after the stunt they pulled."

"Still not a good idea to break the law if we don't have to." Not a single muscle on Desmodian twitched. Not even his tail.

A strange but familiar tension passed through the trio, like a live current bouncing between conductors. Then Brog surrendered the argument.

The doorway emptied of its blockade as Brog finally let Pet into the room and claimed his own chair at the controls.

With the efficiency of cogs snapping into place, a sense of rightness settled over the trio.

It was such a drastic change from just a few minutes ago. His trio had figured something out. Normally he would just ask, but with the agents in hearing range, he didn't want to draw attention to his trio's plans. Instead, he moved to the observation windows for a front-row seat.

They pressed on through the Iota Cloud by following the wake of the nimbus glaukos. Long orange fins swept in front of the window as one of them drifted close to the ship.

Because of the cloud around them, Pet couldn't see all of the creature at one time. The fin disappeared into the white to be replaced with an eye larger than he was tall. It rolled like its own little planet with galaxies swimming in its pupil. For a moment it seemed to look at him.

The first warning of danger came when a sudden stillness fell over the nimbus glaukos.

Its fins hung limp within the mist like flags on a windless day. Then, all at once, it turned and disappeared into the cloud.

"What happened?"

Desmodian sat up from his observant slouch. "Pet, come away from the window."

Pet went to join the Dhen'in at his seat, but Desmodian pushed him toward Xavis.

"Look after him."

Xavis didn't argue with the command. He just nodded and wrapped an arm around Pet's waist.

Lights flooded the window.

Pet blinked through the glare. Oh, those were spotlights from another ship. Static burst through their speakers, loud enough to make his teeth vibrate in his head. He covered his ears and didn't uncover them until Xavis adjusted the settings. The static became an unrecognizable language.

Or at least unrecognizable to him.

For Desmodian, however, it seemed this was not the case. "They want us to surrender."

How could anyone understand such a language? It sounded like someone striking a drum while leaning too heavily on a synthesizer.

From the corner, Nauzeia stepped forward until she stood almost equal with Desmodian's place at the controls. "Who are they?"

More unfriendly noise issued from the speaker, nearly drowning out Desmodian's simple but devastating answer.

"Poachers."

Vige had warned them back at the Gravity Well. Poachers roamed the Iota Cloud hunting nimbus glaukos. They would love to get their hands on décor. There would be no shortage of questionable buyers willing to pay a high price for him. He shuddered and clung to Xavis. Hopefully his trio knew what they were doing.

Something clanged against the hull of the ship, sending a vibration through the floor. A seldom-used screen started beeping from Brog's portion of the controls.

"They've put a magnetic lock on us. We're not goin' anywhere."

"We're going to open the side airlock." Desmodian was already pressing buttons on the console to start the process.

Nauzeia crowded him at the controls as if she meant to slap his hands away. "That's as good as inviting them onboard."

Desmodian stopped and leaned back in his chair. "Most poachers come from the Partition system. Their electronegative pulse weapons are no joke. These people will be coming on board, and we would prefer they don't punch a hole through our ship in the process."

Another *bang* against the hull, this one louder than before.

Brog's fists clenched and unclenched in the silence that followed. "They're on board."

Desmodian stood and brushed past Nauzeia. "Open the doors from there to here. Let's make room for our guests."

His trio vacated their controls and pushed the furniture as far to the side as the tracks allowed. This left the center of the room a desert of empty space.

Xavis stayed with Pet at the side of the room, letting him cling to his arm. "I should warn you. The Sclersy from the Partition system are…very large."

Pet sighed. "Of course. You know, for once I'd like to find a species smaller than me. Just to balance things out."

"They exist. Though they tend to keep out of trouble. There's this race of sentient slugs no taller than your ankles. They get around in motorized wheelchairs. We'll go visit them after this. You'll feel like a giant."

A wing brushed Pet's shoulder, and he calmed down. "Thanks." Getting through their current ordeal seemed much more certain with future plans waiting for them.

A distinct buzzing, like a live wire held too close to a microphone, heralded the invaders' approach. *Large* didn't begin to describe the being that appeared in the doorway. They stood nearly as tall as the ceiling, though stand would be the wrong word as they had no feet. In fact, they had no recognizable appendages of any kind. They resembled a nervous system missing the rest of its body. The tangled mass of organic matter glowed a white so sharp it looked blue.

Pet hoped this was a Sclersy. Anything larger would be a nightmare. The Sclersy had no head, so Pet categorized the denser tangle at the center of their body as the face. This didn't make their synthesized drumbeat language any easier to understand. However, they repeated themselves a moment later in poorly accented common language.

"Who is captain?"

Demands issued in the Sclersy's synthesized voice sounded even more menacing.

Desmodian stepped forward, though Brog and Xavis stayed close at his back. "I'm listed as the ship's captain. Desmodian of the *Vanguard*. This is Brog and Xavis. My crewmates. Why have you boarded our ship?"

He pointedly didn't introduce Pet. This was fine for Pet. He had no desire to be introduced.

The Sclersy ignored everyone but Desmodian. "You are Dhen'in. Are you not of Gonthorn?"

"No. I am not of my homeworld, and it is not of me. I claim only the *Vanguard*."

The Sclersy made another of the strange buzzing noises Pet had heard when they approached. It probably meant annoyance or some sort of equally irritable emotion.

"Ship-dwellers are strange. I am P'pavakass of Ackan. First and primary planet of the Partition system. And the rest of your crew?"

When it came to difficult languages, many species chose to translate their names into something the rest of the galaxy could pronounce. Not the Sclersy. The sound of the intruder's natural name among the otherwise common words gave the illusion of a radio signal that lost connection midsentence.

Desmodian continued ignoring Pet and instead gestured to the agents. "They aren't part of our crew. They're just guests and are here for their own reasons."

With a wave of one fleshy nerve, P'pavakass dismissed Desmodian's explanation. "They are on your ship. That makes them yours. We take your ship. You are ours now."

As décor, Pet had an unusually high level of experience with declarations of ownership. There were only so many ways the statement "you are ours" could be interpreted.

"Come." P'pavakass didn't turn toward the door, but merely started moving in that direction. Pet had been right. Their body had no proper front.

"We would prefer to stay on our ship." Desmodian made no move to raise his hammer, but Brog and Xavis stood a little closer at his back.

P'pavakass glowed brighter and part of their tangled body lashed out. Sparks danced through the air, and the criminal alien put a hole in their wall with the same nonchalance as someone backhanding a pesky bug. Luckily it wasn't an outer wall, or everyone would have been jettisoned into space. "Come."

This time there was no objection. Everyone, including the agents, followed silently. Pet stayed glued to Xavis's side, with Brog and Desmodian completing the triangle around him.

When they stepped onto the catwalk, two more poachers fell in behind their group. They weren't Sclersy, and Pet understood why people believed only criminal ships were crewed by multiple species. He lived amongst a diverse crew, and the combination looked odd even to him.

One of the poachers was of a species he didn't recognize—something purple and gangly—but the other resembled the stranger who accosted him at the Gravity Well. Those four legs, fish scales, and natural jewels were hard to forget. He would much rather be dealing with that drunken idiot than their gun-wielding counterpart.

Across the chasm of the main storage area, the airlock should have opened into empty space. Now it led into a new corridor branching off from the ship. The boxy architecture clashed with the *Vanguard*'s patchwork design. Its chrome surface looked to have once been sleek and reflective, but time and negligence had tarnished the metal like an antique mirror.

Before entering the main body of the poachers' ship, they were stripped of their weapons. The Sclersy collected everything, including Brog's personal arsenal, and deposited it in a bin that look suspiciously like a trash receptacle.

Then the poachers demanded Desmodian's hammer. He never let the weapon out of arm's reach. Yet he handed it over without complaint and watched calmly as it was discarded with the rest.

Once disarmed, the poachers brought them farther inside. The boxy, repetitive architecture made it impossible to tell where they were being led, but Pet had a feeling they were headed for the heart of the ship. Each step into the unknown made Pet's hands shake, and he tucked himself further against Xavis's side to hide his nerves.

To anyone who hadn't lived on a spaceship, metal smelled like metal. Those who did, however, learned that every metal had its own scent. The *Vanguard* typically smelled of clean steel and copper. It was a sharp but warm smell, like steam from a hot bath. In contrast, the poachers' ship smelled like iron and magnesium. The combination created an odd heavy odor that hung in the air like cold oil.

They reached an open room at the center of the

ship large enough to make even the Sclersy's immense size look small. A screen covered one entire wall, mimicking a window to the outside. It showed only the swirling cloud, but that was enough to indicate the ship was moving.

Due to the room's size, the non-Sclersy poachers were easy to overlook. Among the mix of different species, including an Ocan even bigger than Brog, the Sclersy held obvious authority. Wherever the tangled ball of nerves went, the other species stayed to the edges.

P'pavakass approached the largest member of their species at the center of the room.

This had to be the leader. Why else would the smaller Sclersy defer to the larger one in such an obvious way?

P'pavakass and the leader spoke in their humming and drumbeating version of communication, and P'pavakass gestured toward their little group of prisoners. The wave of their nerves perfectly emulated Pet's previous owner when showing off his collection of décor.

It earned a reaction from the leader, but without a face or recognizable body structure, Pet couldn't tell if the reaction was positive or negative.

"Here." All of the leader's nerves rippled as they delivered the order.

Non-Sclersy poachers herded their group forward until they took P'pavakass's place.

"You are captain of this crew?" The leader spoke to Desmodian and only Desmodian.

They didn't introduce themselves before making demands as P'pavakass had, which Pet appreciated.

Remembering P'pavakass's name was hard enough. He was happy to simply refer to the large Sclersy as Leader.

"I am listed as the *Vanguard*'s captain." The careful word choice allowed Desmodian to answer the question without committing himself to a title.

Leader issued more orders in their own language. The synthesized drumbeats sent both Sclersy and non-Sclersy scrambling. A panel in the wall opened opposite the screen-window, revealing prison bars divided into a dozen cells. All stood empty, except for one.

The prisoner held behind the bars resembled folded paper. It was an Oculian.

Wait, Pet had seen this individual before. Their face once stared back at him from the *Trailblazer*'s crew logs, listed as the captain of the ship.

Every Oculian had a different color and folded pattern. The *Trailblazer*'s captain was an unfortunate shade of puce and had long double-jointed knees with a triangular head that extended well below his collar.

His name was Captain Covols, if Pet remembered the logs correctly.

Their captors herded them toward the cells. Since none of his trio protested, Pet went along quietly, but the sight of prison bars pushed the agents past their breaking point.

"Hey, hey, we're not even with them." Irih backed away from the poachers closing in on him. Nauzeia tried to calm her partner, but it was a lost cause.

The gangly purple poacher struck Irih with the same kind of neural disruptor the agent had used on Xavis. Irih didn't fall unconscious as Xavis had, but the left side of his body went limp. He would have fallen on his face without Nauzeia's support.

She managed to keep him upright long enough to comply with their captor's orders and enter the open cell.

Several poachers, including the larger Ocan, crowded Brog and forced him into a separate cell. He snarled and slapped away hands that wandered too close.

Xavis stroked Pet's hair and sent his senses into red alert.

"Pet, we need you to be brave."

Others lined Xavis up with his own cell while Pet still clung to his arm. Before they were forced inside, the poacher with fish scales and jewels stepped between them.

On instinct Pet tried to get back to Xavis, but Xavis pushed him away.

"Pet, calm down. It'll be all right, but you need to do what they say. Calm down."

Strange hands grabbed him. It was normally easy to listen to his trio, but they had never asked him to do something he hated so much. He fought off the unwanted touch, until the stranger's hands wrapped around his neck.

"Let him go. He's just scared."

Desmodian's voice sounded distorted through the rushing in Pet's ears. Unlike the one at the Gravity Well, this attacker had no interest in him. They looked bored as they squeezed tighter, sending black spots dancing over Pet's vision. Then he was abruptly released and dumped inside a cell. He lay where he fell, coughing against the cold floor. Somewhere in the distance he heard his trio's voices.

When he felt strong enough to sit up, he found Xavis straining against the shared bars of their cells, trying to get as close as the unyielding metal would allow.

Brog also called for him from the cell beyond, out of sight but not sound, demanding to know if he was all right.

"I'm okay." He flinched at the rasp in his voice. Even a long night entertaining his trio never left him sounding so abused.

"That was uncalled for."

Desmodian didn't sound happy.

Leader ignored Desmodian's accusation. "You keep strange things on your ship. Government agents that are not of your crew, and a pretty piece of décor. I didn't think they could be owned by ship-dwellers."

The Sclersy had no eyes. Yet the sense of being stared at made Pet shudder. He forced himself to stand, refusing to lie on the floor like a doormat.

"What we own is none of your concern." Desmodian looked unnervingly small next to Leader, but he stood his ground. Only the flicking of his tail gave him away. "We were hired to find the *Trailblazer*. That is our concern, and you seem to know all about it."

The non-Sclersy poachers released the *Trailblazer*'s captain from his cell and brought him to stand beside Desmodian.

Captain Covols looked worn, like paper that had been folded along its creases one too many times. Yet he still managed to stand tall. "My government hired you to find me?" He directed an expression toward Desmodian, which must have meant something unpleasant, because Desmodian's response was decidedly curt.

"Yes. The Oculian government was concerned when you lost contact."

Captain Covols scoffed, a snort of indignation recognizable in any species.

"Great. Well, here you are. Now, who rescues the rescuers?"

Desmodian angled toward the *Trailblazer*'s captain, giving him more attention without visibly turning his back to Leader. "Who says we're here to rescue you? We were hired to find you. Saving you from your own mess was never part of the deal. As you said, here you are. That means our job is done."

Evidently realizing he was on the verge of losing his only potential ally on the ship, Captain Covols's indignation turned to fear. "But…you have to…"

Desmodian cut him off. "You don't deal with ship-dwellers much. If you did, you would know. We don't 'have to' do anything."

Captain Covols took a step back, glancing rapidly between Desmodian and Leader. "Are you siding with these criminals? I should have expected this from ship-rats."

"Careful with your insults, Captain. You also live on a ship."

Pet leaned over to whisper to Xavis through the bars. "Why is Desmodian being so hostile? Shouldn't he be happy we found Captain Covols? It means the *Trailblazer* can't be too far away."

Xavis gripped the bars tighter, his talons sparking against the metal. "That man shouldn't be here in the first place."

In the cell beyond, Brog nodded and clenched his fists.

Leader's body momentarily flashed brighter as they interrupted the exchange between Desmodian and Captain Covols. "As amusing as this argument is, no one is going anywhere until I get what I am due."

P'pavakass floated up to Leader and handed them a box marked "dehydrated rations."

It was a common supply on ships and in poorer areas that couldn't afford fresh food, but Pet doubted the contents would be as ordinary as the label.

Especially when Leader held it aloft the same way someone might thrust a diseased cat toward a veterinarian—with a mix of disgust and a demand to fix the problem.

As ridiculous as it sounded, everything came down to that ordinary yet slightly familiar box. No matter what it held, it wouldn't be worth the trouble. Not worth five hundred lives or dealing with agents on their ship, and definitely not worth discord among his trio.

Nothing could be worth that.

## Chapter Sixteen

*Then*

Cold metal pressed against 2689's temples. His protests went ignored and a helmet dropped over his eyes. Through the dark he heard the auction house staff telling Owner he had to stay until they completed the memory wipe. Once the former 2689 was assigned a new number, then Owner would no longer be Owner. He would be merely Mister Stiril and was free to leave.

Those were their exact words. "Free to leave." This phrase stuck with 2689. Leaving was a freedom. Nothing emphasized 2689's position more. He couldn't leave if he wanted to, and he really did want to. Something in him screamed to leave, but leaving required freedom, and freedom only belonged to people.

2689 retreated to the safety behind his closed eyes and waited for the memory wipe. The machine's whirring drowned out all other noise. It put him into a trance as he waited, and he almost wished they would hurry up. Once his memories were gone, he could stop worrying about things he didn't remember.

A sudden banging overcame the noise of the machine. 2689 flinched and hit his head against the metal helmet.

He couldn't hear anything else, but he felt it, like

the electrical charge of a storm building in the clouds, high above and out of reach. The banging came again. One. Two. Three. The third bang brought more noise with it. Was the machine broken? The disturbance came from the other side of the room, not right above his head, but he could hope.

"Shit."

Someone shouted loud enough for him to hear through the helmet.

"Found him."

The voice inspired humor and relief. 2689 laughed without knowing why.

Protests, yelling, and more banging sounded muffled to him inside the machine. Sounds came and went too quick to make sense of them, but the commotion seemed to be getting closer.

"Don't touch that." That was the very clear voice of the Processor.

The machine whined, and the helmet lifted from his head. 2689 blinked rapidly as his eyes adjusted to the light.

The person standing before him was neither Vunqril nor décor. They were large, grayish blue, and had four arms. He couldn't remember seeing an Ocan in person, yet they felt familiar. Exhaustion swept over 2689 as he tried to parse the nonsense swimming in his brain.

The Ocan looked at him with bright orange eyes. "Hey, Pet. You okay? Say somethin' "

This earned another laugh from 2689. No one wanted décor that spoke. Didn't the Ocan know that? Maybe it was a trick by the auction house to give Owner less money for him.

The Ocan looked upset and called to another person behind him. "Xavis?"

Judging by the feathers, a Scaacax stood at the machine's controls aggressively hitting buttons and sending the auction house staff into fits.

"The memory wipe hasn't been activated yet."

The Ocan called them Xavis. 2689 liked that name. It brought to mind warm feelings of pleasure and fun.

"Well, get him out 'a there."

The Ocan's fingers dented the metal as he gripped the helmet.

With a name assigned to the Scaacax, 2689 found it easier to name the Ocan as well. Brog. A strong, aggressive person who was surprisingly soft at times.

Xavis's feathers stood on end. "I'm trying, but I can't risk poking around while he's still connected."

"Damn it." Brog drew a pair of guns from the holster on his hip and pointed them at the auction house staff. "One 'a you grounded fucks better release him."

Vunqril stood nearly as tall as Brog, but their spindly physique was much more delicate in comparison. Despite their fear and the way they trembled whenever Brog looked their direction, they didn't immediately give in.

"This décor belongs to its owner. You can't just come in and make demands."

For a moment 2689 thought Brog really would shoot them.

However, the Ocan shoved the guns back in their holsters. With all four hands free, he gripped the restraints binding 2689 to the machine. His muscles bulged and light flashed in his eyes. Then, with a shriek of twisting metal, the restraints tore in half.

2689 stared down at his freed arms, ignoring the shock and horror around the room. Was he supposed to do something? They had given him no orders as an owner would.

Brog pulled him from the machine. "Come on, Pet. You don't belong here."

He clung to the forearm around his waist, marveling at the strength that supported him so easily. "Belong? Décor belongs to its owner."

Double shoulders hunched and thick fingers twitched toward his guns again, but Brog kept the weapons holstered.

Whatever 2689 had done to make the other uncomfortable, he wanted to fix it. He tried to stand on his own, but his legs wobbled. The effect of his time in the deprivation chamber lingered, and with the added chaos of the last few minutes, his balance remained lost to him. They gave him one order and he failed.

Yet Brog didn't get angry, and no more orders came. Thick arms took his weight upon themselves and picked him up, ending any chance he had to redeem his mistake.

"They may not 'ave wiped his mind, but somethin' is definitely wrong." Brog brought 2689 closer to the group and farther from the machine. "He's completely out 'a it."

Everything seemed much bigger and more intimidating when he was restrained. From Brog's height, it all looked a little less impressive. This especially applied to Owner, Curator, and the auction house staff who stood against one wall, guarded by a third familiar stranger.

Desmodian. A Dhen'in of confidence, intelligence,

and hidden ruthlessness.

"They may have done something to him back at the estate." The Dhen'in never turned away from the line of people held hostage against the wall.

Owner's laughter made 2689 cringe. That wasn't his real laugh. That was his angry laugh, and it never meant anything good.

"Proper décor are supposed to be like that. Though I understand why you're confused."

No one else laughed with him.

The auction-house staff impersonated statues, and Curator kept looking around like salvation would magically materialize.

The angry laughter only lasted a few seconds, but it felt like it went on forever. 2689 clamped his hands over his ears to block out the imposter emotion. Laughter expressed happy, and yelling expressed anger. When these things crossed, he never knew what to expect.

Brog's hands twitched toward his guns again, but Desmodian acted first. Bracing the business end of his hammer under Owner's chin silenced the laughter with striking efficiency. "He wasn't like that before." The hammer dug a little deeper.

Owner didn't laugh again, but he still looked smug. "A problem I will be addressing with my Curator. She's been too lax with the quality of my décor. Though it's nothing a day in deprivation can't fix. Almost made the one you tarnished clean again."

2689 burrowed farther into Brog's arms to ward off the memories of the dark chamber, the water, and the silence.

Desmodian fell very still. "Deprivation? I've seen

sensory deprivation chambers before. They don't produce this kind of effect."

No matter what 2689 did, the anger around him kept increasing. Décor made their owner happy, and he was failing that. However, Owner was going to sell him, which would make him not Owner anymore. The trio weren't Owner, yet they acted as if he belonged to them. Maybe they were his new Owner. That meant he should listen to them.

Desmodian's hammer dropped from Owner's— Mister Stiril's?—chin down to his chest. The hammer flashed green, and the slightest tap sent Mister Stiril to his knees clawing at his throat. Another tap of the hammer and he could breathe again, sucking in deep lungfuls of air.

"Let's try this again." Desmodian knelt to Mister Stiril's new level. "What did you do to the human? This is not the result of time spent in an ordinary deprivation chamber."

"The water in the chamber is laced with banali root. It increases the effects. Keeps their minds blank. Standard care for décor, like polishing a gem. It makes them perfect."

The spines along Brog's shoulders rose. "Fuckin' slavers." He abandoned the smaller handguns to pull out the larger one strapped to his back.

The weapon's barrel hovered a few inches from 2689's face, giving him a good look down its sights and the fearful expressions people wore whenever it pointed toward them. No wonder Brog carried so many. Weapons meant power, even when they weren't being used.

Before Brog could decide where to aim his

weapon, however, the Processor stepped forward.

"Slavery is illegal. We aren't criminals. No one can be forced into becoming décor. They willingly sign away their living rights. Their planet is dead. They're the ones who came up with the décor industry. This is all according to their wishes. Now please, sirs, the authorities have been called. They'll be here soon. If you'd calm down and leave quietly, we'll call this a misunderstanding and forget all about it."

"A *misunderstanding*?" Desmodian repeated.

He looked toward Brog and Xavis. There it was again, emotions pretending to be other emotions. All three of the trio smiled, but they didn't look happy.

"There *has* been a misunderstanding." Desmodian calmly leaned against his hammer like they had just stopped on the street for a casual chat. "Mister Stiril promised us this décor as part of his payment for our services. We were upset to learn he was selling what should be ours. I'm sure the mix-up can be sorted out if we talk privately for a moment."

"I di—" Mister Stiril fell silent mid word.

Desmodian pulled a small object from his pocket—too small for 2689 to discern from a distance—and held it in a way that no one lined against the wall except Mister Stiril would see. Whatever it was, it made the usually opalescent Vunqril turn a sickly shade of yellow.

"Yes, a mix-up." He looked desperately between whatever Desmodian held and the rest of the trio. "We can settle this without involving anyone else. If everyone would excuse me, I need to speak with these gentlemen alone."

For the first time, Curator stopped looking around

and stared at her employer. "Sir, what are you—"

Mister Stiril cut her off. "If you and the good staff here could wait in another room. I'll come get you once the issue is resolved."

Curator and the staff were reluctant, but with Mister Stiril's insistence and the threat of Brog's gun, they eventually left.

The new cordial attitude between the trio and Mister Stiril brought with it a wave of suspicion. They had switched so quickly from animosity to cooperation. Maybe the trio weren't his new owners. Whatever they intended, he just wanted them to explain it to him. Then he would know what was right and wrong.

Brog stowed the gun and found a seat in the corner of the room. Once there he wrapped all four arms around 2689.

He should have felt trapped, locked in such a strong grip, but it soothed him. It wasn't an order, but he couldn't accidentally disobey or make someone upset if he couldn't move. Left with no other choice, he sat on Brog's lap and let the Ocan coddle him.

The moment they were alone, Owner sneered hard enough to show teeth. "Where did you get that?"

"This?" Desmodian held up the object for everyone to see clearly. "On our ship. Where you put it."

The glass sphere was small enough to hide within a closed fist, with yellow smoke swirling at its core.

Desmodian tossed the sphere toward Mister Stiril.

The man nearly climbed the wall in his panic to get away.

The glass sphere landed harmlessly on the floor and rolled until it tapped Mister Stiril's foot.

It didn't even make a *plink* sound, which 2689

would expect from glass.

The Vunqril barely dared to glance in its direction.

Xavis retrieved the sphere. "Sistat bombs need to be armed before they'll go off." His words didn't say "idiot" but his tone did.

That was a bomb? He'd pictured them to be larger with lots of wires and complicated bits. The simplicity of the small sphere made it even more threatening. It had no obvious mechanisms and therefore no obvious way to be disarmed.

The rhythmic tapping of Desmodian's hammer against the floor set a twitch in Mister Stiril's eye. "You know, this little arms-dealing scheme of yours was almost a good idea. Selling weapons in an active warzone is illegal, so if we're caught, you can claim you had no idea about the bombs. The supplies you gave us even contained food rations. It almost worked, except you should never underestimate ship-dwellers. Nothing comes onto our ship we don't know about. Now, we've made ourselves criminals as well by breaking in here, but I wonder whose crimes the authorities will be more interested in. Our misdemeanor, or your felony."

Holding a staring contest with Desmodian was a futile effort. Having no eyes to stare into gave the Dhen'in an unbeatable advantage, but Mister Stiril tried anyway. It had the expected outcome.

Since he couldn't intimidate his accuser, Mister Stiril fell back on the next logical course of action. "What do you want? You would have already turned me in if that was your intention. You want something in return for your silence. What is it?"

2689 watched with mild curiosity as the trio looked

at each other.

They silently shrugged at the same time, as if ending a conversation that never happened.

"Isn't it obvious?" Xavis's smile almost looked happy. "We want him."

Mister Stiril followed Xavis's pointing talon and gaped. "You want the décor. Fine. Take it. It's yours."

Xavis laughed, and 2689 covered his ears again. Just when he thought it was over, the laughter that wasn't happy returned.

Luckily Brog noticed his discomfort. "Xavis."

The Scaacax stopped laughing and gave a brief apology.

2689 accepted it and settled back against Brog, comfortable once again.

Desmodian stepped closer to Mister Stiril, making the Vunqril flinch. "Oh, no. We take him, you claim he was stolen, we get arrested anyway. No. You will sign legal ownership of him over to us. Everything on the up-and-up. In exchange, we won't tell anyone about your little side business. We'll even deliver the cargo to the Partition system as promised. After all, we're still the only ship that can make the trip."

"Just like that?" Mister Stiril regarded the trio as if they had just broken out into singing *a capella*. "I sign over the décor to you, and you deliver the cargo?"

Xavis started poking around the room, throwing his words over his shoulder. "We don't care about your dealings. The Sistat bombs, the Partition system's war. None of it's our business. A ship-dweller's desires aren't complicated. Give us what we want and we're happy."

He investigated the memory wiping device. Sharp

talons sorted through delicate wires and electronics, occasionally pulling things apart that probably should have stayed together. Between Brog's aggression and Xavis's meddling, the machine would need heavy repairs when they were done.

"And you want décor?" Mister Stiril looked equally perplexed by Xavis's actions and his answer.

Brog surprised both 2689 and Mister Stiril by speaking up. "We enjoyed him and want to keep enjoyin' him."

2689 sat in his lap and even he hadn't realized Brog was paying attention. The trio seemed to thrive on playing into people's expectations, in Brog's case—the mindless brute, just to slap them in the face with their own assumptions.

It didn't take Mister Stiril long to weigh his options and come to a decision. One décor was a low cost for a landowner's reputation. He and Desmodian conversed for a moment over a tablet, each signing something that would start the ownership transfer process.

Once the trio confirmed they would become his new owners, 2689 stopped paying attention. It required too much energy. He would get his orders from the trio. That was all he needed to know to fulfil his role as décor.

Mister Stiril kept talking about documentation and other legal jargon. It would take time for ownership to transfer officially, but unofficially the trio were free to leave.

There was that phrase again. "Free to leave." Except this time, 2689 would be leaving with them. He wasn't sure if it counted as having freedom when he needed someone to help him leave, but it felt like an improvement.

This time, Brog took the initiative and threw 2689 over his shoulder.

It was a fun ride, hanging upside down and staring at the stumpy tail just out of reach while the floor passed several feet below. From his angle, he got a backwards look at the destruction the trio caused on their way in. Doors and security guards lay crumpled on the ground. The doors were beyond repair. Hopefully the people were not.

Mister Stiril stayed behind to smooth things over with the auction house.

2689's last glimpse of his former owner showed Curator and the auction-house staff bombarding him with questions when he opened the door to where they waited. The man was good with words when he needed to be. Whatever he said, they would believe.

They left the auction house and stepped into the open air. Brog hitched 2689 higher on his shoulder. "Hey, Des, we won't really drop a bunch of illegal bombs into a warzone, right?"

From his position, 2689 couldn't see where they were going, only where they had been.

The auction house stood in an isolated area, surrounded by untouched nature. The sun had set while they were inside and thrown the world into darkness. Brilliant lights coming from the auction house made it look like a lone beacon of warmth among a shadowy landscape.

2689 mimicked one of Brog's rude gestures at the building as they left.

Desmodian walked somewhere ahead of Brog and out of 2689's sight. "If we don't deliver them, then

Mister Stiril may not sign Pet over to us."

"Yeah, but, like…we're not gonna do it." Xavis also spoke from out of 2689's sight.

He wanted all his new owners where he could see them. How else was he supposed to know what they wanted? Twisting his body around to get a look at the trio didn't work. The width of Brog's shoulders proved too big an obstacle.

Desmodian hummed in thought, his hammer rhythmically thumping the ground as he walked. "We have to deliver something. Xavis, can you contact your old dealer?"

"Maddax?" Xavis said the name like a squawk, and a bright feather floated to the ground. "I haven't spoken to him since I stopped using, but it won't be too hard to hunt him down. Why?"

They were still talking about someone unknown to him. This must mean they didn't need anything from him right now. He hung limply over Brog's back. The cool air felt nice on his skin, and if he braced against Brog's shoulder blades, he could even look up at the stars. More and more trees blocked out the sky as they moved farther into the woods, but he could still see patches of stars through their branches. It was more than he saw back at the estate.

Desmodian continued talking about this other person. "Maddax can acquire just about anything, right? Can he find us a good forger?"

This got the trio talking in an excited manner, but 2689 couldn't follow the conversation. A lot of times and dates got thrown around as the trio planned out the logistics of whatever they intended to do. 2689 didn't even know the current date, let alone intergalactic dates like the trio used. Hopefully this wouldn't interfere with fulfilling their orders, or if it did, they would take the time to teach him. He liked learning new things.

As they walked, Brog brushed against a tree and a leaf snagged on his shoulder spines.

2689 plucked the leaf free. Staring through the hole in the otherwise smooth surface, he could see the dwindling light of the auction house in the distance. Despite how easily Brog's spines pierced the leaf, 2689 felt no discomfort as he draped over the Ocan's shoulders. The spines lay flat and presented no threat to him.

He let the leaf tumble from his fingers and watched it fall. The hole caused it to turn manic circles in the air. 2689 liked the chaos. Any leaf could journey to the ground in graceful arcs. It took an encounter with his new trio for a leaf to fall in such wild patterns.

The leaf disappeared into the darkness, and when 2689 looked up, the auction house had as well.

## Chapter Seventeen

*Now*

"Fake."

Leader threw the box on the ground. It split open, sending dozens of small glass spheres rolling over the floor. One bounced off the bars of Pet's cell. The yellow gas suspended inside continued to spin even once the sphere came to a stop.

They were the same forged bombs his trio had used to buy enough time to secure his ownership. A quick glance at his trio said they recognized the weapons as well, and they looked shaken. Whatever they expected, this hadn't been it.

Brog said something to Xavis, drowned out by Leader's screeching.

"You promise us weapons and bring us these forgeries. We need the Sistat bombs to hunt the nimbus glaukos. You are trying to ruin us." Part of Leader's tangled body wrapped around the closest thing Captain Covols had to a neck.

He struggled to speak as he was lifted into the air. "It's not our fault. We picked up the weapons from the supplier as usual. They must have been swapped out before we got them."

His pleas cut off as Leader shook him violently. Luckily the Oculi's body only resembled folded paper, or else the violent handling would have torn him to pieces.

"You should have checked them." Leader threw Captain Covols to the floor among the ill-fated forgeries.

Pet flinched in sympathy at the sound of the hard impact and inched closer to Xavis's side of the cell.

The captain staggered back to his feet, hunched over in a protective stance that said he had injured something. "That supplier has never cheated us before. There're so many weapons going in and out of the Partition system, it must have been a mistake."

Leader gave no indication of hearing him, turning slow circles at the center of the room as their nerves all twitched at once. "That batch was worth over a million credits. You will get us those weapons or pay their worth."

Captain Covols gaped. "Pay? You killed every member of my crew not in cryosleep. Twenty-six people. I've paid enough already."

Desmodian stepped between Leader and the injured captain.

Pet's throat collapsed as if he were being strangled again. With Xavis and Brog imprisoned, and his customary weapon missing, Desmodian seemed more vulnerable than ever before.

"I don't care about whatever arms dealing you're involved with. Selling weapons to poachers hardly qualifies as a crime compared to some of the tragedies that go on within the Partition system. None of that is our concern. We're only looking for the *Trailblazer*."

Leader turned away from Captain Covols, who was in no condition to make trouble, and confronted

Desmodian instead. The tangle of fleshy nerves drew itself together, floating a little higher off the ground as they sized up Desmodian. "The *Trailblazer* lied to us."

Desmodian raised his hands in a universal gesture of surrender. "No. Captain Covols and certain members of his crew failed to live up to their promise. And it sounds like they've already been punished. There are five hundred people on that ship that have nothing to do with this."

"And you want us to take pity on them. Let the ship go for the sake of the innocent."

In his place, Pet would have fled, but Desmodian took another step forward, putting himself within Leader's reach.

"The disappearance of five hundred people won't be ignored. The Oculi government will come for them. They've already sent us. If we disappear as well, they'll send others. And next time, it'll be a more aggressive force."

His words had little effect on Leader as the Sclersy gestured toward the screen window. "We're safe here. No one can reach us inside the Iota Cloud."

"We did. If the Oculi government tries hard enough, they can find a way as well. You're facing the resources of an entire planetary system. This won't be a simple battle. It'll be a war. The very thing you left the Partition system to escape."

The mention of war got Leader's attention. A shiver passed through their tangles, as well as every Sclersy in the room.

Pet never wanted to experience war if the mere memory of it inspired such a reaction.

Leader drew their nerves closer together. "I want

what I was promised."

Who were they reminding, themselves or everyone else?

Captain Covols's injuries must not have been too severe, for he found the strength to make his own argument rather than let Desmodian fight his battle. "I don't know how this batch got swapped for fakes, but there's nothing I can do. We won't have any more weapons until we can orchestrate another job in the Partition system. Keeping us here won't get you anything except unwanted attention." It sounded like a well-trod argument. The words knew exactly where to fall and settled easily into their sentences.

Leader rotated to regard Captain Covols with a different section of nerves. "If you can't provide weapons, then I want something of equal value."

Captain Covols made an aborted motion, as if he meant to throw up his hands in exasperation only to be reminded of his injuries. "We've been stuck here for weeks as you've ransacked our ship looking for something worth taking. We had limited room, so passengers couldn't bring much with them. Even the richest landowners left most of their belongings behind, and colonization supplies don't fetch a lot on the black market. I don't know how you're expecting us to magically produce what you want."

At least Pet knew what was going on now. The people on the *Trailblazer* had lain in cryosleep, unaware as the poachers slunk about their ship. He hated being in that cell, but he would take his current situation over blissfully sleeping through danger every time.

Leader rotated again. "It's your lucky day, Captain.

You have something now."

Or maybe not. When one of Leader's nerves pointed toward him, sleeping through the danger suddenly gained more appeal.

"Décor fetch staggering amounts of money. People the auction houses won't sell to would pay anything for one. Give us that décor, and your debt is paid. You can all leave."

Everyone looked at him, and Pet backed away until he hit the far wall of his cell. He wrapped his arms around himself. Why hadn't he chosen a less revealing outfit? His skin prickled under so many hungry eyes and the ghosts of hands that hadn't yet touched him.

Captain Covols and Desmodian responded at the same time.

"Of course."

"Absolutely not."

Brog and Xavis hammered against their cell bars, adding their own curses as emphasis.

Captain Covols pleaded with Desmodian, stressing his injuries and making him double over. "We're not leaving unless we give them the décor. Once we're out of here, my government can reimburse you. With interest."

He reached out as if to lay a hand on Desmodian's shoulder. Before he made contact, Desmodian backhanded him across the face.

Pet jumped. He'd never seen Desmodian strike someone with his bare hands. In moments of violence, the Dhen'in always relied on his weapon. For the last year, those hands had only brought pleasure. To see them causing pain felt like being accosted at the Gravity Well while Brog was in the back room all over again. As if the familiar member of his trio had been swapped for a stranger.

The blow sent Captain Covols to the floor, and before he could get up, Desmodian pinned him with a boot on his chest. "Do not speak as if you have any right to make decisions about the human. He is ours, and he is not for sale. Not for any price."

Leader glowed a little brighter, and their nerves vibrated at the ends like waving flags. "Everything has a price. For example…"

They gestured toward the screen window at the front of the room just in time for the cloud to part and reveal a ship.

It was the very ship the trio had been hired to find, recognizable by its stacked design meant to house hundreds of people. The *Trailblazer* hung dead and motionless in the cloud, surrounded by several poacher ships. It was a massive ship, making even the poacher ships look small by comparison. The *Vanguard* could probably fly through one of its doors with room to spare.

Leader continued their speech, still twitching with manic energy. "Five hundred people on that ship. All asleep and vulnerable. Is one décor worth so many lives?"

It was an obvious answer. Even ignoring the fact he was décor, one didn't outweigh five hundred. Through the bars of the cell, Xavis grabbed him and pulled him close. A talon stroked gently over his cheek, but Pet didn't look up, too afraid of what he would find.

Too afraid to see Xavis saying goodbye.

"I already told you. It's not our job to rescue the ship." Desmodian removed his boot from Captain

Covols's chest and helped the Oculian to his feet. "However, I won't make him live with so many lives on his conscience. I know the weight of one guilty life. Five hundred innocent ones would be unbearable."

Captain Covols dusted himself off with his uninjured arm. "Thank you."

"I wasn't talking about you." Desmodian didn't need to turn his head to keep an eye on both Captain Covols and Leader. He "looked" at Captain Covols solely so he could then dismiss the Oculian by looking away.

Leader's vibrating fell still. "So, we have a deal?"

Desmodian smiled but walked away from Leader over to the cells. He reached through the bars and stroked a hand over Pet's hair. "What do you think, boys? Do we have a deal?"

Brog and Xavis both responded with a resounding "Fuck, no."

"I didn't think so. In fact, I think it's time we left." He leaned in close so only Pet could hear. "Step away from the bars, Pet."

Pet backed up, even though it meant removing himself from Desmodian's touch.

Four identical hands grabbed the cell bars. Pet had seen Brog pull off some impressive feats of strength, but breaking out of the cell with his bare hands seemed impossible.

The poachers thought so too. Sclersy and non-Sclersy alike laughed at his attempt, with Leader the most vocal of all.

"Foolish. Ocans are strong, but those bars are from Gonthorn. They're indestructible."

Brog paid their laughter no mind. He strained

against the metal, and a low growl built in the back of his throat. Muscles pushed to their limit, and an orange light appeared in a halo around him. It emanated from his skin and soaked into the bars, twisting them under Brog's hands. With a screech of tortured metal, he pulled open the cell and stepped out.

Leader dropped from their hover and nearly hit the floor. "What…How…"

Brog cracked his knuckles as he advanced on the poachers, creating little sparks of orange around his hands. Some poachers retreated, but others stepped forward, eager for a challenge. First in line was the fellow Ocan.

If Pet thought Brog was big, the other Ocan was massive.

"Impressive." The poacher Ocan's face pulled into a sneer. "For your size, at least. I'm surprised your matriarch let someone so puny out of their sight."

Brog flexed all four arms to their full length. "And I'm sure your matriarch is thrilled with your life choices. Assumin' she's alive. Though, since you're here, I'm guessin' not."

What little Brog had told Pet about his people put a great emphasis on females. At the mention of his matriarch, the poacher Ocan flew into a rage. Two fists swung at Brog, with the other two ready to follow.

Just like when he fought Desmodian, Brog didn't bother to dodge. Instead he stepped into the other Ocan's swing and caught his fists. The orange light centered around Brog's hands, and he crushed his attacker's fists. The other Ocan dropped to his knees, and Brog slammed a boot into his face hard enough to snap his head back.

The poacher Ocan crumbled to the floor and never got back up.

Panic erupted. Every non-Sclersy poacher piled on Brog, overwhelming him with numbers. He could crush an opponent with one hand, but he only had four arms.

One poacher, the gangly purple thing Pet noted earlier, managed to wrap limbs around Brog's head and block his vision. Brog tore them away, but the distraction allowed P'pavakass to get a grip on him. Even under the Sclersy's full weight, Brog remained standing, but those fleshy nerves twisted tight and cut into his skin.

Pet pressed against the unyielding bars of his own cell in a worthless effort to get to Brog, terrified he would end up the same as their control room wall.

Something crashed through the scuffle. Desmodian's hammer flew under its own power past the poachers and right into his waiting hand.

The hammer glowed with the aqua green light that appeared around Desmodian before.

His fingers had barely closed around the handle before he swung at P'pavakass. The hammer sank deep into the core of the Sclersy's nerves. Green light pulsed and atomized P'pavakass on the spot, leaving a pile of dust slowly floating to the floor.

Leader glowed bright, and their nerves waved wildly like aggravated snakes. "Murderer."

Gripping the hammer in both hands, Desmodian faced the room in defiance. "Yes, I am. But you don't have any right to judge."

With Desmodian and Brog working together, the conflict tipped in their favor. The Sclersy followed Leader's orders and threw themselves into the fight.

Most non-Sclersy fled, probably to the escape pods and the safety of their fellow ships.

Xavis caught Pet's attention as he crouched at the shared bars of their cells. "We need to get going now."

The calm words kept Pet from panicking, and he mutely nodded. His trio had a plan, so he would follow. He could question them later when everyone was safe.

Just like Brog, Xavis gripped the bars tightly. They glowed purple and bent into dramatic shapes, as if they had been crushed in a giant's fist. Not just the bars between their cells, but every bar down the line distorted in a similar fashion. The two of them stepped out of their confinement and into the rapidly dwindling fight.

A nearby poacher decided to turn away from the main fight and attack Xavis instead. It was the same person that had strangled Pet earlier and one of the few non-Sclersy to stick around.

They never got close. Xavis's talons ripped through the poacher's flank. Purple light sparked around the edges of the wounds like fire burning through paper. It spread until every part of the poacher burned. They joined the bodies of their fallen comrades, though they resembled the remains of an aggressive campfire more than they did a living being.

Xavis stepped over the body. "Stay with me."

Pet didn't need to be told twice and pressed close to Xavis's back. Through a gap in Xavis's feathers, he caught a familiar sight. "What about them?"

Xavis followed where he was pointing. "Yeah, I guess we have to."

Despite the crumpled bars of their cell, the DPS agents hadn't emerged.

Their hesitance made some sense. As unpleasant as captivity had been, the chaos churning outside the cell probably seemed just as bad.

Xavis called across the bars to them. "You coming or what? If you want to make it home, get back on the *Vanguard* now."

The agents shared a look of uncertainty, but Nauzeia supported her partner out of the cell. "You're Phazers."

She said it with such weight, the term was obviously important. Unfortunately, it was one that Pet had never heard before.

Xavis kept an eye on Brog's and Desmodian's fight. "We are."

The agents stayed on his heels.

"That's not possible." It took some effort for Irih to walk and talk while half of his body struggled to move on its own, but he managed.

Nauzeia alternated between helping her partner and staring at Xavis in awe. "You can consciously manipulate atomic bonds. It's been theorized for years, but there's never been a successful case. The energy output alone should tear you apart. How did you master it?"

Xavis grimaced. "Not easily. This is not the time to discuss it."

The dismissal was curt but effective. The agents fell silent and followed him almost as closely as Pet did. Together they stayed to the edge of the fight.

After encouraging Pet to stay back, Xavis placed himself in front of the main door. Only a few poachers remained. Leader tried to escape as the last of their people fell, but they found a spread of feathers blocking their path.

A bubble of purple light surrounded Leader.

"You can't be…" Tangled nerves bashed against the side of the bubble to no effect.

Xavis's smile was all teeth. "Yet we are."

With a swing of a hammer and a smash of a fist, Desmodian and Brog finished off the last of the poachers, leaving Leader the only poacher alive in the room.

"We need to get going before the other ships realize what's going on." Desmodian's hammer showed no damage from its vigorous use, but its green glow persisted.

Brog flexed his arms, and the orange light radiated brighter from his skin. "Unless they already know."

"Then we need to move."

His trio led the way through the ship and back to the hallway connected to the *Vanguard*.

The two agents and Captain Covols followed, looking confused but not lost. They, at least, knew what was going on.

Meanwhile, Pet felt more kinship with Leader bobbing along in the bubble, than with his own trio. Neither of them had any control over their situation, and Leader certainly didn't want to be there any more than Pet did.

He trusted his trio. That hadn't changed, but what was he supposed to do with the new information? He had seen demonstrations of Xavis's abilities before, but it had never been explained, and he never knew Desmodian and Brog had power to match. Whatever a Phazer was, it sounded important. Apparently too important for décor to know about.

No one followed them. If any poachers remained on the ship, their fear kept them hidden.

They reached the *Vanguard*, and Captain Covols looked around. "Quaint."

Compared to the Class 1 colony ship he was used to flying, their private transportation ship must look miniscule.

Nauzeia leaned her partner against the wall. "It's not over yet. We're still attached."

Xavis scoffed and fluffed his feathers. "Really? I hadn't noticed."

A wave of his hand sent the bubble flying off with Leader inside. It disappeared into the depths of the *Vanguard*'s primary storage space, and a moment later the slam of a closing door echoed up from the bottom of the ship.

"I locked them in the tertiary storage vault."

"The refrigerated one that keeps leaking?" Brog's vindictive smile looked even more terrifying with a cut across one cheek pulling it lopsided. He was still smiling when he bent to inspect the edge where the poacher's ship connected to their own.

"The cold plus the barrier should keep them out of trouble until our own trouble is taken care of." Xavis ushered Pet to stand on the other side of the hall, equally far away from the trio as everyone else. Then he joined Brog's inspection. "How's it look?"

"Trouble is right. It's a magnetic lock. We can't take it off."

With the help of the wall, Irih managed to take a few steps on his own. "You bashed your way through all those poachers. Yet you can't remove a lock?"

Desmodian ventured a few steps back inside the

attached corridor. "We can't affect anything that generates its own field. Like magnets and electricity." He stopped and knocked at a spot on the wall.

The trio positioned themselves around the edge of the connection.

Xavis knelt on the floor while Brog and Desmodian each took a wall.

Three different colors of light soaked into the *Vanguard* and out to the foreign metal. At first, nothing happened as the light spread. Then the attached corridor writhed like a living creature.

Pet ran to the nearest window. The light covered not just the connecting tunnel, but the poacher's entire ship. Purple, orange, and green swirled together over the hull, entwining but never mixing. Metal fluctuated between states of matter, from solid to liquid to gas, eventually ending in the fourth state.

Plasma.

The ship crumpled beyond dust. Piece by piece, it disappeared as its atoms joined the ionized gas of the cloud.

The tunnel connected to the *Vanguard* disappeared along with the ship, except for the last few feet. The surviving metal ended right where Desmodian had marked.

A moment of fear passed through Pet when the destroyed tunnel left an open hole in their ship. However, the light from his trio formed a barrier over the opening, keeping them all safely inside until an emergency panel engaged.

No one spoke, but his trio panted as they slumped against the newly sealed wall. The light retreated from the ship, but they continued to glow.

They were exhausted. Phazer or not, that much was obvious. The other guests on their ship, Captain Covols and the two agents, stared in obvious shock. Pet took some enjoyment in their awe. They may know about Phazers, but even they hadn't expected such a show of power.

Alarms erupted through the hall. Red flashing lights and blaring sirens filled the *Vanguard*, warning them of immediate danger.

"I think the other ships noticed somethin'." Brog stood and ran to the control room.

Desmodian followed, as did their unwanted guests, but Xavis stopped to collect Pet.

The moment his hand touched Pet's shoulder a sharp spark passed between them. Pet yelped at the unexpected pain and stumbled back, knocking into the railing of the catwalk.

Xavis immediately reached out to stabilize him but stopped and stared down at his hand. The purple light still emanated from his skin. He stayed near Pet without touching him again. "Stick with us, Pet."

The warning sirens shut up when the trio were back at the controls. Beyond the observation windows, all three poacher ships, which had been standing guard over the *Trailblazer*, now faced the *Vanguard*. It looked absurd. Their little private vessel didn't even equal the size of one gun on the poachers' ships.

Brog hunched over a control panel and grumbled. "This had better work."

Xavis kept looking between his controls and the window. "I gave it my best, but it's never been tested."

The two agents entered the room last, as Nauzeia had to help her partner who was slowly regaining his mobility. "Do you have a plan?" Out of habit, she and Irih gravitated toward the extra seats that had hosted them during each of the *Vanguard*'s dramatic maneuvers.

Captain Covols, on the other hand, hovered by the door. The captain looked absurdly lost on a ship he didn't command.

"The poachers' ships are outfitted with electronegative pulse weapons." Desmodian sounded more exhausted than Pet had ever heard him. "Luckily, we had to arm the *Vanguard* against such weapons for a previous job."

No one directed Pet to his antigravity bubble, but his trio may have forgotten in the chaos. He compromised by clinging to the outer frame of his bubble, ready to jump inside at any moment.

The poachers' ships drew closer, looming huge even at a distance. They never tried to contact the *Vanguard* or give any sort of warning before they fired. The only signal came from the way the cloud rippled between their ships.

Electronegative pulses charged them from three directions at once, gaining power the closer they came. Just before the unified pulse smashed against the front of the *Vanguard*, a glowing energy shield sprang to life, swirling with a trio of familiar colors. The pulse broke against the shield, scattering like water droplets in every direction. Almost immediately, the *Vanguard*'s shield also vanished, leaving the space between the ships pristine and undistorted once again.

The poacher ships didn't fire again, but the silence was short-lived.

"You have a shield against their weapons?"

Captain Covols stormed into the control room as if he meant to claim it for himself.

"Something I came up with a year ago. Glad to see it works." Xavis should have been proud of the accomplishment, but he only sounded tired.

Captain Covols's anger almost outshone the glow still trapped in Xavis's skin. "If you're shielded against their weapons, you could have stopped them from boarding your ship in the first place. Why risk all our lives pretending to be prisoners when you had this kind of power?"

In one decisive move Desmodian stood, grabbed Captain Covols, and dragged him across the room toward Pet.

Green sparks tormented the captain wherever Desmodian touched. He struggled against the pain added to the injuries he already bore, but Desmodian's grip didn't relent.

"You don't get to talk about putting people in danger." Desmodian tossed Captain Covols inside Pet's antigravity bubble.

Pet let go of the frame. The bubble would work both ways, keeping them safe from the captain, while also protecting the captain from further injury.

Desmodian turned back toward the controls but was stopped when Nauzeia confronted him in the center of the room.

"He may be immoral, but his question has merit. If you're shielded against electronegative pulse weapons, why let the poachers capture you?"

Desmodian collapsed into his chair in the boneless way only the truly exhausted could manage. "That shield only works once. If they fire on us again, we're dead. We had to play it right. Make a big enough display so they would be too scared to try a second time."

Neither the agents nor Captain Covols had anything to say to this.

Brog, however, was happy to break the silence for them. "Well, we're still alive. So, it seems to have worked."

Desmodian sighed. "Yes. Seems it has."

## Chapter Eighteen

*Then*

The transition from planet gravity to ship gravity nearly upended 2689 as the trio brought him into the *Vanguard*. Everything turned sideways, and he clung to Brog among the new surroundings. The patchwork design of the *Vanguard* provided a comforting familiarity.

Brog carried him to the ship's control room, where he carefully set 2689 on his feet.

He had been there before, but he couldn't remember anything substantial.

At the front of the room nearest the observation windows, Xavis sat in a chair that looked to have been specially made for him.

"Already got the engines going. Two more minutes and we'll take off."

"Good." Brog collapsed into his own chair, the largest of the three. "Though I hate lettin' that asshat get away with his dealin', even if we're only deliverin' fake weapons."

Desmodian took his place as well. "He won't be safe for long. Eventually someone will leave the authorities an anonymous tip about him."

Brog laughed. A real laugh this time, without any traces of anger. "And if that tip happens to come right after we got ownership 'a Pet, even better. Right?"

"Right."

Desmodian's attention stayed on 2689, who was struck by the strange urge to sit on his lap. Décor didn't touch their owners, and certainly didn't cuddle on their laps and beg for attention. 2689 needed to get himself together or risk being resold again.

His gaze fell to the floor and he shuffled his weight from foot to foot. How could he make them happy without any commands? He really wanted the trio to like him, more than he ever wanted his previous owner's approval.

"Xavis." Desmodian still stared at 2689. "What do you know about banali root?"

Xavis pushed a few more buttons, causing the engine sounds to increase, before looking up from the screen. "It's used as a catalyst for other ingredients. I've never heard of it being administered in this way, and it sounds like he was soaking in it for a while."

"Will it wear off?"

"It should be temporary." Fiery feathers ruffled, and Xavis left the controls. "Brog, take over the ship. Get us into hyperspace."

Brog slid his chair along the tracks to take Xavis's place. "You have an idea?"

"Maybe."

The ship moved, and the floor under their feet vibrated as the landscape beyond the windows became a sudden blur of color.

2689 backed into a corner intending to get out of the way but tripped when the ship hit turbulence. Before he could hit the floor, Desmodian wrapped an arm around his waist.

Once they leveled out and flew relatively smooth, Xavis held out a hand to him. "Pet, come over here."

He jumped to obey, desperate to redeem himself after stumbling. "Pet?" He tilted his head at the strange title. They must not know his number, since they hadn't bought him at auction. "I am item number two-six-eight-nine."

"I know." Xavis took him by the hand and pulled him toward the windows. "But we're not calling you that."

A bench was in front of the observation windows, partially sunken into the floor and hidden behind the control consoles.

2689 barely noticed when Xavis fulfilled his earlier desire and pulled him onto his lap. The sight beyond the glass proved too distracting. They had left the planet behind. No clouds or atmosphere lay in sight, only an endless expanse of stars.

It was beautiful.

Long tough hands traced a path up his chest and parted his robe.

"Have you ever seen space before?" Xavis spoke against his neck.

The puff of air tickled the small hairs there, and goose bumps rose on his skin. "I don't remember." His voice sounded breathless, like he'd been running.

A curved talon tipped his head back until they looked each other in the eye. A forgotten instinct in 2689 knew what was coming, and he leaned into Xavis's kiss. However, this didn't prepare him for the hand that untied his robe and slipped between his legs. 2689 squirmed against the attention. The tongue playing between his lips and the hand stroking him created lovely contrasting frictions. He didn't know what to do, or where to put his hands. Frustration mounted, and he opened his legs to invite more.

"This is your plan? To fuck him back to normal?" Desmodian leaned over his control screen, watching them with interest.

Xavis shrugged, and 2689 felt the movement against his back. One hand never stopped stroking him, while the other discarded his robe. "The problem comes from the banali root amplifying the sensory deprivation. I figured we could counteract it by kick-starting his senses with something intense."

"That's why we're going to hyperspace." Desmodian's breathing sped up, and he licked his lips, nodding along with the explanation.

Xavis returned to nuzzling 2689's neck. "Hyperspace heightens the senses. Combined with the effect of my own lubricant, you can't get more intense than that."

Their position in the observation pit blocked off the rest of the room. The stars buzzing past the window filled 2689's vision. Every second they moved faster and faster, and the entire universe became a blur of light and dark. In contrast to their increased speed, the ship calmed until it barely seemed to move at all.

As soon as the shaking stopped, a strange sensation overcame him. His skin buzzed, and each touch felt like a live wire to his nerves. Even drawing air into his lungs made him squirm and caused heat to pool in his belly.

"Welcome to the universe's best secret."

The brush of Xavis's lips against his ear made him moan.

"No better aphrodisiac than hyperspace, but I can make it even better."

Xavis's hands carefully gripped his ass and spread him open. Something hard and slick pushed against him, smearing hot wetness between his legs and over his hole. Everywhere the slick touched, his skin prickled. The heat pooling in his stomach blossomed and spread through his veins. 2689 moaned and gyrated against the member threatening to push inside him. This was something he remembered, and it would be good.

"He's as eager as he was before." Desmodian sounded closer this time.

2689 opened eyes he didn't remember closing to find Desmodian kneeling on the floor only inches away.

He stroked a hand over 2689's cheek. "Come on, Pet. You know what to do."

"You're both assholes." A piece of foil trash sailed over the console from Brog's direction to bounce off Xavis's head. "Havin' all the fun while I'm busy flyin' the ship." A second projectile followed the first, this time aimed for Desmodian.

2689 pressed into Desmodian's hand. The Dhen'in, in turn, stroked a thumb over his bottom lip. "Don't worry, Brog. You'll have your turn. Our Pet won't be satisfied so easily."

Pet.

Their Pet.

That word sounded so much better than an item number.

"Please."

Xavis's hands tightened on him. "Your wish. Our pleasure."

With a quick thrust Xavis's cock shoved inside.

The sudden intrusion made him scream, but the sound caught inside his throat and turned into a strangled grunt. Farther and farther it pushed, spreading him open and stretching inner muscles wide. 2689 trembled against the invasion. He wanted more, but he already felt like he was going insane. Then Xavis's cock hit a spot that made him scream for real. Electric pleasure surged through him. His joints locked and his back arched. Something hot and wet rushed from him, splattering his stomach and legs.

Desmodian gasped as some of it landed on him as well. "Wow, he came already. But look at him. He's still hard."

"H-he'll be like...like that for a while." Xavis struggled to speak as, with one last shove, he settled all the way inside.

2689 writhed on him, rolling his hips in a desperate plea for more friction. The position meant he could do little to help. His legs hung to either side of Xavis's knees, too short to reach the floor and too long to brace against the chair.

This left Xavis to do most of the work. He lifted 2689 up before slamming inside. On each thrust, he pulled those gyrating hips back into him, pushing his cock as deep as it would go.

"God, I'll never get tired of that sight." Desmodian brought 2689 forward into a desperate kiss.

The Dhen'in's long tongue found its way into his mouth, reaching so far it slipped down his throat and fucked him in time to Xavis's thrusts.

Memories flashed behind his eyes. Two days spent in similar intimacy, being filled over and over again until he thought he would burst. Those memories were precious. He had done everything he could to hold on to them. Instead they stole his motivation to recall the very thing he cherished. It was the worst kind of manipulation, to still have what he held dear while forgetting its importance.

Something new rubbed between his legs.

Desmodian's pants lay puddled around his knees, and his dual-shafted cock trapped 2689's arousal between its own. The Dhen'in kept one hand in 2689's hair, but the other stroked their cocks together, straining to fit around all three shafts.

The heat and the friction made his already throbbing cock ache for release.

They found a rhythm, Xavis bouncing 2689 on his lap while Desmodian kissed and rutted against him at the same time. Something inside that had been crying out finally settled.

Their rhythm sped up. Each thrust came faster as the coil of arousal tightened.

Xavis purred against his neck, biting sensitive skin while pressing in harder than ever and staying there. The tight grip on 2689's hips would undoubtedly leave bruises as the Scaacax trembled and came deep inside him.

The feel of Xavis's pleasure flooding him pushed 2689 over his own peak. He came hard, crying out against the euphoria that seemed limitless. It kept pushing further and further until he was left sobbing.

Finally, his body ran out and he sagged in Xavis's hold. Minutes passed before he found the strength to open his eyes. So much mess stained his skin, not all of it his own. Somewhere along the way Desmodian had come too, leaving him covered in three people's pleasure. Soon he would be itching for a bath, but for now he was content.

Though not fully satisfied. One thing was still missing.

Brog shouted from behind the console. "All right, you've had your fun. Someone switch with me."

Kissing 2689 one last time, Desmodian stumbled to his feet. He resituated his pants back into place, then disappeared behind the controls.

Xavis's face was still buried in 2689's neck. "Better prepare yourself, Pet. Brog doesn't like being left out."

Brog stepped into the observation pit. "Damn right. But you knew that."

"He was going to have to learn what a brute you are eventually."

It sounded like a warning. Maybe he should worry, but how could he when everything felt too good? No room remained inside him for unpleasant emotions.

He whimpered in protest as Brog pulled him off Xavis's lap and the softening cock slipped out. His legs shook trying to hold him up, but he wasn't burdened with his own weight for long. The Ocan pushed him against the window, one set of hands pinning his wrists to the glass above his head, while the other set took control of his hips. He stood there, legs spread wide, face-to-face with the stars.

"Look at you." Brog pressed against his back. "They really made a mess 'a you. Got you all nice and slick for me."

The head of Brog's immense cock pushed inside, and 2689 keened against the glass. Xavis wasn't small by any definition of the word, but there was no beating an Ocan when it came to size. Muscles stretched to their limits, straining around the hard flesh spearing him open. He felt every ridge disappearing past his rim and every bump along the knobbed head.

2689's breath came in short pants as Brog drove a little deeper with each thrust. He hoped the window was made of something sturdier than glass, or else the Ocan was in danger of shoving him right through it. Stars glowed seemingly inches from his face, filling his eyes with their light. His strangled moans fogged the glass as he was fucked hard. It was a marvelous view. So much beauty lay at his feet, waiting to be explored.

Brog growled as he pounded 2689 against the window. "Come on, Pet. Let the whole universe hear you scream."

The Ocan hit deeper than ever, stimulating spots 2689 didn't know he had. It was instinct to clench around the shaft that plunged in and out. Each ridge tormented his rim, making him tremble as he humped his own erection against the cold glass.

Somewhere in the depths of hyperspace, he and Brog came at the same time. His release spattered the window, painting his own constellations.

Brog filled him and kept coming. 2689 had no hope of holding it all, and the warm liquid dripped down his legs.

His orgasm didn't last as long as the previous one, though it was no less intense for its brevity. The pleasure left his muscles twitching long after it abated. He collapsed when he tried to move, and only Brog's arms kept him off the floor.

"Easy, Pet, don't push yourself."

The sudden switch between mindless brute and

mild kitten made 2689 giggle, then pitched him right over into joyous hysterics.

Brog took his seat behind the console, two arms keeping 2689 in his lap while the other two attended the ship's controls.

It was mesmerizing to watch him work. Every flashing light and scrolling symbol presented something new to learn. Flying a ship seemed complicated. Maybe they'd teach him someday.

Xavis leaned over from the next seat to check on him. "You'll have to wait a little while, Pet. All non-vital functions shut down while we're in hyperspace. It would be too much strain on the ship. Once we're back in normal space, we'll get you cleaned up."

2689 nodded and let his head rest against Brog's chest. He liked the idea of staying messy for a while. Décor always had to be pristine. One hair out of place would send Owner into a fit of rage. Being allowed to stay messy reinforced the warm feeling that built in him since he first met the trio.

He remembered everything. Every touch and interaction with the trio, as well as the years of boredom he didn't even recognize as boredom. Now that he knew what excitement felt like, he could never be perfect décor again. Not unless they erased his memories—but the trio would never do that.

Because they were his as much as he was theirs.

Desmodian had his feet kicked up on the console, leaning back as far as his chair would allow. "How long will it take to find Maddax?"

Xavis also slouched in his chair, but for him, this entailed perching his feet up on the seat, so his knees were level with his head. "Depends how long it takes us to reach the Penumbra belt. I know a few places on the belt he likes to skulk about."

"And he can find us a forger able to fool the eyes of career criminals long enough for Pet's ownership to transfer?"

Xavis shrugged, moving both wings and shoulders as he did so.

Feathers brushed against 2689's leg, tickling still-sensitive skin and making him squirm.

"If one exists, then Maddax can find them." Xavis repeated the action just to get another reaction out of 2689. "I'm not eager to get in contact with him again, but I guess the past can't stay forgotten."

2689 laughed again, harder and sharper this time. When the trio looked at him confused, he just shook his head. Oh, how wrong they were. The past could stay forgotten. It had happened to him once when he became décor, and it almost happened again.

He never really cared about the memories he originally lost. No matter who he was before, he liked the person he was becoming. In just a few days of knowing the trio, he had developed likes and dislikes, wants and desires. He even had a few aspirations. Those were all necessary components that made living beings into people. He wasn't there yet. Too many décor habits lingered for him to truly be considered a person, but he was on his way.

He couldn't wait to see what he would become.

Chapter Nineteen

"So, you're Phazers?"

Pet waited a few hours to ask this question until after the poachers fled.

The sight of their flagship being destroyed and the *Vanguard* deflecting their electronegative pulse weapons dissuaded the poachers from further conflict. Leader was freed on the condition they left immediately and didn't bother the *Vanguard* or the *Trailblazer* again.

The moment Leader returned to their people, the poacher ships disappeared into the cloud.

Meanwhile, Desmodian struggled to contact the *Trailblazer* over the communication system. "Yes, we're Phazers. But that probably doesn't mean anything to you."

He sounded more brusque than usual. All the trio seemed on edge. The glow in their skin persisted, even hours later. Desmodian slammed his hand against the communication panel, cracking the screen, and collapsed back against his chair.

"Nothing. Those poachers weren't lying when they said they killed the skeleton crew. That ship's sitting dead without anyone to man it."

Captain Covols pounded against the inside of the

antigravity bubble. "Just take me back to my ship. I can wake up the remaining crew and get it going. It should be enough for us to reach civilized space."

They had given him basic first aid for his injuries. The worst problem was his arm, which needed a splint, but it didn't slow him down.

Desmodian's hammer tapped against the floor, barely a touch, but it sparked green and dented the metal. The *Vanguard* would need a long list of repairs when everything was over.

"If you think we're just letting you go, you're more insane than I thought." Before Captain Covols could argue, Desmodian tapped a button on the side of the antigravity bubble and turned its usually clear walls opaque. Faint muffled shouting could be heard inside.

The black bubble looked so ominous compared to the protection it usually offered. Pet caressed the outside of the bubble to see if it felt the same, even if it looked different. To his relief, it did.

"Better stay away from that, Pet." Brog reached out to pull Pet away.

Xavis squawked. "Brog, don't. You'll hurt him."

Brog snatched back his hand before it touched Pet's shoulder and glared at the orange barrier around his skin in disgust. "I'm going to the kitchen." He wrenched open the door to the control room and accidentally crushed the handle. More cursing followed as he stomped away.

Xavis approached Pet but also refrained from touching him. "Sorry, Pet. Everything's just a bit much right now. You should stay away from us until we settle down."

Pet glanced between Xavis and Desmodian, who

still hunched over the control panel trying to contact the *Trailblazer*. Despite his claim that everyone on the ship was asleep, he must have a plan, because he tapped at the screen like he knew what he was doing.

"But why? I don't understand. What's a Phazer? How are you able to do all that?" Pet wildly waved his hands about the air, encompassing everything that had happened in the last few hours. "And why are you still glowing?"

"It's hard to explain."

In an unusual flip of their power dynamic, Xavis fidgeted as Pet stared him down. One of his wings brushed close to Pet. It never touched him, but a purple spark jumped between feathers and skin. The electrical crack made everyone jump and caused a red welt to appear on Pet's arm.

"Fuck, Pet, I'm sorry." Xavis fluttered between his need to check on Pet and the need to stay away.

The handle of Desmodian's hammer shot between them. "Xavis, take care of the ship."

Purple light danced brighter than normal in Xavis's eyes, like two searching spotlights. He wavered between staying and leaving but eventually gave up and left with a huff.

With a deep groan Desmodian ran a hand over his mask. "The *Trailblazer* is open to incoming messages. We should be able to trigger an override. If an emergency hail goes unanswered too long, the ship's backup system should automatically bring the next highest authority out of cryosleep. Assuming the poachers didn't tamper with anything else."

It was a poor attempt at deflection.

Irih had returned to the guest bunks to sleep off the

lingering effects of the neural disruptor, so Nauzeia stood alone as she hesitantly approached Desmodian. "You don't really have control of it, do you? The power output has always been the biggest issue with making Phazers. In every experiment it proved impossible to control."

"We have control." His words were certain, but his slumped posture didn't convey confidence. "It's just difficult. We've each found our own way of coping with the backlash of power that comes from manipulating atomic bonds. Brog is strong enough to internalize it and use it to his advantage. It gives him a hellish metabolism, but otherwise he manages okay. Xavis has to constantly siphon it off. He pours everything into the ship. At this point he practically is our ship's engine. It's problematic, but we manage."

No one would notice if Pet left. They were too busy with their own problems. He stayed, hovering at the edge of the room, because he wanted the answers as much as Nauzeia did.

She stepped a little closer. "And how do you manage?"

Desmodian regarded her coolly and held up his hammer for closer inspection. "I'm lucky. This weapon is a family heirloom. Forged with the blood of my ancestors, so I have a special connection to it. The material is nearly indestructible and conducts a vast amount of energy. It can store surplus power and expel it at a more convenient time for me."

Compared to Brog and Xavis, Desmodian glowed the least. The green hovered only as a faint halo around his body while the glow of the hammer increased in equal measure. He clutched the handle so hard tendons stood out under his scales.

The width of Brog's chair dwarfed Nauzeia when she sat on the edge. She never settled into the seat but instead leaned toward Desmodian.

"You weren't Phazers when you joined Unit 22. Evaluations for joining the Gantry are too thorough to miss such a thing. You must have developed Phazer abilities afterwards."

From her angle she addressed Desmodian's shoulder more than his face. She probably thought it was less intrusive, but she was really looking directly into his eyes.

The wheels of her brain turned, almost creating an audible ticking noise as each word she spoke stitched information into a cohesive tapestry.

"Your last mission with Unit 22. The three of you were MIA for six months, before suddenly reappearing. What happened during that mission?"

Desmodian twitched and held his hammer closer. "Those records are sealed. We were honorably discharged. It's not your concern."

"Do you know how much could be gained with your abilities? The very fabric of the universe would be under our control."

He leaned in until his masked face hovered only inches from hers, the one part of his body he couldn't see from. "No one should have that much power. Not even us. These powers weren't our choice, but they're our responsibility, and we're not going to hand them over for governments to turn the universe into their own personal playground."

With his piece said, Desmodian returned to the *Vanguard*'s communication panel. Lights flashed on the controls that hadn't been flashing before.

Nauzeia looked to be gearing up for round two of her argument when a voice filtered through the speakers.

"Hello?" Interfering static emphasized the voice's uncertainty. "This is Third Officer Molov of the CS *Trailblazer*. Who is this?"

Desmodian spoke directly into the communication speaker. "Third Officer? This is Desmodian of the *Vanguard*. My crew was hired by the Oculi government to find you."

"Well, you've found us." The Third Officer sounded amused in a way that belied his panic hiding just under the surface. "Maybe you can tell me what's going on. Emergency systems woke me from cryosleep to find the ship off course, behind schedule, and the entire skeleton crew gone. Not to sound unprofessional, but what the hell happened?"

"We have Captain Covols on board with us, but the rest of your skeleton crew is dead."

Desmodian went about the difficult task of explaining what happened to the *Trailblazer*, starting from the beginning, with the *Vanguard* having been hired to find the missing ship. The whole story would take a while and wasn't helped by Nauzeia's continued pestering about their Phazer abilities.

She wanted more information, but Desmodian provided nothing else. Pet's trio would keep their secrets. Maybe even from him.

He left to seek his own seclusion. The *Vanguard* may not be very large, but it had enough space for solitude, even with extra passengers on board. He ended up sitting in the middle of a lesser-used catwalk, arms hooked through the railing and legs dangling over the edge.

Blackness spread below him. They rarely illuminated the primary storage space unless in use. When empty, it remained dark, and dark was what Pet wanted. It gave him a chance to think.

Life with his trio turned out to have more complications than he first thought. From the beginning, it had been dangerous as well as exciting, but the excitement had always outweighed the danger. Had that changed?

Footsteps alerted Pet to someone's approach, but he was too distracted to identify them.

Irih sat next to Pet on the edge of the catwalk. "On your own for once?"

The railing didn't allow Pet to scoot away. Leave? No, he wasn't going to be chased away on his own ship.

He kicked his feet through the dark. "I'm never alone. Sometimes there's just a little more distance."

"Even a little distance out in space can be dangerous."

Pet waited for a threat of some sort. He doubted the agent approached him simply for conversation, but Irih seemed content to stare into the abyss with him.

This wasn't the kind of silence Pet wanted. It was anticipatory instead of soothing. "Why are you here? It's not because you're concerned for me. You're too self-serving. But you're not greedy enough to only care about selling décor. I'm not sure why you agreed to come on this trip."

Irih laughed, and it almost seemed genuine. "Agreed? You really don't understand how a job works. My bosses give me an assignment, and I have to do it."

Pet couldn't hear the grinding of his teeth over the furious rush of his blood. "I know all about following orders."

"Décor stand there and look pretty. My job requires doing things. To answer the question you probably meant, I became a DPS agent because I like art. If I had known it would mean traveling outside civilized space, I would have second-guessed my choice of career, but it's too late now. I follow orders or I get fired. We all do what we must to survive. This assignment aside, my job is usually much more pleasant. That's all I want. A comfortable life."

A different expression descended on his face. The Yce narrowed his eyes slightly.

Ah. They had arrived at the agent's real reason for the conversation. Pet braced himself for what would come next.

Irih pulled out a holographic tablet. "I'm not the only one. Most people just want a comfortable life, but not everyone gets it. Décor are lucky that way." He handed Pet the tablet with a video already queued up.

"What's this?"

"Just watch it and you'll see. I think it's something you should know."

Pet's first instinct was to give the tablet back, but curiosity got the better of him. The agent had specifically waited until he was alone to show him, meaning it was something he didn't want others seeing. Not even his own partner. Sitting there on the catwalk next to the agent, he hit play.

It was a formal recording, with multiple angles of a small white room.

Three people crowded around a single table, two

on one side and one on the other. All were human, but with a staggering difference between them.

The two looked older than any humans Pet had ever seen. Wrinkles showed on their faces, and their hair had started losing color. They were no longer in the prime of their lives, but still healthy and robust.

The single human on the other side of the table contrasted with them in every way. Only a year or two into adulthood, they had a hard quality in their eyes which made them look much older. Their skin pinched as if their bones might poke through any moment. The baggy worn clothes and lank hair didn't help the effect. This person probably missed more meals than they ate. They sat with their feet tucked up on their chair and observed the immaculate humans.

Pet couldn't have said if the person was male or female.

The pair were deep in conversation.

*"I don't know. In such a condition, we may not get much."*

None of the multiple camera angles showed the pair's faces. Everything focused on the solitary individual. Since they were in nearly identical outfits and displayed no other identifying marks, Pet called the person who spoke first Number One and the other person Number Two. Number One may have been female based on the longer hair, but other than that, they were unremarkable.

Number Two spoke as much with their hands as their mouth as they argued. *"They always come in looking like this. A few good meals will turn things right around. It's the underlying bone structure you need to look at. My program will show us that hidden potential."*

*Number One shook their head. "I'm still not convinced."*

*"Let me show you. It'll only take a minute." Number Two opened a panel in the table, revealing a keyboard. The tabletop turned into a holographic screen, which showed a loading symbol as Number Two booted up the program.*

*The lone person on the other side of the table kept out of the conversation. They peered at the pair through their bangs every now and then but stayed silent as they scratched at flaky, irritated skin.*

The clear signs of chronic malnutrition made Pet feel ill. Such conditions were common back on Earth. Without enough resources to go around, every day more and more people went hungry. It was the reason colonization was so imperative. As a species, their only hope for survival was to reestablish themselves on a new fertile planet.

Over the noise of Number One and Two bickering, the other sound on the recording almost went unnoticed.

*Huddled in their chair, the lone person hummed to themself.*

It was the same wordless tune that bounced around in Pet's head. He'd never been able to piece the whole thing together. Hearing the complete music from a stranger's lips slotted a new feeling in Pet's heart. It was a longing for something great and a sadness that it could never be achieved.

Perhaps this was the kind of tune a mother would hum to their child just before they fell asleep.

*As they waited for Number Two's program,*

*Number One addressed the younger human for the first time. "You know what this will mean for you, right? If you go through with this, there's no going back. It's permanent."*

*The lone person glanced around the room nervously as if looking for a trap. "I know. It doesn't matter. I have nothing to go back to."*

*"Here, it's done." Number Two brought up an image on the table-screen.*

Pet nearly dropped Irih's tablet. That was *his* face. There were a few differences here and there, like someone had recreated him from memory rather than captured a picture, but it was definitely him.

*Number One studied the image. "You're sure? This is quality décor."*

*"Fix up his health and this will be the end product. He'll fetch a high price."*

*"The change seems too drastic to believe."*

*"I've done dozens of these transformations. Just needs some cosmetic adjustments."*

*As Number One and Two debated over the reliability of the image and what changes would need to be made, the lone person touched the face on the table-screen.*

*"This'll be me?"*

*Number One waved a hand in Number Two's face to shut them up. "Yes, if you agree to become décor, this will be you."*

Pet compared the lone person with the image of his own face. The lone person had freckles scattered over their arms and shoulders, and a mole at the corner of their eye.

He felt the unblemished skin at the corner of his

own eye. They had removed every freckle and discolored patch, like an artist repainting a poor brushstroke. Some of these changes made sense, but others served no purpose other than personal taste. His hair had been altered from medium to light brown, his eyebrows given a more prominent arch, and his cupid's bow emphasized. Only his eyes remained exactly the same. Those were his eyes staring out of a stranger's face.

*"I'll do it." The lone person looked up from the table to face Number One and Two. "Give me the forms. I'll sign them. You make me into this, sell me for as much as you can, and I get to live comfortably. Shelter and food every day. Right?"*

*Despite Number One's earlier arguments, they were quick to mollify the lone person's questions. "Décor contracts ensure they are never mistreated or harmed. You'll live stress free and be provided for in every way."*

*"Then do whatever you need to. I don't care. I just don't want to hurt anymore."*

*Number One looked ready to accept the lone person's declaration immediately, but Number Two had a few more concerns.*

*"You understand that becoming décor means signing away your rights as a living being? You'll legally become an object. Your memories will be erased and who you are right now will cease to exist. And, there's one more thing you need to know about."*

*The lone person nodded. "The* Caducity. *I've heard of it. Sounds good to me."*

*The easy acceptance struck Number One and Two. They shared a concerned look, brows pinched in worry.*

Oh. He knew that word. He had heard it once before, back in his earliest memories. It was the exact opposite of its name.

*"I'm not sure you understand."* Number Two *turned off the table screen. "The* Caducity *is a process all prospective décor must go through to halt their aging. There's no use for art that loses its beauty in a few years. But the procedure is dangerous. Only one in five people survive. If you agree to this, you'll be taking a huge risk."*

*The lone person reached across the table and turned the screen back on. "If I survive, I'll be set for life." They tapped the image of Pet's face. "If I don't..." They shrugged and scratched at flaking arms. "Then I'll be dead, and it won't matter. As it is, I probably won't live long anyway. Twenty percent chance of survival is better than zero."*

*Number Two seemed even more hesitant at the lone person's answer, while Number One's enthusiasm reached insincere levels. "Excellent." They clapped their hands as an added exclamation. "We'll need you to state very clearly, for the records, that you are of legal age, understand the procedure, and are agreeing of your own free will. Then we can get started."*

*The lone person traced the image on the table. "I am an adult and I understand. If I survive, do whatever you want with me. Make me into whatever I need to be."*

"No." Pet threw the tablet over the edge of the catwalk. It tumbled into the dark where it smashed somewhere far out of sight.

"No, no, no." He clung to the catwalk's rail as he shouted, hoping to drive the recorded memory away.

A red hand lightly covered his. It was the only skin contact Irih had ever initiated between them.

"Interviews for prospective décor are always recorded. That person in the video, you don't remember them, but they took the ultimate risk and made the ultimate sacrifice for the sake of their species. All they wanted in return was a life free of suffering." He waved a hand to encircle the ship and everything in it. "All this. Traveling through space at the whim of ship-dwellers. Living inside a metal box. Getting captured by poachers. This is not the life that person wanted. They may have been lost with your original memory, but it doesn't seem fair to deny their final wish just because you don't remember them."

Pet gripped the railing tighter, breathing deeply through his nose. "That person was me. I'm happy, so that person is happy."

"You really think so? You saw the video. Do you really think that person would be happy to know how they're living now, away from the safety and comfort they expected? They were promised a good life in return for becoming décor, and the trio you live with took that away when they brought you onto this ship."

Irih briefly touched the bruise on Pet's neck left by the poachers and the more recent welt on his arm from Xavis. "The person you used to be risked their life for the promise that they wouldn't experience any more pain. You're betraying yourself by being here. Leave this ship and come back with us. The *Trailblazer* is returning to civilized space to refuel. We'll go with them and find you the kind of life your previous self would have wanted."

The whirling thoughts filling Pet's head defied

classification. Guilt over hurting someone, even if that person was himself. Disbelief at seeing the person he used to be, so different from who he was now. Anger over being used against himself, though he wasn't sure who to direct the anger at. Could a person be angry for hurting themself? He wanted to run away from the memory trapped in that video but had no strength in his legs to stand. Nor was there anywhere to go.

Nauzeia appeared at the entrance to the catwalk. "What's going on?"

Desmodian followed right behind her.

Almost immediately, Xavis and Brog entered at the other end. Pet's shouting must have caught their attention.

The light emanating from his trio had lessened, but not completely disappeared. They were finally recovering from their Phazer manipulations. They didn't need to deal with his problems as well, but his rapid breathing refused to calm down.

Irih stood from the edge. "I was just talking to the décor. He seemed upset."

Desmodian gripped his hammer in two hands. "He wasn't upset a few minutes ago. What did you do?"

Flanked on both sides by the trio and his own partner, Irih crossed his arms and stood firmly at the center of the catwalk. "I asked him to come back with us on the *Trailblazer*. Surely that's allowed. You insist on treating him like a person, so a person can give their own answer."

Cool metal felt soothing against Pet's forehead where he leaned against the railing. He could answer for himself, but he couldn't tell what the question was any more. Did he want to live like typical décor? No, but at the same time, yes. Even if he didn't remember, the answer had once been yes. "What was my name?"

Five different gazes looked to him in confusion.

He only took comfort in three of them, and even those not as much as usual. "In that video, they never said it. What was my name before I became décor?"

Of the five gazes, only two changed to understanding.

"It was…"

Before Irih could finish, Nauzeia darted across the catwalk and slapped him. "What are you doing? You don't tell décor that kind of information. Why is he even asking? Did you…you did… You showed him the interview?"

"What's that mean?" Brog reached the agents first as the trio converged from their ends of the catwalk. Everyone huddled together on the bridge over the dark.

When Nauzeia answered, she spoke with the weight of someone sounding out a reality they couldn't believe. "You showed him the recording of his interview before he became décor. That is absolutely forbidden. Décor can never know anything about their previous lives. Facing that lost identity can have severe psychological consequences."

"He will face more severe consequences if he stays on this ship." Irih's facial tubules puffed up in fury. "He needs to come back with us. For his own sake. We'll find him a better owner, away from all this nonsense of poachers and Phazers."

They kept talking about him. Pet kept his gaze on the dark below his feet. It was supposed to bring him solace, instead he felt even more alone.

Over his head, the argument continued. Nauzeia

sounded particularly upset.

"You've gone too far. We've been walking a thin line already. Attacking one of the people we were supposed to observe could be excused since we thought we were protecting the décor. But this can't be excused. Look at him. He's having a panic attack. You've done the very thing we're supposed to prevent."

Panic attack? The title sounded right. It certainly felt like an attack, except his own brain was the one attacking him. It squeezed the air out of his lungs until he wanted to pass out just to make it end.

Xavis knelt at his side without touching. His wings blocked off both agents and the dark depths below. "Pet, you need to calm down and breathe."

"Take in as much air as you can an' hold it." Brog joined Xavis, as close to Pet as he dared while the light still lurked in his skin.

Pet did as they said. He filled his lungs with as much air as possible and held it while Brog counted the seconds. At the number five, Pet was told to exhale, and the abrupt release made the next breath a little easier. They repeated this pattern, adding seconds until Pet could hold his breath for a count of ten.

Desmodian shifted until his body blocked the gap between Xavis's wings, keeping Pet surrounded from all sides and out of the agents' line of sight. "What interview are you talking about? What did you show him?"

Nauzeia held up a hand to silence her partner before he could answer. "Interviews with prospective décor are always recorded to make sure they know what they're agreeing to."

"Show me. Something in that recording upset

him."

An awkward tension hung over the agents.

"That's classified." Before Irih could say more, a strange sound interrupted him. It was like someone had squeezed a half-inflated balloon.

Pet leaned around Desmodian's legs to catch a glimpse of Nauzeia holding her partner by his face tubules.

"You've already gone too far. Now we need to fix it." She handed Desmodian her tablet after hitting a few keys.

The opening scene of his interview showed on the screen. Brog and Xavis stood to look over Desmodian's shoulder, simultaneously blocking Pet's view.

Desmodian hit play, and the familiar sounds of the interview started.

From the outside, the video lacked the same drama Pet had experienced while watching. The first time around, it seemed to go on forever, but in reality, it only lasted a few minutes. Shame set the blood in his face aflame. That video showed not the beautiful décor his trio knew but the half-starved desperate human he used to be. He never wanted them to see him like that.

The video ended. Desmodian shoved the tablet back at Nauzeia.

She clutched it to her chest as if hiding the screen. "He doesn't remember it, of course. That's why we keep these records away from décor. Seeing a version of yourself you don't remember, it's like seeing a stranger wearing your face."

Desmodian touched his mask.

Xavis returned to Pet's side while Brog stayed at Desmodian's back as an intimidating wall that bisected the catwalk.

All four arms crossed over his chest. "What was that word they used? *Caducity*. It sounded dangerous. What were they talkin' about?"

It wasn't the agents who answered, but Desmodian. "The *Caducity* is a highly controversial procedure that stops the aging process. Not immortality, nothing can do that, but it will allow the person to live a very long life without growing old. But like they said, it's very dangerous. Most people don't survive the process. I didn't know décor were put through it."

Nauzeia shrugged, glanced down at the blank tablet, then quickly looked away. "Décor are valued for their beauty. They wouldn't be worth much if they couldn't stay beautiful. That's why we must make sure they're well cared for. Only the truly desperate are willing to risk their lives like that. They shouldn't suffer any more."

Bright wings ruffled, drawing closer around Pet while still maintaining a safe distance. A few feathers floated down into the dark. "Pet's not suffering. At least he wasn't until you showed up. We take care of him."

"For now." Nauzeia tried to pull Irih back, but he shook her off. "Maybe you take care of him. And maybe he isn't suffering. But it won't last. The longer he stays with you, the harder it will be when he's resold."

Pet really hated the word "resold." People kept throwing it around so casually, treating it as both a threat and an opportunity at the same time. Like anger expressed as laughter, something couldn't be both at once.

Brog stomped his foot. "Are you still on about

that?"

The catwalk shook. Pet redoubled his grip on the railing for fear that his trio's out-of-control strength would send them all plunging into the abyss.

Desmodian laid a hand on Brog's arm, reminding him to watch his actions.

It would have made Pet feel better, except Xavis looked ready to catch him if they fell.

"I'm fine, I'm fine." Brog batted away Desmodian's concern. "But we're not sellin' him. Not now, not ever."

Irih eyed the distance to the end of the catwalk, but the danger below their feet didn't stop him from talking. "Maybe not now, but eventually you will. Even if everything you're saying is true and you keep him for the rest of your lives, what about after that?"

"You've said enough, Irih." Nauzeia urged her partner off the catwalk.

Desmodian pointed his hammer in their direction without swinging it. The light didn't spark, but the threat remained. "If he's got something to say, then let him say it."

A whispered argument passed between the agents before Irih pulled away from Nauzeia despite her efforts. "All this time you've treated us like we're idiots. You may know how to survive out in space, yet you're missing something simple. Your precious Pet survived the *Caducity*. He'll never age, and eventually he'll outlive you. What do you think will happen then? He'll get resold anyway, and it'll be even worse after a lifetime of your influence. For his own sake, he should come with us now, while we can still restore him without too much pain."

Pet had always known he didn't age, but it never mattered enough to bring up. The future with his trio had seemed to stretch on indefinitely. Now he was reminded that, like all things, it had an end.

Desmodian's command came swift and merciless. "You're getting off this ship."

For a moment Pet thought Desmodian meant him, and nearly started his panic attack all over again.

However, Desmodian spoke to the agents, going so far as to "look" at them. "Whether or not Pet goes with you will be his choice. He will not be guilted into it with a past he can't remember. As for your concern, a lifetime is a long time. There's no telling how things will play out. We don't even know how our Phazer abilities affect our own aging. For all we know, we may outlive him instead. That's an issue we will deal with when it comes, but whatever happens, we won't let Pet suffer."

Irih tried to protest, but Nauzeia twisted his facial tubules again. "No, you're done. You've already crossed the line. No more."

Once she manhandled her partner off the catwalk, she turned back to the trio and Pet. "I'm not sure what will happen in the future either. But I think at this point two-six-eight-nine will only be happy with you. Any other owner would make him miserable, with or without his memories. It's obvious this is where he wants to be, but I need something I can take back to my superiors. Something tangible to prove you're capable of taking care of décor."

Another conduit of silent communication passed between his trio.

Pet envied them for it.

Bringing up his own holographic tablet, Desmodian touched a few illuminated keys. "Will that work?"

Nauzeia opened the information on her tablet. "What is this?"

The holograph projected a lot of numbers that meant nothing.

Desmodian's tablet showed the same numbers, until he stowed it away. "Our bank statements. Yearly income, to be exact."

"But…this is…" She scrolled through the long string of numerals.

Desmodian shrugged, but it was Brog who answered. "Our clients are mostly rich, desperate landowners. We're the only ones who can fly where they need. They'll pay whatever we charge. Means a lot 'a money in the bank for us."

Xavis laughed under his breath, and it was a real laugh. "That should be enough to convince your bosses we can afford to take care of Pet. Décor is a rich man's enterprise. But luckily we are."

Still looking stunned, Nauzeia closed her tablet. "I think I can spin this in a way my bosses will accept. They love attractive numbers. When the *Trailblazer* picks up their wayward captain, Irih and I will be joining them. Our mission is over. It's time we headed home. I've had enough of space for one life."

She turned to leave the catwalk but stopped and looked back at them. "Oh, concerning the authorities we contacted before we entered hyperspace. I'll smooth things over and tell them it was a misunderstanding. And I'm sorry for what happened. We never meant to hurt anyone."

Then she left Pet and his trio alone on the bridge.

Desmodian and Brog joined Xavis kneeling beside Pet, forming a protective triangle while he clung to the railing. The abyss stretched below.

"Sorry." Pet could barely be heard over the ship's silence. "I didn't want you to see that."

"See what?" Xavis's talons were inches from making contact.

Pet really wanted his touch, but they couldn't cross that line until the light vanished from their skin. "Everything on that video. The interview. The *Caducity*. What I was like before I became décor. It's all so ugly."

Frustrated tears gathered in his eyes. With no better option, he started to hum. For the first time, he gave voice to the tune that had, until now, only existed as fractured pieces in his head. Even without words, he knew it wasn't a happy song. It didn't claim "everything would be all right." Rather, it gave permission to be upset when everything wasn't all right.

His trio communicated wordlessly between themselves. Another moment of understanding Pet wasn't part of.

Then Desmodian held out a hand.

Very carefully, he cupped Pet's cheek without hurting him. At his side, his hammer glowed brighter than ever, illuminating the darkness at Pet's back.

"If you're talking about the way you looked before, don't. We're not going to judge some half-starved soul because their clothes don't fit."

For people who owned décor, his trio were surprisingly dismissive of looks. However, that still left Pet's biggest concern. "But the way I acted. I agreed to whatever those interviewers said, like a doormat. I knew I agreed to be décor, but I never realized I did it so eagerly. I actually wanted the life I had with my previous owner."

Brog's arms wrapped around Pet's shoulders.

"One question, Pet."

Xavis gripped his hands. "And there's no wrong answer."

Desmodian stroked both of Pet's cheeks, banishing the tears that managed to fall. "Do you want to go back with the agents?"

Surrounded on all three sides, Pet finally relaxed. His trio struggled so hard to control the residual power coursing through them, but they did it, just so they could comfort him.

He shook his head. "No, I don't. But the past me would have given a different answer. The person in that video had all their memories, so they're the real me. And the real me wanted the kind of life I had with my past owner. I can't help but think that maybe I owe the real me the life they wanted. I feel like I'm disrespecting their sacrifice by choosing something different now."

Together the trio pulled him away from the edge of the catwalk until he let go of the railing and clung to them instead.

Desmodian let go of his face to lean their foreheads together. "You don't owe anyone anything. Not even yourself. With or without memories, you are just as real."

Talons tickled the inside of Pet's wrist, inspiring a smile on his face.

Xavis smiled with him. "People change their minds

all the time. You know things now that your past self didn't, so of course you make different choices."

Brog held him a little closer. "I'd say changin' your mind proves you're a real person. You gotta have a mind in order to change it."

Their touch started to tingle unpleasantly, but Pet ignored it to remain in contact with them just a little longer. "So, choosing something different is a good thing?"

"It's a natural thing." Desmodian urged Pet to his feet. "Not good or bad. Just a thing that all people do."

After sitting on the hard metal catwalk for so long, Pet's legs had gone numb and it took a few tries before he could stand. His trio reached the limit of their control. They supported him until he felt steady again, but then they had to let go to avoid hurting him. Pet missed their touch immediately but knew it would be waiting for him.

They had time. He wasn't going anywhere, after all.

****

A few more hours passed before the *Trailblazer* took custody of Captain Covols. He would return to civilized space in the brig of his own ship to answer for his illegal arms dealing.

The two DPS agents also joined the *Trailblazer*, and true to her word, Nauzeia didn't let her partner speak to them again before the pair left the *Vanguard*.

By the time the *Trailblazer* was ready to leave, the glow had finally receded from the trio's skins. They were no longer in danger of breaking everything around them and took advantage of their regained freedom.

Pet and his trio lay curled together in a pile in front

of the observation windows watching the *Trailblazer*'s departure.

As the biggest of them, Brog made the base of their pile. "We should demand a bonus. We were only hired to find the *Trailblazer*. Not save it from poachers and its own captain."

Xavis agreed and nuzzled his face deeper into Pet's neck. "Sounds like a good idea."

Pet squirmed when the Scaacax's breath tickled the fine hairs on his nape, prompting Xavis to blow on him again.

At the top of the pile, closest to the windows, Desmodian's tail slid languidly back and forth over the floor. The gentle swishing steadily counted down the seconds until the *Trailblazer* made its exit. "Our last bonus started this whole disaster. We'll have to choose carefully."

Outside their window, the *Trailblazer* turned its nose toward civilized space. The large ship couldn't maneuver quickly, so it was a slow departure. Lights flared in systematic patterns down the ship's sides, signaling the efforts of the *Trailblazer*'s engines. Hyperspace travel was impossible within the Iota Cloud, so the ship had to leave the old-fashioned way— by drifting little by little into the cloud until it disappeared.

Then it was gone, and with it, so was the mission.

The nimbus glaukos had returned once the poachers left. Along with the swirling cloud all around them, it made for a beautiful sight.

"A vacation. As a bonus, I want a vacation." Pet could feel his trio smiling even without looking at them. It radiated from them with the same strength as the light that had glowed within their skin.

"A vacation, huh?"

Desmodian's playful tone warned that mischief was afoot. His trio had something on their minds.

Out of everyone, Desmodian had the easiest time disentangling himself and disappearing behind the control panel.

Pet tried to follow with his eyes if not his body, but he was distracted.

Xavis's talons made quick work of his clothes.

"Vacation sounds like a good idea. Although the ship's going to need some repairs first."

"Oculi government's probably gonna try to cheat us outta our pay." Brog helped by tossing Pet's clothes out of the way. "Thing's didn't exactly turn out how they expected."

Pet squirmed as six hands roamed his skin. He had missed this. Not just the sex, but the freedom to act on their urges whenever they wanted without censoring themselves.

Desmodian spoke up from out of sight on the other side of the room. "It might be a while before we can take that vacation. We'll have to invent our own reward until then."

The ship moaned as if in echo of Pet's arousal. A moment later, the lights dimmed and gravity disappeared.

Pet turned weightless and clung to Brog and Xavis.

Traitors that they were, however, they pushed him off into the air.

"What're you doing?" He flailed in the middle of the room, too far from anything that could support him.

Desmodian watched him from below. "Didn't you

want to try this? Zero gravity can be fun if you know what to do with it."

Experimenting with sex in zero gravity had crossed his mind, but he never voiced those desires out loud. Somehow his trio had known anyway. He may not be a part of their intimate connection, but they still understood him without words.

He understood them as well. Even without an explanation, he knew fulfilling this unvoiced desire was their way of apologizing.

After their incident with the poachers, it hadn't taken him long to retroactively figure out his trio's plan. The same way they transported fake weapons in place of real ones to buy time for Pet's ownership to transfer, they also pretended to be prisoners to buy time to find the *Trailblazer*. All their power would mean nothing against the threat of five hundred hostages, so they couldn't act until they knew the ship was safe. Their plan had worked, but they must have felt guilty for dragging Pet along and allowing him to be hurt.

They didn't say it out loud, and Pet didn't need them to. The apology was unnecessary. He never held the incident with the poachers against them, but he would always capitalize on an opportunity for new pleasure. "I can't even keep myself pointed in one direction." To prove the point, he turned another circle. "You'll have to come up here and show me how it works."

Three bodies met him in the air. The tangle of limbs tested even his trio's skills, and it turned into the most awkward sex Pet ever experienced.

At one point, Xavis's wings accidentally hit Brog in the face, and Desmodian elbowed Xavis's ribs.

The comedy of errors was just as enjoyable as the intimacy. Pleasure could be found in a lot of unexpected ways. Not just the brush of skin against skin but the relief of a completed job and the hilarity of seeing Desmodian scowl when Brog yanked his tail out of the way.

They were all pleasures he never experienced as proper décor, and he looked forward to learning many more.

*Later*

The holographic tablet sat on the table, open to the news article driving her insane. She would swear they left it there just to torment her, but no one thought about her. No one ever did.

A father and son sat at either end of a table long enough to hold a dozen. Since Iknox reproduced asexually, children looked like copies of their parents. The pair were no exception. Most days she struggled to tell them apart. Pale-lavender skin showed freckles in the same places, while long downturned ears and large drooping eyes gave them identical expressions. They looked permanently depressed. Only their upturned tails showed any liveliness, though she constantly had to remind herself not to laugh at the ridiculously fluffy feathers.

Spread on the table between them sat a breakfast far larger than either of them could finish. They wasted so much food, just as they wasted her. She deserved to be appreciated, but the occupants in that room barely glanced her way. They kept her only out of expectation. She deserved more than their token attention.

"Can you believe this?" The father on the left side of the table slapped the tablet as if to punish the article for its words. "Bunch of ship-rats saved that lost colony ship. And not just any ship-rats. I wasn't happy to open the morning news and find a picture of that bastard staring at me. Thought he died in Unit 22, but here he is. Alive. Don't you be getting any ideas."

The father gestured toward the son with the tablet, thrusting it forward like a dagger.

The son kept careful eyes on their breakfast and not the article. "Of course." His words were simple, precise, and exactly what the father wanted to hear.

She knew the son was lying. The father probably did too.

The tablet was set down again. Although the article remained open, conversation drifted toward other topics. Another hour passed before the father and son left.

Once certain no one would notice her, she left her post and approached the table. In an action that would have horrified her a year ago, she knocked the tablet to the floor and smashed the screen under her heel. It took a couple attempts, but she left a satisfying web of cracks emanating from his stupid, spiteful face.

She shouldn't get so mad. The article gave her exactly what she wanted. It wasn't the words that bothered her, but rather the picture. Right at the top of the article was a candid shot of the *Vanguard*'s crew.

He looked happy in that picture, and it made her hate him even more. After he ruined her life, he had vanished overnight. Only later did she learn he traveled on a ship, visiting distant places and finding new things to be happy about. He was far away and out of reach, but now the article gave her a way to find him.

Quickly, before anyone could catch her in the act, she shoved the broken tablet behind a bookcase. Its disappearance would be blamed on one of the staff.

Anyone who included her on the list of suspects would be laughed out of the room.

She would make him pay. She had plans, and now that she knew where he was, she would hurt him as much as he hurt her.

## About the Author

D'Arcy Arden grew up in Akron, Ohio, where she attended creative art schools and was surrounded by beautiful country landscape. This combination cultivated an interest in literature, art, and the natural world around her. In college, she earned a Masters Degree in Fiction Writing, which primarily taught her that there is no one way to tell a good story. So she turned around and went back for a degree in Animation as well. This love for both visual and written stories has given her a preference for stories that are memorable, easy to picture, and most importantly, fun.

That was her main goal when she started writing *The Fourth State of Matter*—to provide readers with a fun story featuring the three S's: Science, sex, and spaceships. It is her first published novel but only the beginning of a great adventure.

Visit D'Arcy at
https://daarden33.wixsite.com/weatheringthestorm

Also Available
from The Wild Rose Press, Inc.
and major retailers.

# Universe Hunters: Taken
## By C.L. Scholey

Being lost in the forest is the least of Cali's worries when she's attacked by flesh-eating creature not of this world. She is rescued by a scorching alien light that kills the creature but inadvertently burns her. Cali wakes to find her body healed but her sanity in question. She can't really be zipping through space on a vessel manned by two light beings who have taken the form of human men—two sexy as hell human men calling themselves…Universe Hunters.

Two male beings, one human female. Life as Cali knows it changes in the blink of an eye, or in her case, a flicker of light.

# Catch a Tiger by the Tail
*One Scoop or Two*
## By Gabbi Grey

Thomas Walsh knows the number one rule in the film industry. Don't get involved with the talent. But resisting the urge to take the big screen to the bedroom can be hell when the lead actor on the set looks good enough to eat…one slow lick at a time.

Peter Erickson's latest role as a gay man hits a little too close to home. He's still in the closet and secretly grieving the death of his lover. Then an enchanting production assistant catches his eye, and he's surprised by the instant attraction that stirs more than his wounded soul.

When the two men are caught on camera in a very intimate pose, both Thomas and Peter are afraid they've caught a tiger by the tail.